THE EMPYRICAL TALES BOOK I

JOURNEY
OF THE
FOURTH
QUEEN

Mark Miller

MillerWords, LLC
PO Box 861074
Shawnee, KS 66286

Copyright © 2017, 2022 by Mark Miller

First Edition

For discounts on bulk purchases, please contact MillerWords Educational Sales at **Sales@MillerWords.com**

Printed in the United States of America

2 4 6 8 10 9 7 5 3 1

Library of Congress Control Number: 2017915457

ISBN: 978-0-9982986-7-2

What others are saying about Mark Miller's writing...

"...a well-crafted piece of literature with many unexpected twists and turns throughout..."
-Amazon Review

"Miller has a lot of whatever it is that makes a good fantasy writer...Whatever the secret is to writing great fantasy, The Secret Queen is the result."
-Reader's Favorite Book Reviews

"There is a musical quality to the way Miller writes that makes the reader want to pick up more of his books. Something else that should be considered is that these books have very strong female protagonists, none of the wimpy ones we see too often nowadays, so it's a great choice for teen girls."
-Midwest Book Reviews

"From trials and victories, battles and moments of heartwarming scenarios, The Fourth Queen is a novel the entire family will find enjoyable... His vivid and descriptive narratives portray him as a master of the craft."
-Amazon Review

Books by
Mark Miller

The Empyrical Tales
Book I: Journey of the Fourth Queen
Book II: Search for the Lost Queen
Book III: Mystery of the Secret Queen
Book IV: History of the First Queen

Dinosaur George and the Paleonauts
Episode 1: Raptor Island

Small World Global Protection Agency
#001 New Kids on the Rock
#002 Bulls and Burglars
#003 The Not So Perfect Game

Promise of Tomorrow

For My Children

Chapter 1

A Bad Night

Two sisters, Zandria and Olena, lived in a village by the sea at the eastern edge of the queendom of Empyrean. Their story starts here.

The hooves of the two horses ripped the ground as they pounded forward, every muscle rippling, every sinew stretching at the speed. Wrath, the lead horse, drove them on side-by-side at this impossible pace with a will more powerful than any driver's whip. The carriage that they pulled bounced and rocked through the ruts left by thousands of years of travel on this ancient path that had only one destination. The Castle Empyrean stood waiting in the distance.

Wrath could see the enormous castle for the last two days as they rampaged forward without stopping. An urgent message was dispatched and carried by the castle's guardian hawks. Wrath knew the four hawks flew in four directions, with scrolls tied to their claws directing each recipient to come to Empyrean. In Wrath's experience, this meant without delay.

After six days with almost no stopping they were now in sight of the main gate, its sheer massiveness was both inspiring and frightening every time he saw it. Wrath looked up to the tallest spires of the castle piercing the night sky and parting the threatening clouds. He sensed the storm coming since only moments before the hawks arrived for his mistress. The whole of the castle appeared to be made of glass, but he knew it was impenetrable to any army and unbreakable to any giant's club. Over the edge, the lowest cellars clung to the wall of the bottomless canyon that protected three sides of the structure and the towers grew out of the top in every direction like a blooming tree. Wrath had seen Empyrean in better times and knew it looked magnificent in the sunlight, but tonight under the full moon, even partially covered by clouds, it looked alive.

The shining, black horses pulled the carriage along the only path leading up to the entrance of the castle. The stocky driver pulled at the reins. Wrath laughed to himself knowing that the human was not trying to control the horses, but was trying to keep from being thrown from his bench.

This face of the fortress was not protected by the canyon, but by an unyielding field of briars and thorns. Although the path was blocked, Wrath did not allow his apprentice to slow.

From inside the carriage, an aged hand pulled back the thick, red velvet curtain. The venerable woman carefully poked her head out the window and whispered to the impending vines. The thorns bowed and retracted, pulling back row upon row, like a theatre curtain at the start of a performance. Not a single twig brushed the carriage as the stallions rushed through.

Wrath knew, once upon a time, this woman was known as Snow White, but for the past two hundred years, she has only been called the Queen of the Northern Wood. He never doubted her intentions and followed every order without question. As they raced toward the thorns, Wrath did not hesitate because his queen would not fail him. He knew that only by the speaking of the magic word from one of the four queens would the floral guardians let anyone pass into this sacred place.

He did not slow as the queen let the night air rush upon her porcelain white skin and ripple through her regal mane of midnight black hair. Her ruby lips parted again as she whispered another magic charm to seal the path behind her. Wrath wondered how long it had been since the first time she came to Empyrean. How long since the noble dwarves saved that young girl in the very forest of which she was now queen? Snow White let the curtain fall closed with what seemed like the weight of those forgotten years and waited for the journey to end as her trusted steeds led the way across the immense drawbridge made from the tallest and sturdiest trees of the Northern Wood ages before she was born.

As the carriage rolled from the wooden planks onto the carved stone inlaid in the great circle courtyard, lightning flashed in the distance. Under the flash, Wrath saw two tiny scratches in the middle of the bridge that he never noticed before. He suspected it was some animal claw marks, but he did not take any more time to think about it. He got inside quickly because the storm was approaching faster than anyone predicted. Still, the two fastest horses in all of the Northern Wood beat it here.

Wrath silently instructed Fury to slow their gait now safely inside their mistress' sanctuary. The elder horse addressed his friend and student, "Fury, I told you we would beat the storm."

Fury, the younger and less experienced of the two Friesians, shook out his mane and turned a wild eye towards his mentor. His ears flitted front to back as he tried to catch his breath, "Come on, old nag. You couldn't have done it without me. And you definitely could not have done it if we stopped at every watering hole you wanted to."

Wrath let out a scoffing neigh at his friend's overconfidence and the two stepped on in silence. The driver leaned back on his bench, looking happy to be at the end of the treacherous ride. Now he calmly listened to the echo of their diamond horseshoes clicking on the stone.

It had been some time since Wrath, Fury or even Snow White came to the castle, but both horses knew to stop where the engraved stones gave way to the sculpted glass staircase. The stallions twisted their necks around to watch the driver climb down from his perch. The man was new to his post, but Wrath could tell that he took great pride in his work. He watched the man fold the steps into place and then check to make certain they were secure. Then the man held his breath as he opened the door. This caused Wrath to suck in his own breath and Fury took the cue to stand at attention as well.

Snow White, the Queen of the Northern Wood, emerged from the carriage. She was an old woman, but time had been generous to her. The vestige of her throne instilled her with power, but underneath was the pure and simple beauty to which so many innocent men fell victim. The driver looked at the ground, afraid to stare at her radiance and she touched his shoulder as she stepped past him, trailing the green velvet of her robe across his arm. Even Fury dared not gaze.

But Wrath watched her. He carried her on his back many times since he was a young colt and became one of her most trusted advisors, as his father was before him. Their eyes met and she blew him a gentle kiss. The enchanted breath swirled and sparkled faintly as it drifted over to the old warhorse. It filled him with the minty smell of fresh evergreens and a musical *thank you* danced at his ears.

The queen turned and made her way to the stained glass doors where an elven butler waited to escort her inside. Wrath knew that not one of the four queens dared the mazes of the castle without a guide who had been born inside its walls.

Wrath stood, watching his queen for a moment longer, while the driver busied himself with unbridling the amazing animals.

As soon as Wrath and Fury were loose of the leather straps, they both shook their entire bodies and stretched their legs, glad to be free of the oaken carriage. Both knew where they would spend the night, but waited for the driver to lead them across the courtyard to the stables. Wrath watched his young friend staring up the castle walls.

Fury responded without being asked, "You know, I thought I could see the top."

Wrath looked up into the darkness. He could make out the shapes of the circling hawks, nested in the highest peaks of the castle and slightly beyond that, more of the curved crystalline wall that reflected the last of the moonlight. On the brightest summer days, he never clearly saw the opening, so far beyond even the reach of the guardian hawks, which marked the top of Castle Empyrean.

The handcrafted diamond shoe embedded in Wrath's hoof clicked sharply on the glass surface at the entrance of the stable, so he waited to respond to Fury.

Fury was still craning his neck skyward when his front hooves left the stone to meet with the glass pathway and he lost his footing sending him hard to the ground. His legs slipped out in front of him like a newborn deer's first time walking on an icy pond, but he recovered and was standing upright before the driver could react.

Wrath did his best to hold back his laughter. "The top, huh?" he asked. "It seems to me that the only thing you could see was the bottom. And so, you are still my student."

"Hey, I passed your tests, old nag." Fury was as indignant as the day he first set hoof into the academy.

"If you are so wise, then tell me what two lessons did you forget?" said Wrath.

Fury seemed annoyed, "I give up. You tell me."

"First," Wrath was using his gentle, teacher's voice, "Your mind was on the future and objects in the distance and not where it should have been, on the events right in front of you. Second," he switched to his rough military voice, the one Fury hated, "never look like a gelding in front of the ladies."

The driver led them beneath the pointed archway, directly in front of six glistening, beautiful, golden Andalusians. Their long, braided tails swished gently in the awkward silence, while Fury attempted to recover from his misstep. Wrath nodded and issued a polite greeting to the mares, until he could move closer to the only one he knew. Fury was now trying to posture for the two fillies and they seemed to be excited in the presence of a soldier. Wrath moved close to his friend and she whispered something in his ear. They shared a quiet moment and then he gestured to Fury that it was time to move down to their stalls.

Fury began to canter down the hall, showing off, as he turned into what he thought was an empty stall. At the last moment, Wrath blocked him to keep him from crashing into the massive black shape that filled the stall. The shape, like a boulder larger than Wrath, heaved and fell with the steady breath of a creature deep in sleep after a tiresome journey.

"That is Apis. You do not want to disturb him," said Wrath.

"Apis the bull?" Fury sounded excited by this.

"The one and same."

Fury understood the implication, "With the girls back there and the black bull himself, that means almost everyone is here. The four queens haven't been together at Empyrean since before your time, old nag."

Wrath started to answer, but was interrupted by a muculent snort from Apis.

"Sorry, big fella," Fury was trying to be friendly.

"Don't expect a reply. He never speaks." Wrath turned away from the stall.

Neither horse wanted to wake this hulking beast, so they continued to the far end of the stable.

The two soldier-horses positioned themselves in silence for their hard-earned rest, quietly hoofing the straw into the shape of a bed. Wrath slept on hard ground many times and found a comfortable spot more quickly than his partner.

Fury, despite being trained as a warrior, was used to the pampered life in the stables of the Northern Castle and so there was much stamping and brushing of the straw in his stall.

This gave Wrath time to consider what was happening tonight. He knew the six mares were responsible for the pumpkin coach of the Queen of the Western Sun and Apis in his many reincarnations was solely responsible for guiding the chariot of the Queen of the Southern Valley. The only queen yet to be present was the Queen of the Eastern Sky. When she arrived, Fury was right, that would be the first time all four queens met at Empyrean in all of Wrath's eighty years. That meant only one thing to Wrath, some great evil was rising across the land, something so powerful that the Empyrical Wizards summoned the queens from their four realms.

If there was to be a war, no one was prepared. Only the Northern Friesians and their men were trained as an army. And of those, only Wrath had seen an actual battle and that was when he was still a colt. Peace reigned for so long under the skies that Castle Empyrean touched that perhaps even the queens forgot the old wars.

Wrath was going to warn his young friend of the threat that he suspected, but Fury fell asleep almost as soon as he made his bed. Now Wrath would wait for the twin Alkonosts to arrive with the Queen of the Eastern Sky or any news from the halls and chambers in the glass towers above him.

He only met the Alkonosts once and tried hard to remember what they looked like. He pictured their feathered wings and fanned tails, identical down to the pointed black claws ticking against the tempered floor. Even he was struck by the beauty of their human heads, both young, vibrant females, who were truly as old as the mountains that marked the gateway to the East.

Wrath was used to the dwarves and occasional trolls that inhabited his country, but he was not so experienced to know the many creatures of this world. He knew that the Eastern country was by far the largest of all the domains and he knew that was where the last few dragons had been hunted, but he never imagined the possibility of so many amazing creatures sharing the same sun. He came to know a few. Aside from the extinct unicorns, the Alkonosts were his favorite.

Wrath drifted into sleep, with the sweetness of their long forgotten voices easing his worries of the impending storm.

Somewhere above the stables, the Northern Queen followed her guide. They moved quickly, but without a sense of urgency. The elf knew his course, but the queen could only follow.

She was dazzled by the shimmering walls, as she was every time she entered Empyrean.

Moving past the growing crystal, up small steps, sometimes ducking through short hallways and turning through doors that only appeared a moment before, they hurried along. In her mind, Snow White was transported back to her youth. There was old magic buried deep in the foundations of Empyrean and it affected everyone who passed through its gate.

Mostly, she watched the elf's feet and which way they would turn. Then she would look at the back of his head, his silky blond hair falling in braids past his shoulders. He was silhouetted in a warm, comforting light and his pointed ears stood out clearly above either side of his head. Their path was lit by the glowing amulet hanging from the small gold chain around the elf's neck. His narrow, ageless face was illuminated from below his chin causing him to look far more sinister than his pure heart would ever allow.

In front and behind them was darkness, and in the darkness, the magic did its best work. Even when they neared an outer wall or a window, no light could break through the threatening cloud cover. The queen could see the light reflect off the walls when they came to a sharp jagged turn, but otherwise the walls were smooth and she would run her hands along them like a child running past a picket fence. She could feel the magic inside the walls and she could feel it enter her as her fingertips brushed against its coldness.

Even if the heavy velvet of her robes did not wipe away their footprints, the castle would not give up its secrets. No one could follow them or guess at the labyrinth long enough to find where the elf was taking her. She tried to imagine in her mind which part of the castle they were in, but it was pointless. Suddenly, in her memory, she was in the forest again.

She was lost among the trees, swallowed in the blackness, fierce branches grabbing at her with their gnarled hands. The wicked queen's Hunter fell at her feet. He was begging forgiveness and weeping uncontrollably. The queen, her stepmother, instructed him to cut out her heart, but he could not bring himself to do it, so he sent her racing into the forest.

Snow White was terrified and everything in the woods was trying to get her, to deliver her to the evil queen as a sacrifice. Her blind panic kept her moving forward, ripping her simple dress, scrapping her arms and face. Her hair snagged on a moss covered limb and she yanked free, leaving a few bloody locks behind. Then she tripped over a rotting log and dived face first into a cold, sucking well of mud. Crawling onto the wet grass, she collapsed in the darkness and sobbed.

Then she was back in Empyrean. She was on her knees, alone in the darkness and she was crying.

The elf did not realize she stopped. He did not realize that the old magic was awakening her buried, painful memories. The castle would do that to people, even the queens. The old magic would challenge its inhabitants to prove them worthy.

Snow White sat on the floor, gathering her composure, mad at herself for falling into this trap. Faint golden light slipped around a corner and then a moment later, the elf was back at her side, holding her hand.

He looked at her knowingly and reassured her, "There has never been a Queen of the Northern Wood as fine as you. In all the years of your reign, no maiden has been mistreated and no stepmother has held cruelty in her heart."

She wanted to tell him thank you, but her heart was too heavy to bring herself to speak. In the days of her youth, Empyrean's power did not reach to every corner of the land and smaller regions were left to their own rule. Evil had time to fester and find hollow places to dwell. She was afraid those days were coming again.

The woman and the elf continued in silence.

Then the sound started that both comforted her and terrified her all at once. It came first as an echo and then built into a wave until it vibrated the floor beneath her feet. She could even feel it coursing through the walls and was frightened that they might begin to shatter around her. She was certain that it was an earthquake, but apparently, the elf was not slightly concerned as he kept moving up the hallway, so she decided it was something else. Then the pulsing and thumping began to take shape and there were smaller sounds mixed in, some clanging and even smaller chiming.

Bells!

The bells were ringing for midnight. When the initial shockwave passed, the air, the walls, the floor and even Snow White's head were filled with a melody so peaceful and calming that she wanted to drop to the floor again and sleep. However, she knew if she did that, this sleep would be almost as deep as the one caused by that poison apple so long ago. The elf turned and grabbed her under the arm as she began to lean against the wall and slide down.

It was so tempting. That is what frightened her, the lure of the melody. She knew she had never seen a bell tower or even a pull-rope for a bell in the castle. Her mind drifted to the thought of where the bells could be and then as quickly drifted on to other thoughts.

The song called to her again, bidding her to sleep. The elf was mouthing words that could not be heard and he was urging her, pulling her along. His amulet flashed in her face and now it seemed so bright. She wanted to close her eyes. She wanted to be an old woman and not a queen. She wanted to sleep.

Finally, they reached a door at the end of an unbelievably long hallway. She had no idea how long the elf carried her or how long since they turned down this hallway. But here he let her slump into the corner as he fumbled for his key. It was in a pouch secured to a rope under his tunic and now she could feel the faint onset of panic radiate from him as she started to slip away.

With what seemed to Snow White as unbelievable dexterity, the elf jammed the key into the star shaped hole and twisted it hard. When the door swung inward, the bells stopped, no fading or trailing off, they simply stopped in the middle of a chord. She could feel the elf pulling her to her feet and lead her into the throne room. Once inside, he collapsed. She could vaguely feel the waves of anxiety falling off him.

The Queen of the Northern Wood's eyelids felt so heavy and even though the song was gone, she still wanted only to sleep. Through the haze that became her vision, she could make out the shapes of two other people closing in around her and she could hear the elf's voice so far away as if she was at the bottom of a deep well and the water was splashing in her ears.

"The bells. I forgot she never heard the bells."

Then she drifted into blackness.

Chapter 2

A Bad Night Gets Worse

When Snow White awoke, she was certain that she was lying across several uncomfortable miniature beds. Her body ached all over and the way she was laying only caused her more discomfort. As soon as her eyes focused on the high curved glass ceiling, she knew she was not in any dwarven home. She was at Empyrean.

Instead of being surrounded by a group of little men that looked as if they were carved out of the very stone which they mined, there was an old woman on either side of her, pressing cold rags against her wrists and forehead. These two ancient ladies seemed familiar, but the deep wrinkles in their skin and silver hair hid their true identities from Snow White. The woman to her left laid a fresh cloth across her forehead and the icy cold sent goose bumps down both arms.

With each chill, Snow White regained consciousness and her memory returned with it. She remembered that she was the Queen of the Northern Wood. To her right, draped in red robes and dangling golden jewelry from her neck and ears was the Queen of the Southern Valley. Her dark skin was tanned even more by the burning sun that showed no mercy to her land, but through her dry, hard features, her kindness flowed out of her like the river that once issued from her palace into the desert valley.

Then the great grandmother on her left removed the rag and she could see her face, beaming at the top of her sparkling white dress, greeting her with a smile. It was the face of her oldest and dearest friend hidden behind several hundred birthdays. It was the Queen of the Western Sun.

A long time ago, in a far away land, the Queen of the Western Sun was called Cinderella and her slippers were cut from the same magic glass that grows in this castle. And, Snow White knew, history had another name for the Queen of the Southern Valley. It was Isis.

Snow White tried to stand, but fell back into her throne under the weight of Cinderella's welcoming hug. The two women moved as gracefully as their worn frames would allow. Snow White returned the hug and then clasped both of Isis' hands in hers. Three of the four queens were reunited and overjoyed to be together even under these dire circumstances.

"But the bells...what happened to the elf?" Snow White was still a little confused.

"Tym has gone off to tend to other duties," Isis answered. "He is fine."

Cinderella locked arms with Snow White and helped her from the ornate chair, "The bells you heard were the midnight chimes from the heart of the castle."

The three ladies moved over to the wide door and onto the balcony that looked down hundreds of feet to the courtyard below. Cinderella continued, "Part of their magic is to keep intruders away and since you never heard them, you almost fell under their spell."

Snow White saw movement below, a speck, like an ant wondered into the center of the courtyard. Even from here, she recognized her new coachman. He must be watching for the arrival of the last queen. Lightning snapped outside the main gate and stretched his shadow longly behind him.

The warning of the storm brought the women's attention back to their task and Isis spoke, "As Queen of the Southern Valley, I call this meeting to order."

"But we have to wait for the Queen of the Eastern Sky." Cinderella was clearly concerned for their missing friend.

Snow White said, "No. The Southern Queen is right. If the storm is this close, then we can wait no longer. I hope that even my delay has not been our undoing."

The three queens stepped to the center of the room, each in front of their own throne. When they quietly joined hands, the floor inside their circle dissolved into liquid and a crystalline pillar rose from it.

Each in turn placed her right hand on the pillar and each in turn said her verse of the incantation.

Snow White went first, "As Queen of the Northern Wood, I bring my fertile soil from which all things grow."

"As Queen of the Southern Valley," Isis spoke second, "I bring my precious drop of water from which all things live."

And Cinderella finished by saying, "As Queen of the Western Sun, I bring my righteous flame, from which all evil is purged."

A light began to grow where their fingertips touched on top of the pillar. All of Empyrean shook and two new towers grew instantly on the canyon side. Snow White felt her horses and the other animals jarred from their sleep. The black clouds above the guardian hawks swirled and parted as the light shone and refracted from the tallest spires. The storm was being pushed back.

Then a bolt of lightning broke straight into the center of Empyrean, through the open balcony and shattered the pillar, knocking all three women down and into darkness.

"It's no use." Cinderella was crying, which she professed she had not done since the night that she lay sobbing at her fairy godmother's feet. "Without the East Wind, we are not powerful enough to stop this."

Isis struggled to her feet and grabbed her sistrum-headed cane from beside her throne for support. "What evil is this that can stand against even one of us, let alone three?" She looked outraged and the little brass rings on her cane jingled as she shook.

Snow White watched the shards of the pillar melt back into the floor. She was sure that Empyrean was not damaged, but had no good answer for the Southern Queen. "I believe that we are safe here. Even if we cannot stop this thing, it cannot harm us inside these walls. Otherwise, we would all be dead now."

The ladies looked around the large empty room and suddenly felt alone and vulnerable with no courtiers or advisors to keep them company. Then, as if they could feel that they were needed, a door burst open that was not there a moment ago. Several wizards led the way, followed by Tym the elf, two women with cat's heads and at least a dozen mice scurrying at their feet.

The queens were now surrounded by people checking on their well-being. The elf dashed about the room relighting torches and the wizards were arguing with each other. Isis' servants were preening their mistress and Cinderella's mice were careful to stay clear of the feline-like visitors.

One of the smallest mice, brown with ears as large as his head, sneaked over to the balcony.

This poor creature looked deathly afraid of heights, but Snow White suspected his curiosity forced him to find out exactly how afraid he should be.

When the daring mouse peaked between the rails and saw how impossibly high up he was, he tipped over on his back and stared up at the sky, swooning. That is when he saw it!

With the speed capable of only a determined mouse, he skittered and slid across the glass floor, dodging giant feet and his fellow mice. Almost slipping past her, Snow White watched him snag Cinderella's silken gown with one tiny foot. In an instant, he dashed from her hemline to her shoulder and was squeaking in her ear and pointing outside.

Cinderella moved to the balcony. The rest of the party followed. Everyone was looking skyward in different directions. Then Tym, with his deep evergreen eyes, spotted it too. A lone hawk was attempting to fly through the storm.

Snow White saw the hawk being dashed about by the unrelenting lightning strikes. Every time he would regain his course, another bolt would blast him in a different direction. His body looked like the last leaf falling on a windy autumn day, whipping and swirling, with no good probability of reaching the ground safely.

When the hawk realized he had spectators, he did his best to fly towards them. And the lightning kept striking, singeing his feathers and swatting him away. What made Snow White feel worse was the ominous black shape that was outlined with each intermittent flash. Something, some beast, was gaining on the hawk.

The weary bird came near enough to the balcony that he folded his wings and dropped. Snow White stretched out and caught him as he fell past. One of the cat women pulled the queen back before she went over the rail.

Still, the black, shapeless monster was coming straight at them.

Tym yanked the amulet from around his neck, spoke in his native Elvish tongue and threw the glowing charm into the air. The magical light hit the beast and both exploded into wisps of black smoke.

Everyone moved safely back inside.

Snow White was cupping the tiny wounded bird in both hands.

Isis said, "Is it a baby," revealing that her servants probably received her messages for her.

"Um, no. All of our guardian hawks are miniature. It makes the castle seem taller." The wizard looked embarrassed to admit it and changed the subject, "He's trying to speak."

The tiny hawk coughed and stretched its wings across Snow White's palms. "Your majesty, I..." more coughing, "I am sorry."

He paused to take two deep breaths.

"The Queen of the Eastern Sky is dead." He exhaled a final breath and his eyes fell closed.

"How could he know this?" Isis looked like she did not want to believe the news.

Cinderella was crying again as she plucked loose the small scroll that was tied to the bird's leg. It was the undelivered request for the Eastern Queen with the same message that the three other queens received.

The eldest wizard read the message over the Western Queen's shoulder, "Then this is Aeran, the captain of the guard, who I personally dispatched to the East. He would not have failed to deliver the message unless his last words were true."

Snow White carried the captain over to her throne and rested his body on the cushion of her seat. "Without the Eastern Queen, I fear we do not have the power to stop this approaching storm. Whatever evil is hiding behind it, we can only hope to hide ourselves in here."

Tym rebuffed her, "I hoped to have lived never hearing words like that from one of my queens. To admit defeat already, when you know that even at the moment of her death, the new queen was called."

"I'm sorry, my friend. It is far too easy to surrender when you are frightened." Snow White was regaining her composure. "I thought I lost my girlish fancies long ago, but even at this age I would feel safer with my covers pulled up over my head. You speak the truth better than the wisest elves of the Northern Wood. Nevertheless, we are trapped here with no way of following the signs to the new queen. We will have to wait here for her to come to us."

The wizards nodded in agreement with the Queen of the Northern Wood. Tym bowed to

Snow White. The mice were busy cleaning the scarred and broken body of Captain Aeran.

Isis, known for her benevolence, showed an aggressive side that Snow White did not know she possessed.

"There is something we can do." The Queen of the Southern Valley strided to the balcony as if the past six hundred years had not affected her body. She whistled sharply to the courtyard below. The shrill sound bounced off the walls and curved around the circle of the courtyard until the ears of its recipient perked at its sound.

The bull's eyes popped open.

The massive Apis hoisted himself onto his hooves and lumbered out of the stable. Wrath and Fury had not gone back to sleep from the earlier disturbance and followed Apis into the courtyard. As Wrath passed the Andalusian mares, he reassured them, "Stay here ladies. I'm sure everything is fine." He trotted to catch up to Fury.

Apis stood in the center of the courtyard and looked up in the direction of the balcony. Fury and Wrath stood behind him and were completely hidden by his hulking mass.

Another whistle drifted down from above and the bull turned toward the front gate. Apis moved incredibly slowly as if time did not matter to him.

Wrath and Fury looked at each other, not sure what to make of the unintelligible instructions.

The coachman sat by the door to the guest quarters. Not quite giving up on the late arrival of the fourth queen, he kicked off his boots and lit his pipe before the storm started. When he saw the animals moving about, he ran first toward Apis and then to the stable. He grabbed some rope and came hobbling back, his bare feet sore from slapping on glass and stone. He stopped, looked at the length of rope in his hand and then at the gigantic bull and apparently could not figure out what to do next.

His dilemma was solved by a meteorite crashing to the ground a few feet in front of him. A moment later, two more fell inside the courtyard. The coachman ducked safely into the guest room.

Wrath looked up and saw a few more meteorites heading toward them and Fury whinnied. He turned and saw Apis continuing towards the gate although one of the burning rocks skinned his side. The meteorites were not actually damaging the castle, they were cracking and breaking into pebbles on impact. Wrath knew the real problem was when the super-heated space debris hit the wooden drawbridge. The bridge was catching with small fires on each impact.

Wrath looked up to the distant balcony. He could almost make out Snow White and Isis up there. The horse waited for the orders of his queen without fear of the falling sky.

He pricked up his ears and could barely make out her words, "Isis, do you have a plan?"

"Not really," Isis replied. "Maybe they can find the new queen, or at least bring us an army."

"Good enough, old girl," he heard Snow White reply. Then she leaned over the rail and blew another kiss to him.

When the kiss reached Wrath's gray-tipped ears, the message was complete and the scent was enchanting. He understood and galloped after the bull, "Come on, kid."

Fury stood, snorting. Wrath knew the scent of the pine needles reached him as well and tickled his nose. Fury doubled his gait to catch up to his superior officer. An instant later, three meteorites hit the ground where they had been standing.

Apis already crossed the bridge by the time the two horses made it to the gate. The small fires were springing up across the entire span and the meteor shower was gaining in intensity.

Wrath and Fury raced the length of the bridge. Rocks smashed the wood around them and flames licked at their hooves. One meteor as big as the carriage they pulled tore a hole directly in front of them. Wrath slid to the edge and stopped before skillfully maneuvering around it. He looked back to make sure Fury made it.

The younger horse leaped the gap, yelling, "Yeeeeehawwww!"

The three animals were clear of the chasm only seconds before the flaming timbers dropped into the void below, tumbling like a spilled box of lit matches. They stood with their back hooves on the edge of the bottomless pit and their muzzles tucked into the briar patch.

Wrath watched the collapsing bridge for a moment and then looked up to see the main entrance of the castle transform into a solid wall. He knew that Empyrean was defended and no one could pass in or out until the new Queen of the Eastern Sky was found.

"Well this was a good idea," said Fury.

Apis snorted.

Then Cinderella's voice drifted from above and the curtain of razor sharp branches parted for them. They passed through onto the muddy road and the thorns grew impassably closed again.

Wrath stopped to catch his breath and give some instructions, "Alright, I'll go with the big guy to see if we can gather an army to defend the castle. You go and see if you can find her."

Fury was at a loss, "Uh, find who?"

"The new queen. Didn't you understand Her Majesty's instructions?" Wrath was flustered.

"Ohhhh. That was the pine fresh scent. Nope. Didn't get a word."

Wrath stuck out his chest and put his head above Fury's so that his mouth was next to the younger stallion's ear, a technique that intimidated all of his students. "You are to go east. The Queen of the Eastern Sky is dead. You are to find the new queen. Apis and I are going to raise an army. Until you return with the queen, we have little chance of winning this battle and the other queens will be forever trapped inside Empyrean."

"You got all that from a puff of wind?" Fury gazed admirably at his old teacher.

The bull was already heading south and gradually picking up speed on the open road.

Wrath stamped with impatience. "You have to go now!" He started after Apis then stopped. "Fury, be careful."

The younger Friesian was still waiting, "Yeah. You too, old nag."

The two friends galloped off in opposite directions as the first meteor shower died out.

Chapter 3

Ten Days Earlier

The hawks' nest at the top of Empyrean was windy and straw constantly fluttered through the air in small cyclones. The room at the top of this tower had an open window in each of the four compass directions so that on the calmest of days, the tiny hawks gripped their perches tightly to keep from being blown out.

The birds managed to keep the room clean and the glass walls and floor stayed bright with their best efforts. Piled in the corners and draped from various roosts were prizes and souvenirs that the hawks collected in their time of service.

The hawks favored jewelry and their nest showed it. More than any other thing, necklaces hung everywhere. Some were simply gold or silver chains, others were embedded with diamonds or sapphires. Sometimes, only the pendant made it back and so there were piles of rubies, pearls, amethysts and the like.

Besides the jewels, there was a wide assortment of pocket watches, two doorknockers, a few wedding rings, small ornate knives, feathers of other brightly colored birds, and a glass eye. Not a single thing in the nest had been stolen in the history of the Empyrical Guard. Everything that was collected was either given as a gift or received as a reward.

First, they were messengers, but sometimes they had other tasks. They were guardian hawks, but they were not trained soldiers. The nest of the Empyrical Guard was a place of honor and tradition. Their skills were bred in hundreds of years of instinct.

Aeran, the new Captain of the Guard, could remember stories that his grandfather told of his nestling days that were already legends then. The hawks were the first creatures to settle in the castle when it grew out of the side of the canyon wall.

Of course, they were much larger then. The hawks descended from the great predator birds of the Northern Wood and ruled the Central Plains until the day the bottomless canyon split open.

The cataclysm split the land in four directions and a monstrous beast was trying to claw its way out of the pit. The hawks that survived the disaster flew off to the North, South, East and West to find help. By coincidence, or some say fate, the first human they found in each direction was a beautiful maiden.

Without cause or trepidation, the girls followed the hawks to the edge of the canyon. Peering into the abyss, they could not see the behemoth, but could feel its searing heat and smell its rotting flesh. The four young misses joined hands and offered only what they brought with them from their four homes: Earth, Water, Fire and Air. When the elements joined together, they formed a crystal that dropped to the ground at their bare feet. From the magic that was born that day out of their courage and beauty, the creature was banished in a glorious flash of light and Empyrean took root.

As the castle grew, so did the girls into women and the hawks proclaimed to all the lands of their deed. Humans and animals alike agreed that they should be the first queens of a newly united queendom and that the once separated countries should pledge allegiance to Empyrean.

Aeran was proud of his heritage and to hear his grandfather tell it, the hawks played a significant role in every major event in the history of Empyrean. Therefore, it was no small honor when he was named Captain of the Guard, the first in his family.

This post was not assigned by the wizards who ruled Empyrean when the queens were absent. It was a position nominated and voted by the hawks themselves. The previous captain succumbed to a flesh-eating oak root when he stopped to rest on a hunt.

It had been some time, and not at all in Aeran's short tenure as captain, that the hawks had been given a message to deliver or any other task. So it was a great surprise when the floor swirled in on itself and the spiral staircase appeared from below. A moment later, the oldest and wisest of the wizards climbed up into the aviary.

"Where is the Captain?" called the old man.

Aeran fluffed his chest and alighted on the top of the wizard's crooked staff. "Here, sir. What is your bidding?"

Now that Aeran was close to the man, he could see the sweat on his forehead and the genuine fear in his eyes. The staff trembled under the wizard's grip. Something terrified him.

The ancient sorcerer produced four tiny scrolls from inside his dingy black robes, "I need you and your three swiftest fliers to deliver these at once."

"As you wish," Aeran was exhilarated to be taking his first command. "Who are the recipients?"

The wizard paused, gathered his thoughts and put both hands on the staff to keep it from shaking, "The four queens."

Some of the closest birds let out audible gasps. Everyone in the nest knew what it meant to deliver a message to one of the queens, but to have a message go to all four queens at the same time could only mean that all of Empyrean was threatened.

The wizard continued, "Captain, it is my wish that you personally take charge of the message that is to go to the Eastern Palace by the Sea. It is by far the longest and most treacherous journey and if the guardians of Empyrean feel that you are worthy to be their captain, then I can trust none other to do this most dangerous of tasks."

The horror that the old man was feeling could not reach Aeran's heart. He was too excited and too proud. The honor of being given the most important mission of the most important missions caused his head to swim. The rewards and treasures that would be awaiting him on his return would bless his family's name for generations to come. Then he felt a pinching on his leg.

The wizard was attaching the scroll with a bit of leather strap. Aeran decided quickly who the other messengers would be, who were the fastest. He let out a sharp caw and the nest fell silent, the birds came to rest on their perches and the squawking died out. The only sound was the wind cutting through the tower with a shrill whistle.

"Habrok to the North, Derek to the South and Bellevue to the West." Aeran's hubris was at a peak. He made the decision of the other flyers in an instant and no one second-guessed him. With the power going to his head, he was starting to believe that *his* hawks were invincible. The wizard shook his staff to break the captain from his reverie.

"I will prepare the others, but you must leave now because you have the greatest distance to travel." The wizard pounded the staff on the floor and Aeran took wing. The bold captain circled the roost once, imagining the glory and praise that would be waiting for him and then shot out of the Eastern window.

Glass and crystal surrounded him as he spiraled up to the top of Empyrean. Then Aeran did something that no other hawk claimed to have done before. He cleared the top of the highest towers, then continued straight up, no longer circling, and beating his wings furiously. He never attempted to go this high before, his joints were burning and his breath was short. He could go no further and turned to look down. Even at this height, the castle tower seemed so close, as if it was reaching for him and trying to pull him back down.

Today was his greatest day, his crowning moment and nothing was going to stop this golden-brown guardian from completing his mandate. Aeran folded his wings and tucked his body into a power dive. He was speeding back toward Empyrean.

Below, he could see the wizard at the Southern window, holding what must be Derek out on one boney extended finger. Aeran plummeted down, as close to the outer wall as possible, almost letting his claws skim the surface. He whisked past the man and bird, startling both. The massive wooden drawbridge was directly in his path and it came closer and closer, faster and faster. Aeran's speed was immeasurable and he was getting to the point where even he did not know if he could pull out in time. He momentarily doubted himself and imagined smashing into the wood.

At the last possible moment, the captain opened his wings, swooped up across the length of the bridge and curved to his left. His claws nicked the wood. Several days later, as Wrath and Fury pulled their carriage into the castle, Wrath would notice the two small claw marks scraped into the surface of the wood and wonder what could have made those.

Aeran was now heading due east and laughing with joy. He stretched his wings and the wind shifted. Soon, Empyrean was only a silver needle poking out of the horizon and grassy plains spread out all around him. The grains and grasses swayed and rolled in the breeze like waves on the ocean.

Without growing weary, the Captain of the Guard pressed on and the gateway to the east gradually appeared before him. First, there were small mounds rising out of the grass and then actual hills broke through the rows. As the hills drew their strength from the earth over thousands of years, they grew into mountains.

The Euphoric Mountains marked the true passage into the East. At the base of the tallest peak, Fervent Point, is where the legend says that one of the great hawks found the first Eastern Queen. She was named the Queen of the Eastern Sky because when the hawk sailed to the top of the peak, sky was all he could see. Even the plains below were so far down that they were hidden by clouds. It is said that the hawk came to rest on Fervent Point, heard her singing carried on the wind and dove down to ask for her help.

There is one clear pass that goes directly under Fervent Point and all other ways are nearly uncrossable. Guardian Hawks do not even attempt to fly over the top for fear of being driven mad by the cascade of euphoria rushing down like a continuous emotional avalanche.

Coasting on the air current that rushed through the pass, Aeran could not help but marvel at the historic landmark. Already, he traveled farther from Empyrean than ever before in his life. He did not have to flap his wings for so long that he found himself dozing. His tired eyes dropped closed and he fought to keep them open. Only the threat of smashing into the dull gray rock walls kept him conscious.

Other than almost slamming into the slate and granite, Aeran found himself dreaming. He was dreaming of becoming one of the greatest hawks of all, even greater than the Queen Finders. He was bursting with pride and elation so much that in his dream he was growing. He felt his wingtips brush the wall and assured himself that was only because he had outgrown the narrow crevasse between the mountains. Soon he would be large enough to carry Apis the bull.

Another near collision with stone jutting out snapped him wide-awake. The Euphoric Mountains were weaving their spell on him and he moved faster to escape their effect. Finally clear of the mountains, Aeran sailed over the Dead Forest. He knew this was once called the Royal Forest and now everything appeared as the newer maps showed. He could not understand why this was called the Dead Forest, because he could clearly see things moving beneath the leafless branches of the dry, rotting trees. A feeling in the back of his mind urged him not to go down for a closer look. The woods were not teeming with life, nor were the trees as impressive as the part of the Northern Wood he saw once. These trees were small and depressing, dense in some areas and open to swamps in other areas.

Occasionally, the forest would open into a clearing and these clearings were spotted with caves. He imagined nasty yellow eyes staring out at him.

As much as the Euphoric Mountains elated him, the Dead Forest wringed sadness out of his heart. His travel could not be quick enough to carry him beyond this place.

His spirit picked up only slightly when he saw the start of the wasteland that separated the Dead Forest from the coastal jungles. It was empty and desolate, yet a far more welcome sight than the dread of the forest. What he had not expected was the maze that grew out of the cracks in the ground.

From above, he could see the correct turns to navigate through, but anyone on foot could easily be lost. Many of the passages ended in dead ends or tunnels down into darkness.

As Aeran continued eastward, he now understood why the Queen of the Eastern Sky was carried by the Alkonosts. No one with their sanity would cross this treacherous land on the ground and even if they tried, it would take too many days.

He appreciated the Alkonosts for their beauty and their strength, but it was their hidden power that made them wanted and needed. The enormous birds with women's heads could instill hope in the most forlorn. Their mere presence raised the heads of the lowliest and gave purpose to those without.

The captain gave no thought to their human features. He admired their form in the air from afar and worshipped the hypnotic layers of color in their feathers when near on the few occasions he had seen them. The twin Alkonosts were too big for the aviary, so all except the oldest guardian hawks would perch in the stable on their visit. Aeran was aware that their power affected all of the beings, bird, animal and human.

All of the external exquisiteness paled however when they opened their mouths. The bird-like songs that issued from the perfect full lips of the female faces were enchanting and inspirational. It was as if the voices of a hundred gods flowed through them and comforted all creatures no matter what their belief or passion. On their last visit to Empyrean, the only time Aeran heard them sing, the entire castle paused and all worries were forgotten. That was the kind of hope he needed now and thinking of soon being in their presence drove Aeran onward with renewed strength.

The wasteland ended suddenly at the edge of the old forest, which quickly turned into jungle.

Before he was over the tops of the palm trees, he could smell the ocean. It was a smell entirely new and yet somehow familiar. Rising above the thick saltiness of the air was the smell of fish swimming and dancing about the sea.

Aeran loved fish as a rare delicacy brought to Empyrean by gracious pilgrims. His meals usually consisted of worms and field mice. Never had he imagined the heady aroma of fresh, live seafood.

Instead of looking for the Palace by the Sea, he followed the scent trapped in his beak. The Captain of the Guard had not stopped for six days and his hunger far outweighed his sense of duty. He was going to feast like never before in his life.

Aeran was surrounded by the bright colors of birds that he should have thought of as brothers. They flashed around him and rose in greeting out of the lush greenery beneath him. He ignored them all and darted forward. He could see the waves rolling onto the shore, white foam swishing back and forth.

Then he was surrounded by brilliant white seagulls. They hovered above the jostling brine and then blasted down when an unsuspecting sea creature came too near the surface. Mostly he saw an amazing display of blue, red, or yellow fish being hoisted into the air, but some of the gulls pulled out hard-shelled creatures as well. The victorious birds carried their prizes back to dry land and the banquet raged. Aeran was surprised how easily the seagulls cracked the rusty red shells with their glistening beaks. Then he found himself in the torrid frenzy, slapping wings with other birds, trying to stay in the air and watch the water for prey at the same time.

Now it was his turn. A fat round fish with orange stripes criss-crossing its body slipped its dorsal fin out of the water. He dove. His small body easily dodged the larger gulls and he neared his target. As he drew nearer, he realized that his selected victim was actually more than twice his size. His greed got the better of him and he drove on.

Suddenly there was a shattering cry.

Aeran knew the sound and pulled out of his dive immediately without even touching the water. The seagulls scattered and a flock of curly-tailed parrots burst from the foliage.

Every winged creature of the avian world knew the sound of a dying bird, but there was more to this sound. There was a human quality to it. Aeran knew instantly, but did not want to believe it. The wail continued as if the dying creature or creatures were being tortured. He prayed it was not true, he prayed it was not the Alkonosts.

The captain bolted in several directions trying to discern where the gut wrenching sound was coming from and then settled on following the coastline northward. He spotted the palace standing proudly on a rocky pier, waves dashing against its enduring seawall.

Aeran circled the palace, but the Alkonosts were not there. The weakening cries were coming from the nearby jungle. He passed unnoticed over the heads of the concerned people rushing around the small market at the entrance of the palace.

A moment later, he was cutting through broad leafs and vines. He had forgotten his duty, but now instinct was taking over. Aeran was an Empyrical Guard, the Captain of the Guard, and he pledged to protect every living thing in Empyrean. He let greed and pride steer him off course.

Now the pleas for help and mercy brought him to task. He knew the voices, even on the brink of dying, could instill hope. Aeran hoped he could save them.

His mind did not register the extent of the carnage until it was over. As he neared the wailing sound, entire trees were torn in half, sharp bamboo sticking out between frayed palms. There was a clearing here that was rent out of the jungle only moments before.

Whatever had caused this chaos was now gone. A few feathers and dander drifted in the air above the wrecked grass and trees. He saw the devastated sleigh first, but was more concerned with the shredded feathers pounded into the ground and gooily sticking to the husks of trees. Never had he seen so fine a feather, so sleek like it was oiled, so vibrant as if it were infused with the sun. Even plucked from its owner by the very root, the feathers still seemed alive. He knew the pattern, the way the gold faded to silver and tipped with red. He knew the curved jet-black claw although it was broken and stuck in the ground.

Whatever attacked the Alkonosts was so devastating that there was almost nothing left of the bird-women or the sleigh that carried the Eastern Queen. The sleigh! Aeran darted over to the remains of the sleigh and found its passenger in the same condition as the twins. The steel runners were twisted from the impact and the thick blankets that normally comforted against the wind were unraveled.

The old woman had been beaten severely, partly from being knocked out of the sky and crashing. Something pulled her apart and crushed her bones. Already, her remains were evaporating into golden dust.

The captain understood what it meant to lose one of the queens, but he was furious about the death of the magnificent twin Alkonosts. They were the last of their race and they were needed so badly in the world, and in his life.

He shot into the air, straight up, high enough to see what he was hunting. The assassin was moving west in the direction of the Castle Empyrean. It was not speeding on its way, simply moving ahead.

Aeran began soaring after it, trying to identify the beast. It seemed to be shrouded in a black smoke and skimmed so close to the top of the canopy that he could not pick out a definite shape.

At first, he thought it was a small dragon, but he was sure those were eggshell stories meant to keep the hatchlings from straying. Then he thought it was some other bird, a giant hawk or maybe a condor. He had seen a couple condors' nests in the Euphoric Mountains. Why would a condor come all this way to kill *his* Alkonosts or the Queen of the Eastern Sky?

It did not matter what the monster was or why it committed this vicious atrocity. He was going to punish it.

The shapeless entity did not seem aware of him as he gained on it. Aeran thought it was flapping wings, but the movement was lost in the black cloud that eeked off it. They continued past the edge of the jungle and over the wasteland.

Now the creature moved lower searching for something in the barren labyrinth. Aeran peered ahead and saw a wide opening at the end of a windy vein. The monster was moving lower still, ready to sink into the tunnel.

Aeran thrust forward and stretched open his claws. Seconds before they disappeared into the ground, the captain sank his claws into the beast. He must have caught it by surprise because it let out a thunderous roar. Then Aeran tried to pull away, but now the creature was retaliating. The hawk's claws sank into the putrid cloud like quicksand. Even as he pulled one claw free, the other leg sank in deeper. As he frantically beat his wings to pull away, his feathers became sticky and weighted with the burning tarry flesh. Then they dipped below the surface, into the cave.

If the creature was black, then the inside of the tunnel was a lightless void that made even the hollow eyes of Death seem welcoming to the hawk. Aeran was a prisoner and he had no idea where he was being taken. He could not feel himself sinking into the creature any deeper. He was simply being dragged along like a short-stringed, tattered kite. Even with his acute vision, the captain could not make out anything around him. The entrance had long since faded away and there was no sign of light in the direction they were going.

At least he thought they were moving. It was impossible to tell, but he did not feel closed in and a slight occasional ruffle of wind in his feathers made him think they were still going forward.

The darkness felt like it lasted for a full day. Hunger bounced around the pebbles in his stomach. He was aching and his buried claws were numb. More than that, he had an overwhelming sense of guilt. His own foolishness caused him to fail the queen, his mission and worst of all his fellow hawks. He realized his stupid behavior from the moment he received his orders and he treated it like a game.

Perhaps if he had been more determined and not trying to show off, he could have made it to the eastern palace a day earlier, or at least an hour earlier. If he had not gone to play with the gulls and fish, he could have been there to do something. He did not know what he could have done, except be obliterated along with the Alkonosts, but he would have died in the course of duty. His captor was one hundred times bigger than he was and he knew that any fight would result in his death.

Then a searing pain drilled through Aeran's eyes and bore into his brain. The bird and the beast had been in the dismal cave so long that the approaching daylight was excruciatingly painful. When they rose out of the ground, his lungs tingled with the clean oxygen and he exhaled the acrid smoke that was seeping from the formless beast. It took a moment for him to realize how far they had gone, but then he saw the looming mountains.

The creature moved swiftly underground and they were now rising above the western edge of the Dead Forest. Aeran looked back at the cave they exited and then ahead to the Euphoric Mountains. They were still flying toward Empyrean.

The Captain of the Guard understood now that the monster intended to go after the other queens. He knew it was possible that since the other hawks left the same day that he did, one or two of the queens could already be at Empyrean. This shapeless horror could swoop right over the top of the impenetrable walls. The queens would not even be safe in their sacred towers. Aeran flapped and pulled with only one thought, escape. He had to get free, had to warn someone.

They were now entering the pass directly through the mountains. Aeran, weary from starvation and fear, rested in the vile grip. His mind reeled searching for an opportunity to break loose, but kept returning to a single question, why was he still alive?

Then he felt a crunching, gnashing sensation inside his head. He thought it was supposed to be laughter, but it was full of hatred. Then it occurred to him that the creature was inside his head, reading his mind. Not only did he not warn the Eastern Queen in time, now he was responsible for dooming the remaining queens as well. His thoughts betrayed their location.

In the distance, Aeran spied a condor nest on an outcropping. The mother bird was huddling over her eggs and the father circled, watching the oncoming spectacle. Aeran began screeching for help, but the male condor would not respond. Instead, the father tightened his circle and landed on the precipice next to the mother. Aeran understood that the great bird would be no match for this killer and he had a family to protect.

He decided the eggs would be his rescue. Of course, the condor would not challenge the monster, but a scrawny hawk could be easily dealt with.

"Hey," Aeran shouted one last plea to the nest fading behind him. "Those look like vulture eggs to me."

The protective father was insulted. The mother condor began crying that there was no way they could be vulture eggs. There was only one thing for the male condor to do, Aeran knew he must restore his mate's honor. The condor stretched out his wings, each as long as a horse and cawed once to announce his attack.

Aeran braced for the collision as the condor barreled towards him. Now, the condor was not concerned with the creature, but only wanted to damage the foul-mouthed runt. The condor slammed into Aeran with his beak and knocked him loose, except for two talons on his right claw.

The Captain of the Guard plummeted unconscious to the rocks below. His little body was spinning out of control and his wings were dragging behind him like a cape in the wind. The condor received justice and returned to his nest, unaware of the beast turning back to recapture its guide and prisoner

Tumbling wildly, Aeran awoke. Free of the creature's grasp, he was able to feel the power of the Euphoric Mountains and he was revived. With a hundred feet to spare, he regained control and dove lower into the jagged pass. The beast would have a difficult time following him through the narrow cracks. Instead, the creature kept pace several feet above him where the mountainside gave it room. Once or twice, Aeran was pelted with pebbles and dust as the thing brushed the sides without slowing.

It was a race to the Central Plains, but what then? The captain had no idea how to escape or defeat this monster. When he cleared the mountains, he thought his troubles lessened. A storm formed inside a massive cyclone directly in front of him. Lightning snapped at the hills and mounds around him, setting the dry prairie grass ablaze. There was no way that his enormous pursuer could avoid the deluge of electricity. He thought he might fly straight up into the eye of the storm and have a chance of being safe.

Then he saw how the storm responded to the beast. They moved together, the storm now following in the monster's wake. Aeran pushed on with the last of his strength, barely staying ahead of the tempest. His diminutive heart beat twice as fast as his wings.

In the distance, Empyrean radiated beneath the rising moon. He could see it breathe in rhythm with his own straining lungs. It had only been ten days since he left his perch, but his entire life was gone. In its place was a soul of dedication and honor who only now understood the true meaning of sacrifice. His blood soaked wings flapped slower under the weight of the pouring rain. The storm surrounded the castle and spread out across the surrounding plains.

He had to go up, over the top of the wall. He climbed, veins pulsing in his neck, broken talons throbbing. The beast was toying with him now. It drifted back as the gale began a volley of thunder and lightning that swatted Aeran around like a stick caught in a river's current.

Aeran was moving only on instinct when he could control his own movements. He believed he would be safe within the boundaries of the ancient castle. There was no way the monster or storm could hurt him here. One quick bolt of lightning burned off his tail feathers proving him wrong. He felt like the black beast was savoring its deathblow, waiting for the perfect moment.

On the balcony, Aeran saw a varied group staring back at him. He recognized the old wizard and the three remaining wonderful queens. He knew that he would only have one last chance. A second before the creature snatched him, Aeran closed his wings and fell, aiming for the balcony. He dropped instantly out of the creature's grasp.

His last coherent thought was that he missed the landing. He never really felt the soft gentle hand pull him out of the air. He was only vaguely aware of the dazzling flash of golden light that defeated his tormentor. The captain did not even have a recollection of his final words. He could sense the people around him, but he could only see the pointed face of his grandfather. The old bird was welcoming him and assuring him, "You've done well. Now it's time to rest."

Aeran, Captain of the Guardian Hawks of Empyrean, slipped into darkness.

Chapter 4

A Day at the Beach

The village by the sea where the two girls lived was called Banookanook.

It was built on the sand at the edge of the ocean. The front doors to some of the handmade huts opened onto the surge of the highest tide. The Nookans who lived there would rise in the morning and step outside their home to wet their feet at the start of the day.

Every part of their life was the water. The ocean gave them food, shelter, clothing and protection when they needed it. The few dozen huts that made up the village were spread out across an isolated beach. To the north and south were high rock walls, to the west was a dangerous jungle and to the east swelled the never-ending, life-giving sea.

For the Nookans, the ocean was everything.

It did provide their shelter in the form of the large, spiked shells that lined the walls and roofs of their homes. These shells, so big that it would take two grown men to carry them, would wash up onto the white sand on nights when the moon was full. Almost perfectly round, the dark green shells were studded with razor-like barbs. It would only take four shells to make the simplest huts, three walls and a roof, but over time, the oldest families created four and five room dwellings. In the hundreds of years that Banookanook stood waiting for each morning's sunrise, not a single Nookan claimed to have seen the animal from which these shells were shed.

Their food and clothing came from the bountiful water as well. A myriad of vegetables and seaweeds grew near the shore where the ocean was only knee deep. And in the eddies, near the rock walls, smaller creatures were trapped and deshelled or skinned to make the most rudimentary clothing. The Nookans were modest and had no shame in barely covering their healthy, dark-skinned bodies. It was only in the last five hundred years when explorers began frequenting their shores that the Nookans began wearing clothes at all.

The explorers were looking for a new place to build a castle for their queen. That is when the Queen of the Eastern Sky came to the Nookans' beach. To the north of Banookanook, she ordered her palace to be constructed. Before that, she held her court in a place far to the west called Soria Moria. The Nookans told stories to their children about Soria Moria, the castle hidden below the magical mountains so far away that they could walk for their entire lives and never get there.

When the Palace by the Sea was finished, more strangers came from the west, building their own small village at the castle gates. Soon the village grew into a small town and it was called Edge Town.

The Nookans did not understand the names or the customs that the strangers brought with them. These new people loved Banookanook and treated its inhabitants with kindness. They loved the white sand that swayed back and forth with the waves because outside of that beach, the rest of the coastline was covered in a dull brown shale that was always ripe with algae. The queen herself said there was no more beautiful place in all of her queendom and then the strangers became family.

Westerners shared their foods, clothing and building secrets with the Nookans. The ancestors' homes were torn down and rebuilt with the shells, but also with the wood of the nearby jungle. The fish they caught were mixed with the filthy animals the Westerners so proudly hunted on the land. Finally, a western man married a Nookan woman. Under the reign of the Queen of the Eastern Sky, the true Nookans came to an end.

Most of the time, the village of Banookanook was quiet, except when the queen brought guests for a holiday. Most of the time, the mixed race still practiced the old traditions. They still took their bounty from the sea, but used boats and spears instead of their hands. Instead of taking what they needed, the husbands and fathers would catch their fill and take the butchered fish to the market at the gates of the palace.

Most of the time, it was the perfect place to be a child.

At least, that was how Zandria felt. She was left to care for her younger sister, Olena, every day when their father went fishing. The two Nookan girls would play by the water's edge, building their own castles out of the soft, warm sand. They would take turns being the queen or the sea monster, but some days, they both wanted to be the monster. Their mother died six years ago when Olena was born, so the girls spent most of their young lives alone.

Their father, because he was almost pure Nookan, was one of the most successful fishers in their village. He would work the longest hours and spend the most time at the palace market. He was well compensated and always brought presents for his daughters that would be waiting for them when they awoke each morning, even when he was not. Zandria and Olena wore dresses that were traded in the market, unlike the other Nookan children. They played with brushes and hand mirrors and jewelry which did not make them very popular with their neighbors either.

Despite what their father gave them, the girls did not favor him. They were told by everyone that they took their features and temperament from their mother. Both of the sisters had such natural beauty that the queen left a standing invitation for them to live at the palace. And when they refused at their father's instruction, the queen instructed all of her guests to visit Banookanook and stand in their presence.

Olena, with her bushel of tight curly hair and deep innocent eyes, said the visitors were so funny when they would come and stare at her and her sister without saying a word and then leave. She announced that she did not understand why they were there or what made her so special.

Zandria, with four more years over her sister, was realizing she was someone important. Then the games changed and everyday Zandria was queen and Olena was the monster. And the water monster had many more chores than the queen did.

Under Zandria's careful instruction, Olena learned many skills like cooking and cleaning, so her older sister could dedicate more time to their guests. While Zandria primped and preened, the onlookers still found Olena the prettier even with fish grease on her face. Zandria was certainly a pretty girl, but she was stuck at that awkward age. She was tall for a ten year old and Olena had the advantage of still being very much a child. In a few years, there is no question, Zandria would become quite beautiful.

The two girls spent every waking moment together and grew further apart. Zandria, as the make-believe queen, did her best to hide her jealousy, while pure Olena became the willing servant. Zandria found it easy to talk down to her sister. This did not make her feel especially good, but it did make her feel important.

However, sometimes still, when they were on the beach under the bright morning sun with only the two of them, they were happy. They were two little girls enjoying life and laughing with someone they loved.

This was one of those days. They found something to laugh about. A tiny bird, like none they ever saw before, was trying to cut in among the seagulls. The little brown feathers kept disappearing behind the white flapping wings. Olena was digging a moat for Zandria's newest palace when she looked up to see this poor bird in such a predicament.

"Ka!" said Zandria. *Ka* was a Nookan expression that had as many meanings as the mouths that uttered it. Normally, Zandria used it to express her anger or disbelief. "Why have you stopped digging, servant?" Zandria finished still in character.

Olena smiled and pointed up at the confused looking hawk. Zandria brushed her wavy brown hair out of her face and cupped her hands around her eyes to block the sun.

"What is that fool doing?" Zandria scoffed. She was not concerned for his safety. The outcome would be far more entertaining to let him mingle. The other gulls were busy feasting before the late fishing boats made it to this end of the beach, so they were content to let the stranger join in as long as he did not interrupt the meal. The girls laughed together, the same laugh from each mouth that would be a song to any father's ears. The bird looked lost, but ravenously hungry and to the girls' sheer delight he looked like he was going to dive into the water.

Zandria laughed harder when she saw the fish that the gulls were pulling up, "It's a school of spotted regins. They're twice the size of that stupid bird."

Olena joined with a chorus of giggles, "You don't think the bird can pick one up?"

"Ka, a regin could probably swallow something that small in one bite." Zandria pointed, "He's diving."

The hawk was now in his descent and an instant before he hit the surface, a horrible scream split the air. The smile left both girls' faces, first because they did not get to see the battle, but then because there was something nauseating about the scream. Something in the dreadful voice left a pit in Zandria's stomach.

Something terrible happened.

The girls scrambled up the shore. Zandria noticed that Olena trampled through her sister's sandcastle, probably on purpose she thought. They rushed in among the huts, but nothing seemed to be wrong there. Then they spotted the silly little bird again, he was flying desperately toward the Palace by the Sea.

It did not take long for some of the Nookan men to come running from the market. They spoke to the elders and some of the nearby women.

Neither Zandria nor Olena could hear what happened, so they waited for their father. He already caught a full boat that morning and left for the market when they were coming down to the beach.

Finally, he came running. When he saw his girls standing safely in front of their home, he ran even faster and scooped them up together in his arms. He hugged them painfully tight. Zandria saw a look of fear and sadness on his face.

Almost together, they asked, "What happened, father?"

He was trying to catch his breath and gather his thoughts when Olena interrupted him, "Your squeezing too tight, Pop."

The sun worn man faked a laugh and set his daughters back on the ground. He knelt in the sand in front of them and leaned against their doorpost. He was a strong and healthy man, but whatever happened shocked him badly.

He was beginning to breathe normally, "Girls, something has happened." He paused, fighting back a tear, "We think...we don't know for sure, but we think the queen is dead."

"What do you mean?" Zandria knew the legends, "The queen can't die, can she?"

"Something flew over the palace. She tried to get away. I watched the Alkonosts pull her sleigh right over the top of my head. Whatever the beast was that was chasing her, it followed her straight into the jungle. Did you hear the Alkonosts' cries? Some of the men went into the jungle, but I had to make sure you two were alright."

He hugged them again so tightly that it was their turn to catch their breath.

"Listen, I have to go back to the palace and find out for sure. But if the Queen of the Eastern Sky is gone, we will have to leave here immediately."

Zandria asked, "Why? What do you mean?"

"I will explain it to you when I get back. For now, pack some clothes and food and I will bring back a cart from the market." He kissed each of his daughters on the forehead for the last time and headed toward the rock wall and beyond that to the Palace by the Sea.

To Zandria, it now felt strangely dark inside their low-ceilinged home despite the bright sun outside. Still, neither Zandria, nor apparently Olena, felt like lighting the candles. They remained silent and followed their father's instructions.

Moving from room to room, the cool sand inside was soothing to Zandria's feet after being on the beach all morning. She went to the kitchen area and started putting a variety of fruits into a small net. As she stuffed it full, she remembered tying this net for her father, hoping he would use it on his boat. Instead, the handmade gift was hung on the wall and soon forgotten.

Their father was a distant man. Zandria was sure that he loved both her and Olena, but it was difficult for him to show it. She suspected it was because they reminded him of her mother. Both were fair skinned, not nearly as dark as he was or thick boned like true Nookans. Even among their family, both girls sometimes felt like outsiders. Zandria remembered one other thing, today was the first time he kissed her since Olena was born.

Olena wandered into the back bedroom and began sorting through their dresses. The bright colored ones were always her favorite, especially the few with ruffled collars and sleeves, but she grabbed the simple white work clothes for the trip. The young girl had to dig down deep in her clothes box to find the old dresses. It had been a long time since they were worn.

Olena confided in her older sister that she liked when the queen sent them gifts. She even noticed that none of the other children in the village had clothes like theirs or any of the other presents. She was a smart girl and it irritated Zandria that she noticed things quicker than her. At first, when the clothes came from the palace, Olena wanted to share them with the other girls, but Zandria would not let her.

Zandria realized that they were the queen's favorites and although they never visited her, the two sisters received very special treatment. Olena openly worried that none of the other Nookans were liked by the strangers, but Zandria assured her that they were treated better because they were better. Even when someone from the village married someone from the palace, the children would be the same stocky, brown as anyone else born in Banookanook.

Zandria would tell her younger sibling that they were special and that they should act like it. Olena said she wanted to believe it, but still looked guilty because of it. Olena wished aloud too many times that she had met her mother. Zandria did not know that her little sister often pretended that

Zandria was her mother. Everyone said they both looked like her, so in Olena's mind it made her happy. One time, she did announce that it would be easier for her to do chores for her caring mother than her bossy sister.

Olena did sneak her favorite purple dress into the bag with Zandria's pink pants and shirt. She tucked the purple cloth deep beneath the dingy work clothes that used to be bright white and tied the bag closed. She slung the heavy bag over her shoulder and wobbled back and forth trying to regain her balance. The sack was now almost the same size as her. She spun around once and then angled for the door back into the main room. Before she was halfway, Olena gave up on trying to carry the bag and let it plop to the ground. She dragged it behind her, erasing her footprints as she joined Zandria, already seated by the cold fire pit in the front room.

It was too early in the day to light a fire, but Zandria huddled close to the stones as if they were giving off heat. Olena put the clothes bag next to the food net and sat beside Zandria. Still, neither of them spoke.

The quiet waiting was broken by a noise from the back of the house. It was a scratching sound on the wall that worked its way up to a clicking noise on top of the shelled roof. Whatever was making this noise, it was coming closer. The girls watched the smoke hole above them, waiting for the sound to reveal its creator. The rapid clicking dashed around the roof and grew slightly louder as it neared the hole directly over the fire pit. Glaring sun spilled into the otherwise dark room and a shape appeared in the opening.

At first, neither girl could identify the shape outlined by the bright sun, but they could tell it had a small round head with a wild puff of hair shooting out in all directions. Then the creature dropped in the hole, falling towards last night's ashes in the pit, but stopped in mid-air. Now they could see it. A quzzak was dangling by his tail from the smoke hole. He was swinging in front of them, his crazy white hair looking even crazier for being upside down.

"Kez!" Olena cried.

"Why you little quzzak! You almost scared us." Zandria wanted to discipline him.

As a response, Kez swung his gray and white body like a pendulum on a clock until he had enough momentum to flip over and land on his feet in the sand. Without a word, he dashed into the kitchen area, leaping from the floor, scrambling up a support post to leap onto the table. Olena shook uncontrollably with giggles. The small, monkey-like quzzak ran in circles on the table looking for something. Not finding it, he grabbed the edge of the table and leaned over as if he expected the object of his search to be stuck to the underside.

"I say," Kez was trying to be proper as he straightened himself to face the girls. "Where exactly are the tangerines. I know they were here yesterday. I should know, I brought them." He shrugged, flashing a bit of black fur hidden beneath the gray that ran down his back.

Olena shrugged back gleefully.

Kez continued, "You don't suppose I've already eaten them do you? No. I should know that as well."

Zandria was not in the mood for games. Still seated, she hoisted the fruit bag for him to see, "Ka, they're right here. We're going on a trip when father gets home."

Kez eyed the bag stuffed with tangerines, plantains and half a loaf of market bread. He did a quick back flip and then dove off the table. Rolling head first across the floor, he made it to his feet and jumped onto the net before Zandria had time to move it.

"Bravo," Olena was clapping at the performance. Kez was picking at the knot, but Zandria shooed him away.

"Alright. Easy girl. You do know I was teasing?" Kez scooted back making himself comfortable at their feet. "I would not eat any food except that which I could get my hands on." He began grooming his irrepressible mane. "Now tell me about this trip."

Zandria wanted to start, but Olena blurted out, "I don't know where we're going, but father says we have to take a trip and after the big noise in the jungle he said maybe the queen was dead, I hope she isn't dead, she's awfully nice, but if she is, he had to go back and find out and then we are going to take a trip." The only reason she stopped talking was that she was out of breath.

Kez licked his paw again and ran it down the part on the center of his head, "I have no idea what you said, my dear. However, I suspect it has to do with the Queen of the Eastern Sky being dead."

Both girls gasped.

"It is true," he went on, "but it means very little to us tree dwellers. Should mean very little to you Nookans either. Still, I have one of those feelings. We here by the sea have no real thing to do with the rest of the world and your queen was very much part of the rest of the world. Most likely, they will pick a new queen and life will go on. The saddest part is that you two will have no one to send you trinkets for a while." He stopped talking to pick at a burr on the end of his tail.

Zandria looked at her sister and then into the quzzak's face which looked like an old man. In fact, she knew he was the oldest and wisest of his tribe. He was the quzzakian Storykeeper and learned all of their languages and histories passed down through the jungle branches over the generations.

"Kez, you have been our friend for a long time and I don't think you would lie to us, but there is something you're not saying," said Zandria.

"I told you I have one of those feelings." He let his tail drop and snake around behind him. Then he leaned in close, "It may be nothing, unless...."

"Girls. Zandria. Olena." Their father's voice called from outside.

Kez glanced at the door and then back to the waiting faces of his audience, "Unless the queen was murdered. It would take something quite bad and quite powerful to do that."

The girl's father swiped back the curtain that marked their front door, "Why didn't you come when I called...." He saw Kez scrambling out the kitchen window. "Ka, that thieving pest. At least that will be the last we see of him." He saw the two bags the girls had prepared, grabbed them and turned back outside.

Zandria followed, but Olena watched at the window for a moment longer. Zandria did not see Kez poke his head up and give Olena a wink. She winked back and then ran outside.

Olena popped out the front door to be face to face with a gigantic toad. The enormous red amphibian was harnessed to a two-wheeled cart made of bamboo and leather straps. The beast of burden was ready to carry them on their journey and their father already put the sack and food net in the cart.

"Father, do you expect us to ride with that?" Zandria was disgusted. The jungle frogs were far bigger than what made her comfortable.

He reassured her, "The ride will be a little bumpy, but this was the fastest thing I could get. We have to leave now."

"I don't want to go." Olena moved behind her sister.

Zandria, used to being the boss, took the lead in talking to their father. Since she felt he was practically a stranger to them anyway, she said frankly, "We are not leaving our home because some stupid queen died. If you don't tell us what's going on, then we are staying right here."

The fisherman looked surprised by Zandria's commanding presence and must have decided it would be best to explain everything. "Look, I know

I haven't been there for you a lot. It's been hard for me. You are your mother, both of you darlings. You look and sound like her, you even smell like her. When I lost her, I lost the part of me that knew how to love and I couldn't stand to be around either of you. I was wrong, but it's not too late to try to make up for it. Now I have to get you out of here before I lose you too."

He was weeping, but continued his story, "Your mother was from the west, you know that. She was the most beautiful woman I have ever seen, but I was only a villager. She would come down to the beach every day to watch me fish. I still don't know why she picked me."

Zandria, thinking about her lost mother, started crying with their father. Olena joined her.

"Now she picked me and not long after you came along, Zandria. I was so proud and suddenly I was an important man at the market and the palace. The old queen was always concerned for your mother and took an interest in you before you were out of the cradle. Four years later, I was blessed again. Only a week after your birth, Olena, your mother was called to the palace for a private audience with the queen. I didn't find out what happened until it was too late."

"You told me she died giving birth," Zandria was angered by the revelation.

"I never told you the truth, because I still don't quite believe it. Your mother chose not to tell me, but the queen herself told me later. The old wizards at Empyrean. They say it's a castle to the west. The Empyrean wizards believed your mother was an heiress. They believed she could be the next Queen of the Eastern Sky."

"I never filled your heads with the strangers' fairytales, but they say there are four queens, not only ours. They say that the queens are chosen by fate and live for hundreds of years to rule over the four queendoms of our world. I never gave any thought to the rest of the world. That isn't our way. But your mother was part of that world and when the queen learned of the possibility of your mother being the next queen, she called her to the palace. The queen told me that she was not ready to pass on the throne, but your mother chose to go to Empyrean for training."

"She left when you were a week old, little one, but she never made it to the castle in the west. To this day, the queen still has men searching for her. And every day, I go to the market and wait by the gates for her to return."

The father and daughters hugged and kissed as never before in their lives. Zandria hated the man for lying about her mother's death. She was not ready to quit blaming Olena for it, but loved the man for searching for her.

"But why do we have to leave?" Olena asked, looking confused.

He tried to explain without sobs clogging his throat, "My child, don't you understand. If your mother was to be a queen, then it is possible that your big sister is the next in line. With the queen dead, Empyrean needs a new queen right away."

"Ka, I knew it. I knew I was meant for something more than salt water and sand." Zandria slapped her fist into her open palm.

Olena said, "But didn't you say the queen was picked by fate?"

"I did, little one. There is no family line or way to predict the next queen. Sometimes, the wizards can read signs and guess. But the new queen is not found until she stands in the Great Hall at Empyrean with the other three queens. That is why we have to go. There will probably be others, but if there is any chance that my girl is the next queen, we have to take it."

Kez listened to the whole story from the edge of the roof, "But why must you go in such a hurry?"

The fisherman snatched up a shell to throw at the quzzak, but Olena grabbed his hand. "He's our friend, daddy."

"Why?" The father glared at the quzzak and continued, "I'll tell you what the men at the palace told me. The Queen of the Eastern Sky was attacked and murdered. The four queens are the most magical, powerful people in all of our world and if someone or something could do that to one of them, then they are very dangerous. If there is any chance that Zandria is to be queen, then it is likely that these evil beings know of her already. That is why we have to leave right n........"

His last word was cut short by a muddy dog-like creature pouncing on him. In the fray, Zandria could see teeth and claws ripping at her father. He was fighting back until another of these beasts walked around the corner on its hind legs. When the frightening thing saw the fight, it dropped to all fours and charged in.

There was nothing that could be done for their father. Besides seeing him clawed and bitten in front of them, it hurt Zandria worse to know that she only now truly loved him.

Then it was too late. The fisherman was still and quiet. The two animals circled back around blocking the girls' escape in either direction.

Zandria thought they were saved when three more men climbed down the rock wall and ran towards them. She watched them running and thought it was strange that they only wore cloth around their waists and nothing else. Maybe if they were Nookans, they might dress like that, but she knew these were not Nookans.

Then, as they ran, the men began to change. Each in turn fell to their hands and knees, but continued heading forward. From the shortened distance, she could see their fingernails turn into claws and their ears stretch out on their heads. Hair covered their bodies in an instant and tails uncurled out of nowhere. Beyond belief, the newcomers transformed from three men into three more of these vicious monsters.

Olena grabbed her sister's arm so tight that the older girl's hand was turning blue.

The giant toad panicked and began violently trying to hop away. The cart was whipping around behind it. The two girls pressed against the wall of their house avoiding the spikes on the shells. The attackers were jumping out of the way each time the cart thrashed past.

Kez took the opportunity and dropped down on top of Olena's curls. "Werewolves! We have to get out of here! This way!" He pointed into the jungle behind their house. Olena heard him and pulled her sister along.

The werewolves were too busy dodging the frog to notice their prey escaping. Zandria watched over her shoulder at an absurd dance of wolf, toad and cart. One of the wolves was smacked in the face with a cart wheel and his own blood splattered on his filthy brown fur. The giant flippers were more than a single hunter could handle and it eventually took all but the wounded monster to bring the creature down. Leaping and scratching, the wolves avoided the cart. Then two of them made it onto the frog's back. Then they were out of sight.

The wolves continued to gnaw and dig at its back until the toad collapsed. The wolf with the broken nose was the first to turn back into a human. With blood still dripping from his flat, twisted nose, he kicked the dying toad in the head.

The other werewolves transformed and began searching the surrounding huts for the girls. In Zandria's memory, the five men could have been brothers. They were all short men with broad shoulders that skipped the necks and turned directly into square-shaped heads with the same angry expressions. They were supernaturally strong, but did not have much muscle to show for it. They had the bodies of men that ate too much and worked too little. And none of them spoke a single word.

Zandria would never forget the face of their leader. Now with a broken nose, he gave hand signals for which houses to search. He bent over to examine the net of food and the ripped open sack of white clothes that were tossed from the cart. Then he walked down to the beach to check a couple of idle boats.

A commotion started on the north end of the beach. Some Nookans ran to the palace for help and were now returning with palace guards. The leader of the wolfmen ran into the center of the village. He gave one short whistle at a pitch that could only be heard by his assassins and they came running to him. He gestured for two of them to go into the jungle, noticing the two small sets of footprints that led in that direction. He signaled for the other two to follow his escape to the south wall of the beach.

The girls were running desperately through the short palms and bamboo, with Kez barley holding on. Zandria did not have time to look back again or even think about their home or their father.

Olena was still holding Zandria's hand and they were running as fast and crying as hard as they could. Olena was holding onto Kez with her other hand like holding onto a hat on a windy day. In Zandria's free hand was a bundle of clothes that she managed to save as they slipped away. It was nothing fancy, a sleeveless purple dress and a pair of long pink pants. She did not have the foresight of needing new clothes, but simply grabbed them in her panic.

Kez was watching for a tree big enough for all of them. When he saw one rapidly approaching, he leaped onto one of its lower branches and called to them, "This way!"

Zandria stopped in her tracks, looked around on the ground and realized he was up in the tree. She boosted her sister up first and followed close behind. She would not let her stop climbing until they were as high as they could go. Hidden above the foliage, she sat in terror, tears streaming down both her and Olena's faces. Kez was trying to comfort them, caressing their arms and patting their hands.

Zandria started to talk, but Kez hushed her. Down below, she could hear the snapping of twigs and rustling of leaves. Something was moving around under them. She knew it had to be the werewolves. Olena's eyes grew wide as the sound grew nearer. Her breathing was shallow and she hugged Kez closely. Zandria leaned over the edge of the branch and could see one of them in human form. He was looking for them and she thought the others must be close by. The low-browed man leaned against the tree they were in and recounted his trail. He must not be able to see where they climbed up, thought Zandria.

Then there was a fluttering that caught his attention. A few feet away, the bushes wiggled. The bad man stealthily dropped to the ground and changed into his wolf form. Like the best of predators, he eased toward the bush without a sound. The green leaves moved again and the werewolf sprang in. An instant later, he bolted out yelping with a flock of parrots on his tail. Zandria thought there must have been a hundred of them. Brightly colored feathers of green and red and blue gushed out in every direction. The normally peaceful song of the lone bird was a cacophony of shrill noise. The girls clapped their hands over their ears and Kez buried his head in Olena's lap.

Parrots were flying in fear without a unified course. Most were spiraling between the trees, driving the wolfman further away. Then some started to break through the canopy. The frightened birds smashed the leaves and branches around the sisters and Zandria could feel their hiding place collapsing. Before she knew it, Zandria, Olena and Kez plummeted to the hard ground.

The last of the parrots hurried off and the peace of the jungle returned. Kez pulled himself up to a low branch, scanning for any sign of the wolves. They were alone.

"I don't think we should stay here," Kez was urging the girls to get up. The girls stood up, their dresses ripped and tear-streaked faces covered with dirt. Kez walked by their feet urging them in the right direction. Then he jumped up to swing and flip from branches and vines to lead the way. "We can spend the night at my place and figure out what to do in the morning. At least, you can get cleaned up and rest safely."

Olena skipped behind Kez, already in a better mood because of his acrobatics. Zandria walked a few steps behind, constantly looking back over her shoulder. The girls spent an uneasy night in the treetops of the quzzak village somewhere far from their home. Zandria was somewhat comforted by Kez standing guard as they tried to sleep.

In the morning, the girls washed in the nearby stream and dressed in the clothes that Zandria managed to save. Olena seemed excited to have her favorite dress, but Zandria only had a pair of pants. She ripped the tattered hem off the dirty dress she was wearing, turning it into a shirt. Her pink pants contrasted with the blue remains.

Kez was foraging for breakfast and returned with two bunches of grapes. The girls ate on the bank of the stream.

"I think we should go back to the palace. We should be safe there," said Zandria.

Kez did not look too sure about that idea, "Zandria, if the monsters that were chasing us were the same ones that got the queen, then maybe the palace isn't too safe. Still, maybe we should at least go there to find out what's happening."

Zandria agreed and did not give Olena any other choice. When they were done eating, they immediately started back toward the shore. As they were finding their trail, they came upon a clearing. Zandria thought this strange because the jungle did not have natural glens as far as she knew. Something happened here.

Zandria saw palm trees smashed and broken in half. The underbrush was trampled and pounded into the ground. She could not identify the remains of the animal or animals strewn all over. At one end of the clearing, she saw a pile of rubble that looked like a crushed sleigh. Kez darted back and forth picking up feathers and smelling snapped limbs. Olena went to the sleigh and pulled up a shredded blanket. Where Aeran the hawk had seen the queen's body the day before was now only a faint outline of gold dust that whisked up into the air when Olena moved the blanket.

"This is it. This is the queen's sleigh. This is where the werewolves attacked her." Zandria was mad and scared at the same time.

Kez hopped up on the front handle bar of the sleigh, "I don't think those wolves did this. I'm afraid it was something much bigger and much worse."

Olena moved closer to Kez and he squirreled up onto her shoulder.

"Then we definitely have to go to the palace," Zandria said. She was determined and started walking without waiting for a response from the other two. Before she was at the edge of the clearing, a man came charging out of the brush and ran straight into her. They both toppled to the ground.

The man looked terrified and was back on his feet in an instant. He did not even check to see if she was all right and started running again. Zandria called after him, "What's your problem?"

"The palace is under attack. There are werewolves everywhere and the ground opened up." The man finished talking, looked around, apparently decided on a new course and ran off.

"Now aren't you glad we didn't go there last night?" Kez asked.

Zandria was annoyed at being proved wrong, "What do you suggest then?"

Kez bounced to the ground and stood at Zandria's feet. "There's only one choice that I can see. We try to find Empyrean."

"What!" Zandria shouted. "Are you crazy? Even if it's real and we could find it, it would take forever to get there, especially dragging this baby." She pointed at Olena.

"I am not a baby!"

Kez stood his ground, "You heard your father. You may be the new queen. Why else do you think those werewolves were after us, after you? It won't be difficult for them to find us again. We don't have any other choice."

Zandria looked in the direction of the palace and then to the west. "Fine, but you're responsible for her. I can't be queen and worry about a baby sister."

Zandria stomped off with Kez and Olena following.

Chapter 5

The Morning Started with a Hole in the Ground

The Palace by the Eastern Sea formed when the East Wind blew. The Queen of the Eastern Sky asked the wind to build her a castle on the shore in this newfound paradise. The result was a sprawling palace of curves and pillars, balconies overlooking the ocean and spiral staircases that started in the middles of rooms then swirled up to nowhere. Its magnificence and mysteries were second only to those of Castle Empyrean itself, although it was the youngest of all the castles in the land. Its youth made it weak.

The expansive courtyard always remained clear for the latest flying vehicle or creature that would catch the queen's fancy. It was in this wide-open space that one of the traveling merchants noticed it. On the same morning that Zandria and Olena were watching Aeran attempt to fish with the seagulls, a single dark crack split the hardened sand. It was no longer than an average man if one would lie next to it. The unusual thing about it was with all the wind and water, the palace did not have a single crack anywhere else.

While the merchant ran to tell someone, anyone, the crack doubled in size. By the time the merchant returned with two of the palace caretakers, the crack was venting a noxious steam. One of the caretakers remained at the site and the other left to inform the queen's advisor.

As advisors are inclined to do, this one inspected the crack and decided that it was nothing with which to bother the queen. No sooner had he issued this statement, then the ground vibrated beneath their feet and the crack opened up to become a small crevasse. Black slime was bubbling from the new cracks around the edges of the new hole. The merchant turned to the caretaker for an answer and the caretaker turned toward the advisor. The advisor was already running back into the palace.

No time was lost in harnessing the twin Alkonosts to the queen's sleigh. They had been bathing. Their long locks of hair were freshly braided and their feathers were preened. The human face on either bird showed no sign of worry, but they understood that they must take the queen away until the hole was determined to be dangerous or not. They served the Queen of the Eastern Sky since they were old enough to fly. As the last of their race, the twin sisters performed their duty with honor and grace. The Alkonosts represented the Eastern Sky and were as much a part of the throne as the woman who sat upon it. The queen was loaded into the sleigh as quickly as the caretakers dared jostle her aging joints. A thick blanket covered the old woman to comfort her from the cooler temperatures in flight and the Alkonosts took wing.

The Alkonosts pulled the sleigh over the smooth sand, gradually flapping their long wings faster. After a moment, they were in the air and the harnessed sleigh followed. They pulled the sleigh directly over the growing hole and continued higher to clear the arcing palace wall. Then a murky, black, shapeless cloud leaked out of the hole, spinning almost in a ball as its tail spilled out behind it. When the entire mass was free of its underground home, it followed the queen's path.

Not all the speed and power gifted to the Alkonosts was enough to outrun the smoky monster. They barely cleared the palace wall when the beast hammered the rear of the sleigh. The twins tried to maneuver, but the sleigh was too heavy and they were out of control. The creature rose above them and dived down, knocking Alkonosts, sleigh and queen to the jungle below. That was the last time that any of her subjects saw the Queen of the Eastern Sky.

Amidst the shattering cries of the Alkonosts, the Palace by the Eastern Sea shuddered and rumbled. Five thick-browed almost naked men climbed out of the hole. They spoke to no one and walked past the onlookers, intent on their target. A nearby child thought one of the men had a tail, but when he rubbed his eyes, it was gone.

People began running in every direction as panic took hold of the palace. No one knew if the queen was alive, but they suspected the worst. Nookans fled back to Banookanook. Merchants scooped up what they could and ran towards the jungle. Caretakers and advisors retreated into the palace hoping to find somewhere to hide. Chaos and fear eased into the peoples' hearts. The peace and security that flowed from the living queen was gone.

As the sun set, the five wolfmen, who could not find Zandria or her sister, returned to the hole. They dropped over the edge and disappeared from sight if anyone had been looking.

When the next morning came, the hole that released the queen's final fate peeled in on itself. The ground caved away and the hole became a chasm. Almost the entire courtyard fell into a hole twice the size of the Nookans' village. The frightened people inside the palace could not see past the billowing smoke and ash to the front gate. Most of the people in the market scattered, but a few greedy men remained looting the small stores.

A horn blared from deep inside the ground. It was a signal that marked the departure of the werewolves from their underground lair. Twenty-five wolfmen clawed their way to the surface. Each, in his human form, clambered onto the ledge and stood near the front gate. A few took to their wolf form and scaled the walls to either side of the open doorway. They were scanning the jungle for their prey. The looters turned their attention to the palace at the horn blast and were now face to face with the emotionless men. The bald headed man with the broken nose stood in front of the pack as their leader. He raised an eyebrow at the thieves and casually waved a pointing finger in their direction. Two men to his right acknowledged the order and headed toward the former merchants. As they walked, they fell forward and changed into wolves before their front feet hit the ground. The amateur crooks turned to run, but only one of the three got away. He sped into the jungle unknowingly in the direction of the queen's crash site. This man would quickly run into Zandria.

The men who had not changed shifted partially into wolves. With animal heads and human bodies, they began to howl and wail at their innocuous victory. Finishing their cry as wolves, the assassins formed hunting parties and crept into the jungle in different directions.

After the werewolves scattered and the only sound was the escaping poison gas, one more pair of hands appeared on the ledge. The hands were small and the splintered fingernails were black with filth under the tips. These were not the hands of another wolfman, but the hands of a dirty, lost boy.

The boy, about ten years old if anyone had ever celebrated his birthday, pulled himself up out of the hole. His body was covered in grime and chains dangled from his bruised wrists as well as his ankles. The chains had been broken off short, but the manacles were still tightly in place cutting into his arms and legs. Whatever clothes he once had, he long since out grew and now only a tattered, yellowing rag dangled around his waist. He squinted his eyes in the unfamiliar sun and tried to stand upright against the fresh scars on his back. The boy was dark, not like the Nookans, but dark around the edges like he had not been above ground for most of his short life. His nappy, uncut hair hung in his face and he pushed it out of his eyes with one scraped hand. He surveyed his surroundings as best he could while he adjusted to the bright light.

"Well, it can't be any worse," he said to himself. As an afterthought, he added, "Stupid werewolves."

He was exhausted, so he sat down on the edge of the pit, letting his legs dangle into the void from which emerged. He leaned over forward so that his chest almost touched his knees and peered down. He snorted hard once, again and then spit a large wad of snot and saliva into the hole in a defiant gesture of farewell. The abused boy crawled away from the edge, rolled over on his side and fell asleep.

The ball of spit dropped down into the darkness and continued falling long after it seemed a possible distance for a human or animal to climb. Finally, so far down into the depths that the sun directly over the chasm could not penetrate, the phlegm splattered on the bottom. The wet sound echoed in the enormous chamber and the echo danced around the mouths of the caves that emptied into it.

In the darkness, a lone creature supervised the werewolves' departure. This being was small, no bigger than a Guardian Hawk of Empyrean, and he had a bulging shell on his back. His slug-like body poked out from under the shell, little antennas on his head sensing vibrations as a replacement for sight. From four small holes on the top of the shell, four spindly legs sprouted out and bent down to the ground. The legs pushed hard and lifted the grotesque snail a few inches into the air, breaking his suction from the ground and leaving a trail of slime. He turned and retreated down the largest cave that intersected the chamber at the bottom of the pit, all the while working his mouth as if he was chewing on something.

His blue antennae issued a faint glow that reflected palely on the carved stone around him. There was constant movement in the shadows at the edges of the glow. Something stood in the dark, waiting.

The snail marched down the tunnel almost a mile until he came to a rotting wooden door set into the flat rock. Two claws poked out from the bottom of the creature's shell. The left was smashed and useless, a souvenir from a long forgotten encounter. The right claw was lethal, honed sharp everyday like a ritual. The snail knocked the backside of his right claw against the door.

After a moment, the rusty lock clicked loose and the door squeaked slowly open. A wild looking, but short, man stood in the doorway.

"General Gusk," he growled, "come in."

General Gusk's claws retracted into his shell and the snail tiptoed into the room on his thin legs. Gusk knew the dwarf that opened the door. His antennae could not mistake the rotting smell of raw eggs that poured off the unpleasant man. This was Lord Vanril, who long ago ruled the Northern Wood.

Gusk moved past him, sensing the heavy boots at the bottom of the thick, dirty legs. The snail, even as General of the Rockhorn army, feared a wayward stomp from the angry little man. He made his way to the center of the room, spidered up the pile of rocks and took his seat on the edge of an old, wooden table.

Gusk heard the door swing shut and sensed Vanril moving toward the only piece of furniture in the room. That was not all he sensed. There was another person in the room, waiting silently in the corner. It was Sasha, the gypsy witch. General Gusk could feel his antennae shrivel slightly when she was near. The coldness in her heart seemed to spill out of her and Gusk could never quite get used to it.

Sasha spoke in a crusty voice, "Have my pets gone to do their job?"

"I supervised their departure, yes," the General replied. "However, if they had not failed yesterday, we would be continuing with other plans right now."

"Do not speak badly of my darlings. Their fangs and claws could easily crack your hull," she threatened.

Lord Vanril laughed at this, but it sounded more like he was choking on gravel. Then the gypsy witch turned on him, "Would you stop that before I cut them off."

Gusk could not see, but knew that Vanril was twirling the two long braids of his beard like a schoolgirl's pigtails. It was a habit that annoyed everyone including Gusk's sensitive antennae.

Sasha continued, "My werewolves will see to it that no heir lives to fill the Eastern Throne."

"I'm sure that is true," agreed Gusk. "In which case, we should turn our attention to the Rockhorns."

Vanril spoke next, "My dwarves have carved five thousand stone soldiers to your specifications, General."

"And your spell will hold?" Gusk asked the gypsy witch.

"I have given the Rockhorns life and they will do your bidding," she said.

Gusk took a moment to suck back the slime gathering at the corners of his mouth. When he swallowed enough to speak, he said, "Then the Rockhorn army will march on the Castle Empyrean in ten days while the three remaining queens are at their weakest. When victory is ours, we will seize the power to awaken our Master."

Gusk sensed Sasha make a prayer gesture with her hands, then Vanril slammed his fist on the table causing Gusk to bounce. The dwarf bellowed in the small, subterranean room, "May the Forgotten Evil rise once again."

The three conspirators were satisfied with their plans and an uncomfortable silence hung in the room.

"What about the boy?" Sasha whispered.

Gusk dismissed her, "The boy is nothing to worry about. He has his instructions. Perhaps we should turn our attention to the troops?"

This suggestion must have appealed to Vanril. He quickly grabbed a torch and flung the door open. He led the way down the long corridor followed closely by Sasha. General Gusk followed behind as quickly as his spindly legs would allow.

The red glare of the torch lit the narrow tunnel far better than Gusk's phosphorescent antennae. Sasha and Vanril inspected the monsters that lined this hall as they made their way to the main chamber. Carved from the rock walls where they stood, each one was at least six feet tall, some taller. These behemoths were living stone and they were the perfect army. The hand-chiseled granite required no food, no rest and no emotion. They were alive only in the sense that Sasha's spell animated them.

The Rockhorns were all basically the same shape, tall with a pointed horn or horns where the nose or forehead should have been. Each had one hand shaped for smashing and the other for stabbing. The smashing hands varied from clubs to war hammers to small, rounded boulders. The stabbing hands were sharp, some flat like swords, some pointed like spears.

However, the Rockhorns were not identical. Every dwarven artisan left his mark on his creation. Some of the Rockhorns were inlaid with precious gems, others adorned with gold, and others still with intricate designs engraved into their bodies. Most of the horns were the same, leaving the mindless soldiers looking like upright rhinoceroses. Yet, some of the dwarves took extra pride in their work and created some frightening displays of horns. Vanril stopped to admire one that seemed to have spikes coming out in every direction on its skull.

Gusk, Vanril and Sasha finally emerged in the main chamber of their subterranean lair. The cavern was immense, so large that hundreds of torches and large bonfires could not light the roof or the distant walls. Thousands of Rockhorns filled the room, scattered around the dancing flames. The bonfires cast random shadows giving the silent creatures an eerie look that obscured their faces as the light reflected from shiny metals, diamonds and topaz.

Waiting near the bloodstained altar at the head of the Great Hall were the twelve dwarves responsible for this army. Vanril approached them, shaking hands and hugging them.

"My brothers, a job well done," Vanril exclaimed. "Centuries ago, seven of the ten heads of the Dwarven Council betrayed us and cast our three families out of the Northern Wood. Those seven traitors pledged our wealth and land to a scared, human girl. Now, we are all that's left of our three families and we have made a pledge of our own. We have labored long these past hundred years and our time is at hand. We pledge to smash Empyrean. We pledge that Snow White will cry at our feet with her last breath. And we pledge to take back the Northern Wood and make slaves of the Seven Families."

The dwarves cheered and yelled, screaming war cries that made Gusk pull back into his shell.

Then Sasha spoke, "Mind ye, little men. This is not all for you. When all four queens of the world above are trampled beneath stony feet, then my Master, The Forgotten Evil, shall reign again. Four little girls sent him to a prison fathoms below us. After a lifetime of searching and the stories of my mother's mother, I have found the secret that bars him from our world."

Lastly, Gusk raised himself as high as his spindle legs would allow, still shorter than the shortest of the dwarves. He added, "When I lead this army to victory, our Master shall take his rightful place as ruler of Empyrean and so will begin an eon of darkness. Do not underestimate the size of my body and quiet voice. You see, the size of my desire for chaos and death could not be contained in this room. My greatest pleasure will be to serve as General of the Army of our Master. And at the whim of the Forgotten Evil, I will lay waste to any that do not bow in fear."

The dwarves cheered again. One of them broke open a barrel of ale and the drinking began.

"That's right, my brothers. Drink deep, for in ten days, we begin our march to war," said Vanril. "When the glass castle is shattered, our allies will crawl out of the dark places and be without number. They wait for us, but tonight they will have to wait for me to drink another pint." Lord Vanril joined his kin in their drinking. Gusk and Sasha left the dwarves to their party as slave-children, walking in chains, carried in a feast. The General and the witch spent the rest of the night reviewing their plans.

He had no idea how long he was asleep, but he awoke to the feeling of being watched. Instead of jolting upright, Adam slowly opened his eyes and peered around without even moving his head.

With the warm morning sun and nearby swooshing of the ocean, Adam slept without having nightmares for the first time in years. The sleep was so peaceful that he almost forgot where he was and where he had come from.

The boy looked at the smooth sand beneath him and only a few feet away, the wide, beckoning chasm that was his former home. Across the chasm, through the rising mists, Adam could see a bearded man in a torn robe peeking out from the castle door. Adam did not know or care that this was one of the queen's advisors. He jumped up and let out a low growl that sent the scared man back inside. Adam laughed at this and turned to leave the courtyard.

Outside the palace gates, he found the remains of the merchants' carts. Jungle fruit and strange colored fish, fresh only yesterday, were already starting to putrefy in the early morning sunlight. This did not stop Adam from eating his fill. He was ravenous and had not had a full belly in a long time. He grabbed and tore at the food with bare hands and yellow teeth, not taking time to peel oranges or spit out fish bones.

After a few minutes of gorging, the raw fish turned against him and most of the food came back up in a splash of vomit. Adam stopped eating long enough to wipe his mouth with the back of his hand and move to the next cart. When his belly was full again, he moved away from the palace toward the Nookan village.

He stood at the top of the rock wall, looking over the ancient huts at the vast ocean. He never imagined anything like it, the waves swirling and collapsing on each other, the steady heartbeat rhythm slapping on the shore and the shining reflection of the sun hiding any hint of how deep the water could be. Adam could happily sit here all day, but that was not why he was free from his underground prison.

Banookanook was deserted. At least that is what the hidden villagers wanted any strangers to think, but Adam could sense them. Spending his entire life in darkness, his hearing and sense of smell grew strong. He knew people were watching from behind window curtains in the small huts and spying from the lush cover of the jungle.

He walked through the center of the village and stopped at the remains of a giant red frog. The frog had been torn to pieces and nearby was a dark-skinned man that suffered a similar fate. Adam suspected that no one would be inside this man's house and went in.

Even with the bright sunlight outside, it was dark inside the hut, which was a relief for the boy's eyes. He let the curtain close over the opening of the doorway and stepped inside. Adam could tell instantly that the werewolves had been here. Tables were turned and bed mattresses were slashed. The few cabinets stood open and their contents spilled to the floor.

Adam examined the broken shells that once served as dinner bowls and found a knife buried under the fragments. He immediately plopped down in the center of the room where Zandria and Olena sat only two days before. It did not take long for the boy to pick open the locks that bound his wrists and ankles. After a moment's concentration, he was free. Finally, he was loose of that underground prison where he spent his entire life as a slave to those wretched dwarves. But Adam knew that his freedom came with a price.

He stared at his hands under the light streaming in through the smoke hole, not really recognizing them as his own without the rusted bracelets. He saw years of grime embedded in his skin and decided to do something about it. Adam tucked the knife into his waistband and ran out of the hut. Not minding the hot sand on his bare feet, he dashed across the beach and leaped headfirst into the churning water.

The ocean was warm and drenched him in a soothing wave. Before it was lost to the sea, Adam tossed his knife onto dry land. Then he snatched off his only piece of clothing and used it like a rag to scrub his body. Soon, his dark skin was red from the abrasions, but he felt good. He felt clean.

Adam dove under water and instinctively swam away from the shore until his feet could not reach the sandy bottom. He could feel the red and blue and yellow fish brushing past his legs. Then he swam back and crawled out of the water. His wet hair slapped against his shoulders as he rolled over onto his back. Adam let the sun dry him as he lay on the beach while he used his knife to dig ages of filth from under his fingernails.

When he was satisfied with his work, there was one more thing that needed doing. Adam strolled to the nearest hut. He walked in, past the cowering Nookans tucked into the corner and straight to their bed area. Adam began searching through their clothes and found a plain white shirt that was a little large and a pair of pants that barely went past his knees.

"Close enough," he said, dressing himself. As he turned to leave, he noticed a leather belt hanging beside the door. There was a knife, twice the size of his original, in the holster, so he took the belt. Once he strapped it on, he slid his smaller knife in alongside the new one. Now he was ready.

Adam stopped in front of the frightened family. He asked, "Do you know who the werewolves were looking for?"

They did not answer, but stared at him, their eyes straining wide open in fear.

Adam pried again, "There was probably a little girl. Which way did she go?"

The father, trying to protect his family, pointed to the back of his hut. Behind his hut was the rest of the village and beyond that was the jungle that led to the west. Adam knew the trail would lead him toward the great Castle Empyrean as General Gusk had told him.

Adam ran out of the hut and sprinted through the village.

"I hope I'm not too late," he said as he charged into the thick green of the jungle.

Chapter 6

A Rainbow
on a Sunny Day

They spent the last several hours marching through the jungle. Zandria was in the lead with Kez and Olena bringing up the far rear. Olena did not want to be close to Zandria until she had time to calm down. Maybe she was sometimes a little bossy and occasionally rude, but never mean like this morning. So, until she was back to her old self, Olena decided to leave her alone.

Once or twice, Zandria dipped out of sight as she pushed through a cluster of bushes or down into the bed of a creek. Her sister was fast and she was determined. Now they were crossing another creek. Each time the ground went down, Olena watched Kez go up. He would scale a tree and cross where the branches mingled without the risk of getting wet.

When Olena reached the bottom of this creek, Zandria was not climbing the bank ahead of her. She looked around for her sister, instantly fearing that the werewolves caught them. After a frantic moment, Olena saw Zandria sloshing down the creek. She was heading towards a clearing where the creek fed into a wide river.

"Kez, this way," shouted Olena as she chased after Zandria.

They arrived next to the older girl, watching the flow and churn of the water. This river was nowhere near as big as their ocean, but it was far wider and faster than something she wanted to swim across.

Kez surveyed their surroundings. He offered, "This river seems to be heading in the direction we need to go."

Zandria stared at him with pursed lips. Maybe, Olena thought, she was still mad. Then Zandria spun around, grabbed a smooth, brown stone from the muddy shore and cocked it back as if she was going to throw it at the little quzzak. Kez reeled back as she threw the rock. It splashed into the water at his tiny, black feet and he was soaked.

Zandria exploded in a fit of laughter. Then she snatched another rock and tossed it in the water in front of her younger sister. The juvenile frolicking seemed to wash away the stress of recent events. Olena had not seen Zandria this happy for a while. The two girls began splashing water at each other, giggling and sloshing in the shallow mud. Kez scampered up to dry safety.

He watched the girls as they momentarily forgot their impending danger. The fun did not last long.

Zandria stepped up on a large rock, worn round from years of rushing currents. Either from the wetness of the stone or the mud on her feet, she slipped and fell backwards into the river.

At first, this was funny to Olena, until she realized that Zandria was swept up in the flow and moving away from her quickly. Kez and Olena raced along the side as Zandria fought to swim back to the calm waters near the shore.

"Maybe we should get a branch," suggested Kez. Olena nodded and he scurried into the underbrush. While Kez was gone, Olena tried to keep pace with her sister, but the gap was widening. All the while, the roaring sound of the river grew louder.

Olena kept looking from Zandria to the path in front of her, making sure her way was not blocked. In the distance, she saw Kez coming straight towards her. He must have gone ahead to find a rescue spot. As he came nearer, she saw a panicked look on his face.

He was panting and the words came out in gasps, "Have...to stop...her...no more..." Olena did not think he was going to get it all out, then he finished in one big breath, "Nomoreriver."

Olena was not sure what this meant, but after a few more steps, she found out. The ground suddenly stopped and went straight down. The river turned into a magnificent waterfall, dropping out of sight. The spray of the cascading water created a vibrant rainbow that fell with it to a small lagoon hundreds of feet below.

Kez forced Olena to stop at the edge and they watched with horror as Zandria spilled over the side. The river was so loud here that they could not even hear her scream as she fell.

It took Olena, with Kez's help, the rest of the morning to climb down where the ground was not too steep. At the bottom, the jungle was so much more dense because it was joining with the forest that grew from the west. Even Kez found it difficult to climb through the tangles of vines and sharp leaves.

Eventually, they made it to the lagoon at the base of the cliff. The massive waterfall punched a hole in the jungle canopy that formed a perfect circle around the lagoon. The water thundered down on the far side, but by them, it was still and calm. Kez clung to Olena's shoulder. He whispered in her ear, "There is some magic here."

Olena glanced at him. The only magic she ever experienced was one performance by a traveling minstrel who came down to the beach from the Palace by the Sea. She tried to picture someone wading in the water, making a piece of rope change lengths. She did not realize that Kez was talking about real magic and not party tricks.

He must have interpreted her expression, because he continued, "My child, you know in your heart that our world is made of magic. Some good, some terrible, and some that you don't know until it's too late."

"Is this place good or bad?" asked Olena.

"I don't think we'll know until it's too late."

Kez's tail curled around her head and they moved forward to look for Zandria.

There was no sign of her sister and Olena's heart filled with dread. There was no body, no blood, not even a shred of her favorite pink pants. The only thing they could see was the intense glare of the rainbow.

The brilliant colors should have faded beneath the shadow of the surrounding trees, but it was brighter here than above. The colors sliced through the water and reflected off a myriad of rocks that looked like gems scattered at the bottom of the clear lagoon.

Kez and Olena made their way around by the waterfall. From the side, they could see a grotto hidden behind the pounding flow. The colors of the rainbow reflected off the gems beneath the surface and flashed back into the little cave in hundreds of separate colored beams. Kez studied the beams closely.

"I don't think the rainbow is shining into the cave," he said.

"What do you mean?" Olena asked.

"I mean, I think it is coming out."

"Magic?"

"Yes, magic," Kez answered her.

Then, as confirmation, a voice echoed from inside the grotto.

"In here," it said, "I'm in here."

Olena recognized the voice and rushed forward. Kez almost fell from her shoulder.

"Wait," he shouted, "What are you doing?"

"It's Zandria. She's in the cave."

Kez started to look concerned, "Hello? Remember magic? It could be a trick. I hate to say she couldn't have survived that fall, but..."

"Olena," the voice called again, "Come inside. I'm in here."

Olena was certain that it was her sister even though the voice was barely audible over the constant drone of the waterfall. Against Kez's warnings, she stepped behind the water and into the cave.

Walking carefully over the wet, jagged stones, Olena carried Kez gradually deeper and away from the rushing water. The colored light danced around them and seemed, to her ears, musical. As the light bounced off the walls, floor and ceiling, it chimed and rang like thousands of tiny bells swaying in a gentle breeze. Soon, out of sight, the waterfall was no longer audible. They were surrounded by a chorus with no tune, punctuated only by their breathing.

Then, one by one, the colors faded away. Without even a chance of running for the mouth of the cave, they were trapped in darkness.

Olena screamed, "Zandria!"

"I knew this was a bad idea," Kez added, being no real help.

Olena swatted his tail out of her face, but could not bring her feet to move. They went so far in and so far down that no outside light was visible. Her bare feet were planted on the cold stone almost as if they were part of it. Fear tightened the muscles in her body so that only her eyes could dart about hoping to see something.

She uttered one more scream that came out more like a sobbing whispered question than a yell, "Zandria?"

Silence.

Darkness.

Laughter.

Only faint giggles at first, echoing from somewhere deep below them where no sunlight had ever reached. Olena did not think about how far in she was going to go to find her sister, but she knew there was no way she would go that far.

The giggles grew to chuckles, drifting closer on warm air that issued from beneath. It grew louder and surrounded them.

Kez whispered in Olena's ear, "There are at least four of them."

"Four what?"

"I don't know, but I can discern four distinct laughs. Possibly more." He shifted position to listen better.

The laughter buzzed to uncontrollable fits and Olena strained her eyes, trying to see anything. Then she was blinded. Bright white light exploded in the chamber and at the same instant, the laughter stopped. It took a moment for Olena to regain her sight, but the new light adjusted to her. She could not tell where it was coming from. The light seemed to pulse out of the rocks and it responded to her thoughts, first dimming and then rising back up until she could see comfortably.

Six women formed a circle around them, almost close enough to touch. At least, they looked like women. Their faces and shape of their bodies assured Olena that they were much older than she was. However, they were all shorter than she was. In fact, they were very close to Kez's height. They were perfectly proportioned miniature women, much like the porcelain dolls back at the Palace by the Sea.

Now Olena knew where the laughter was coming from. Several of the women were still tittering and all of them were smiling as if they had been playing a delightful game with their new friend.

Olena was furious. If they were friendly, it was a horrible trick. And if they were not, what did they do with Zandria?

It was as if they were reading her mind and the strange women stopped laughing at once. All six stepped back three times in unison and a wave of relief washed over Olena. When the two women in front of her moved, they revealed Zandria sleeping on a pile of the fluffiest pillows she had ever seen.

Olena wanted to rush to her sister, but Kez pulled hard at one of her curls.

"Ouch."

"Wait, girl. It could still be a trap. We need to find out what they want." Kez was trying to be a voice of reason.

Olena was going to ignore him, but one of the women spoke before she could move.

"We don't want anything from you," said the first woman.

Olena looked at the one who answered and realized something. She, at first, thought that all six women were identical, even wearing matching white dresses. But, she saw now that this woman's dress was actually a faint pink color. She watched for a moment longer, saw swirls of red turn around the dress, and emanate from her. How could she have not seen it before? This woman looked nothing like the others. She had chestnut hair, blood red lips and matching fingernail polish.

Something moved behind this woman's back. Olena stared for a moment and saw the flutter again. A pair of large, glimmering butterfly wings unfolded from the woman's back.

She glanced around and saw similar wings sprouting from each of the women.

"Fairies," Kez uttered.

Olena watched as the red fairy's sanguine dress brushed the ground when she stepped backwards to sit on a small stone chair that was not there before.

"What have you done to my sister?" Olena demanded. She was still too worried to be in awe.

"She's resting. She had a terrible fall, you know," said the red fairy. She continued, "My name is Ruby, and these are *my* sisters."

Ruby gestured to each and Olena saw that none of them were dressed in the white she first imagined. Even their shiny wings danced with their own individual colors. Ruby introduced each sister.

"Coral." She was orange.

"Saffron." Yellow.

"Beryl." Green.

"Ultramarine." Blue.

"Lilac." Purple.

Olena gazed at the fairies and the glorious, vibrant colors returned to the cave. Each sister outshone the other in her turn and the lights churned peacefully.

"You may have heard of us. We are known in most places as the Rainbow Princesses. Except in the East, we were once called the Prismata."

"Ka," interjected Kez. "The Prismata are a myth from my grandparents' days. They don't exist. I told you this was a trick. Bad magic."

Ruby answered, "Why do you say such things. Are we not here in front of you?"

"There is evil at work, determined to stop these girls," explained Kez without giving away everything.

"That is why we are in hiding and why we decided to help you. It was an accident that your sister fell in the river, but when we saw who you were, we knew we must help."

Kez interrupted, "If you are the Prismata and not some wicked little fairies, then your power should be great enough to withstand any enemies."

Ruby responded by addressing Olena, "Wake your sister and we will explain the rest."

Olena sat gently down by Zandria and caressed her shoulder. She awoke with very little effort and did not seem to remember anything.

"What...who are..." mumbled Zandria. Kez scrambled over to her and briefly reintroduced everyone with an audible note of doubt.

"If they were helping the werewolves, I think they would have hurt us by now," said Olena. "Besides, we need all the help we can get."

"Thank you," said Ruby. "As I said, we are in hiding. We do not have the power to stand against the coming evil, only the four queens together can. However, we have always been loyal to them. We know of your quest and wish to aide you as best we can. With the small, but good, magic we have," she glanced at Kez, "we wish to give you these gifts."

Coral stood and glided over to the two girls. She pulled a mirror from her sleeve by its ornate handle and laid it at their feet. The carved wood that surrounded the oval of glass amazed Olena. The handle seemed to change shape to fit perfectly in her hand where it had only a moment before been a perfect fit for the Orange Princess. Leaning forward, she could see no reflection, but only a blue sky dotted with fast-moving clouds.

"It is a magic mirror and will reflect only the truth," said Coral.

Before Coral was back to her seat, Saffron moved up with her gift. She lay what looked like a glass axe before them. "This is not a weapon, rather something you must save for when the time is right," Saffron warned.

Olena was comforted simply to enjoy the fairies flying back and forth as they presented their gifts. For her, now, a wonderful puppet show came to life. On the beach at home, she and Zandria often pretended to be fairy princesses. Despite her continual wishing, Olena never dared to believe they were real. Now they were treating her like long lost family.

Next came Lilac. She looked embarrassed as she spoke, "My gift has no physical form. Instead, it is a single spoken word meant to save you from a dire fate. I wish I could give you something more, but this one word is all I have. Because it may only save you once, I choose to tell it to the quzzak. His wisdom will know how to use it best."

Now it was Kez's turn to be embarrassed as Lilac whispered in his ear. Olena guessed that Lilac's purple lips must have tickled Kez's ear as he squirmed with delight. She saw that he was convinced of their sincerity now and he was trying to hide his proud face.

Ultramarine waited for Kez to recover and then presented a bronze ring. It was a plain, flat piece of bronze, bent into the crescent-moon shape of a ring. There were no designs or engravings or mounted jewels.

The Blue Princess explained, "Some things are not as they look. What is hidden inside is often more valuable than the appearance on the outside."

She laid it next to the mirror. For an instant, Olena thought she saw a face reflected out of the ring. She tried to show Zandria, but it was already gone and Zandria was focused on the next present.

Beryl was holding a dagger flat across both hands out in front of her. She was deliberate in her actions to avoid being cut on the glistening edges.

She laid it down tip first and let the leather wrapped handle slide from her fingers. It was another gift without decoration. It was a knife and that was all that it needed to be. Olena did not want to have to use any weapons.

Answering Olena's thought, Beryl said, "This is an enchanted knife. It will serve its purpose as a blade. However, it can be much more if you need it to be."

Zandria snatched it up and sliced at the air. Then she picked up the glass axe and held the two side-by-side, comparing their merits. She started to swing the axe-shaped present, but stopped with a stern look from Saffron. Zandria laid it across her lap and held the knife close in her right hand. With her left, she reached across and pushed the mirror and ring over to Olena.

"These are yours," Zandria said.

With that, Ruby stood. She spread her wings as wide as she could, floated over in front of the girls and said, "I have my own gift to give, but I wanted to see how you reacted to the others first. That way, I would know which of you to give mine to."

She opened her empty hands to them, palms out. Then she closed them together. When Ruby opened her hands again, the most beautiful flower Olena had ever seen was nestled between her gentle fingers. The bud had three large red petals that split open to reveal a cluster of soft, pink petals inside. Six stamen poked out of the center like long bug antennae. The strong aroma reminded her of everything good in her life and happy days of playing on the beach with their father watching from his boat.

"Olena, this is the mayblossom," Ruby said as she laid it in her hands. "You will find it to be very responsive to your gentle nature. As with all of the gifts, you may not discover its purpose until you need it most. Protect these items and they will serve you. However, if you brandish them foolhardily, then you will fail along with them."

Kez climbed onto Olena's lap and examined the flower. He sniffed it and sneezed so violently that he rolled over backwards. Olena, Zandria and the fairy princesses laughed together at this.

"Now," finished Ruby, "we must get you some traveling clothes and food for your journey."

Kez recovered from his fall and ushered the Red Princess aside. He said, "I apologize for misjudging you. It's my nature to be skeptical."

"No. It is your nature to be protective. You do a great service to these children that will be honored by all future generations. Your wisdom, your skepticism, will keep them safe. They need your help and appreciate your help more than even they know," said Ruby.

"I won't let them down. I'm their friend."

"I know." Ruby turned back to the girls, "Now you must rest. In the morning, you will resume your quest. And the dangerous part is yet to come."

Chapter 7

At Noon
Comes Winter

Despite being a cold, wet cave, there were enough pillows and cushions and blankets that Zandria slept quite well. She awoke rested, having nothing but pleasant dreams about beautiful queens and magical horses in a far off land.

Zandria stretched and rubbed her eyes. Then the smell of food snuck up her nostrils and filled her head, alerting her stomach. Her first thought was to rush to the cooking breakfast, then she turned to wake Olena.

Olena was not there.

Panic quickly took hold and Zandria jumped up from her bed. She did not know in which direction to go. Her mind raced with the possibilities of what could have happened during the night. She feared the wolves found them. The monsters must have tracked them to the cave.

Zandria stared into the blackness behind her, straining her eyes. She knew the wolfmen were there, waiting in the darkness. She knew at any moment they were going to spring from the shadows.

Then she heard laughter. Zandria knew that laugh. It was Olena. Zandria turned toward the entrance of the cave. She started to make her way to the bright morning sunlight, leaving the dark thoughts behind with the darkness of the cave.

As her eyes adjusted to the brightness, she could make out Olena and Kez sitting beside the pool watching what appeared to be miniature dolphins putting on a show.

Olena was safe.

More so, she appeared to be delighted. She was cheering and giggling as the miniature dolphins did back flips and criss-crossed through the air each time making tiny splashes as they plopped back into the water.

Another great relief awaited Zandria at the entrance to the cave. Ruby and her sisters were preparing breakfast. At the sight of this, Zandria could think of nothing else.

The Prismata made food, both hot and cold, that Zandria had never seen before. Her stomach growled loud enough that everyone turned and looked at her. Ultramarine quickly handed her a steaming plate of food. Zandria did not even take the time to look at the dazzling assortment as she frantically gobbled it down. She did not know what she was eating and did not care. She did know that every colorful bite was delicious.

Within minutes, her plate was clean and Zandria sat to join Olena and Kez at the water's edge. When the miniature dolphins finished their show, the Rainbow Princesses served a second course of breakfast, mostly consisting of desserts.

Zandria and Olena ate their fill of creams and fruits. Zandria saw Olena sneak several handfuls of hard candy into her pocket.

When the feast was finally over, both girls and Kez helped clean up. They washed the plates under the rush of the waterfall. Once everything was dry and stacked, Beryl waved a hand and everything disappeared.

"If you were going to do that anyway, why did we have to wash them first?" asked Zandria.

"We always clean up after ourselves," started Beryl.

Ruby interjected, "It is a responsibility. This is something that you will learn. We all have responsibilities, which are why we do things that we seemingly don't have to or especially don't want to."

"Still," Zandria complained, "why couldn't you wave your hand and clean them too."

"It is a reminder. Sometimes, we have to rely only on ourselves. Magic cannot help us every time," explained Ruby.

Zandria could not help but still be disappointed. She decided not to continue the argument. Then Lilac emerged from the cave carrying two small pouches. She passed them to Ruby.

"Oh good," said Ruby. "These are for you girls. We have packed all of your gifts along with an extra set of clothes and some food."

Olena spoke faster than Zandria could, "They're too small to fit all that stuff!" She appeared quite amazed, but Zandria did not believe it.

Ruby opened one of the pouches and showed it to the girls. "They are a little bigger on the inside," she said. The pouch on the outside was no bigger than Kez's head, but Olena stuck in her arm up to the shoulder. She pulled out the mayblossom, smelled it and dropped it back inside.

Ruby waited for Olena to finish her investigation before speaking again. This time, she waved her hand across the small lagoon. On the opposite side, a rainbow painted a path off into the forest. She spoke, "This is our last gift to you. We will guide your way as far as we can and our magic will hide your scent from the assassins."

Zandria was upset again, "Why can't your magic send us to Empyrean?"

"This is one of the things you have to do for yourself," answered Ruby. She handed the pouches to Zandria and Olena and hugged them. Ruby barely came up to Olena's waist, but wrapped her arms tightly around the girl all the same.

Once all of the Rainbow Princesses gave their farewells, Kez led his two friends in the direction of the rainbow path. They were only a few steps into the woods and Olena turned to wave bye once more. To their surprise, all six Prismata were gone and the cave vanished. Zandria noticed that even the path where they already walked was slowly disappearing too.

A strange sadness fell over the group and they walked on in silence for a while.

Even with the thick undergrowth, the going was easy. The trail of shimmering light seemed to push back the weeds and branches.

Zandria debated quietly with herself. Why did Ruby not simply send them to the castle? Why did they have to walk all the way? Not even Kez knew how far it really was. Zandria was sure that Olena would be annoying when she got tired of walking, or worse, if she got hurt. "I'm not going to carry the little pest," she said to herself.

Olena must have heard her mumbling and walked up next to her. "Are you talking to yourself again?" she asked.

"No," defended Zandria.

"Oh," Olena paused. "It's okay if you do. I know I'm not that interesting to talk to. But if you want to talk to somebody else…"

Zandria did not know what to say. She knew her little sister could be irritating, but she never meant to hurt her feelings. She said, "Well, let me know if anything interesting comes up."

"Actually, I do have one interesting thing."

"What's that?" scoffed Zandria.

"Well." Olena paused to tisk her tongue against her teeth, giving emphasis to her next statement, "I don't know how long we've been walking," she tisked again, "but I think the rainbow is fading."

"What?" Zandria stopped in her tracks.

Kez dropped down from a nearby branch and examined the path. "I'm afraid she's right."

Zandria saw it without Kez's confirmation. The blue was almost completely gone and red was looking more like light pink. She scanned ahead and only a short distance away, she could not see a difference between yellow and orange.

"Wow, that's great magic," said Zandria sarcastically. "I think it lasted for almost two whole hours."

Olena added, "And it's getting colder."

Zandria was beginning to get upset again, "That's impossible. We're in the middle of a jungle and the sun is directly above us. Now come on before this worthless trail completely disappears."

Kez took his usual place on Olena's shoulder and they followed Zandria in the direction of the coming evening. Zandria knew it would not be too long before the sun dipped below the eastern edge of the sea back home.

Zandria did not want to admit that Olena was right about the weather, but after a short while, she was wishing she had a blanket or something. She looked back at Olena a few paces behind her and could see her breath coming out in little puffs into the chilly air.

Soon, the last ray of green blended into the vegetation and their rainbow path was gone. At the same time, Kez noticed something overhead.

"Look up there," he said. "One of the branches is covered in ice. I don't think the Prismata's magic ran out. I think someone else's magic took over."

Zandria did not process Kez's statement completely. Neither girl had ever seen ice before and they were both enthralled. Zandria could still see the branch, but it reminded her of something else. She remembered swimming around her father's boat and she would look up at him from under water. She could see him, but it was blurry and hard to reach.

This unexpected thought of her father brought a tear to her eye. Before it rolled all the way down her cheek, it froze, stinging her soft skin.

"Ow!"

Kez jumped to Zandria, "What is it?" He saw the frozen tear and said, "There is some enchantment here. I think we should do our best to remember the direction of the path and keep moving."

Zandria nodded in agreement, grabbed Olena by the wrist and took off at a fast walk.

The further they went, the more ice there was. The more ice, the faster Zandria felt compelled to go. The whole thing made her feel uneasy and she wanted to get quickly through this part of the forest. Soon everything was covered in ice. The trees, the bushes all shimmered under the late afternoon sun. Even the path beneath their feet was white. Now Zandria was at a full run, dragging Olena behind her.

As they rushed forward, the ground sloped up, but Zandria kept her pace only slipping once on the dangerous surface. At the top of the rise, she saw they crested some kind of mound and everything ran back down towards a strange cluster of trees at the center. She decided to cut across instead of going around and in one step, slipped and fell flat on her backside.

Olena did not have time to laugh because an instant later she joined her sister with a hard thwap. Kez climbed off of Zandria and moved towards Olena, but even he could not keep his footing. His four paws shot out in different directions and he ended up flat on his belly.

At this, the girls did laugh, but only for a moment. Zandria saw that Kez, unable to regain his feet, was sliding down the hill. Before she could control her laughter, he was out of reach, whisking down the hill towards the trees. Her shift in weight caused her to start sliding too. Zandria grabbed for a branch, but the frozen stick broke off in her hand and then she was following Kez. Zandria watched Olena give herself a push, laughing all along.

The sensation of spinning and sliding uncontrollably scared Zandria, but apparently not Olena. The younger girl giggled as they zipped down the hill, past the trees, until they came to rest on the smooth flat surface inside the ring of trees.

"Is everyone alright?" asked Kez.

"I'm fine," answered Zandria.

"Can we do that again?" was Olena's reply.

Before Zandria could tell her no, she looked back at where they came from and there was no sign of an entrance. The trees closed in, leaving them trapped with only a large block of ice in the center of the ring.

The girls carefully got to their feet, each checking their balance and gently sliding their feet instead of taking actual steps. Kez remained on all fours.

Zandria wanted to find a way out, but Olena only seemed interested in the large block of ice.

"I think someone is inside here," she said.

Zandria made her way over to Olena, "What are you talking about?" She rubbed the ice as if she could clear it away to see inside. She started to say, "That's imposs..." and then saw a man's face. There was no way to tell how old he was, but he looked ancient.

Olena was peering in too, "He looks so sad. I wish there was something we could do for him."

"I don't think we should. Somebody froze him up for a reason. Maybe he's a bad guy," said Zandria.

"I don't think so," said Olena.

"What makes you think that?" asked Kez. "If you feel it in your heart, then maybe we should help him. Is there something in your pouch that will help?"

"You're right." Olena started digging in her pouch.

"This isn't a good idea. We shouldn't let him out," demanded Zandria.

"Sometimes, Olena can be right too, Zandria," said Kez. "Listen to your instincts when they tell you to trust or help people."

"Aha!" shouted Olena. She pulled out the mirror. For a moment, she looked at her own reflection and then her eyes got wide. She turned the mirror in different directions, looking at everything but herself in it. She turned it to Zandria and Kez.

At first, Zandria saw only her own face and the red blister on her cheek where her tear had frozen. Then she looked past her reflection at the woods behind her. There was no ice, no frozen trees. In the mirror, they were at the center of a beautiful garden. Zandria could not believe what she was seeing.

Kez suggested, "Turn it so the man can see his own reflection."

Olena adjusted the mirror hoping that the man's eyes were pointed back at himself. Inside the block of ice, Zandria thought she saw the old man blink. She decided it was her imagination and then he blinked again. Then she noticed the ice starting to drip.

"It's working!" cheered Olena.

As quickly as she said that, the few drips turned into streams and the streams became one big rush of water as if thousands of gallons had been dropped on them all at once. The rushing water rapidly seeped into the ground and a breeze whipped through drying everything almost instantly.

The old man had been kneeling, propped up by a rusty sword. He closed his eyes, took a deep breath and collapsed.

Zandria's first thought was to rush to the old man, not knowing what she could do to help. Before she took a step, she looked around and was amazed. The bleak, lifeless part of the forest that was only recently covered in ice was coming back to life. Leaves were budding from vacant branches. Vines spiraled up the trees. And a hundred varieties of flowers popped up out of the ground and burst from bushes.

She did not notice earlier, but to Zandria's right, at the northern edge of the ring of trees, was a small stone fountain. It was not ornate or decorated, it was simply a brown stone almost as tall as her. Now that the ice was gone, water bubbled up out of a crack in the top and ran down the sides of the rock back into the ground.

Zandria let her amazement overwhelm her for a moment and then she noticed Olena kneeling by the old man, gently pushing at his shoulder. Zandria knew this was her way of waking someone up as it happened to her many times before.

Zandria decided that the old man needed water and moved to the stone. She cupped her hands and tipped them into the rivulet. When Zandria's hands were full, she knelt beside her sister. Kez saw what she was trying to do and carefully pulled the man's mouth open. Zandria slowly poured the water into the unresponsive mouth.

After a moment of quiet anticipation, Zandria began to wonder if the old man had died. There were no clues to show how long he had been frozen. Maybe thawing him out killed him, she thought.

Then, as if to prove her wrong, the old man coughed, sputtering out some of the water. He rolled onto his back and slowly opened his eyes.

In a cracked, quiet voice, he said, "It's been so long since I've seen the sky."

Zandria looked to Kez and Olena. She saw her surprise mirrored in each of their faces.

"It's the same old sky as yesterday," comforted Olena.

"Yes, but I have been staring at that tree," he gestured weakly in the direction his frozen body had been facing, to the East, "for...for...I can't say that I know how many days have passed."

Kez asked, "You mean you've been awake inside that ice, but don't know how long?"

The old man tried to sit up, but did not have the strength. Olena moved to help him and put his head in her lap. He finally settled on a combination of propping himself on his elbows and resting his head in her comforting lap. He said, "At first, I tried counting the sunsets. Unfortunately, I lost track after about ten thousand."

"So you were only a boy when you were frozen," surmised Zandria.

"Oh, no. No, I have not been a boy for quite some time," his voice was still barely more than a whisper. He continued, "A prince, yes. But I have not been since well before I came to this spot."

"You're a prince?" asked Zandria incredulously.

Olena seemed more ready to believe it, "You're the oldest prince I've ever met."

"He's the only prince you've ever met, if he really is one," retorted Zandria.

"I assure you, I am," he said. At that, the old man seemed to gain some strength and lifted himself up to a sitting position. "I am Prince William, squire to the Queen of the Eastern Sky."

Kez gave a quick bow.

"What's a squire?" asked Olena, not trying to hide her excitement.

Prince William sat upright with his legs sprawled out in a giant V and his hands resting on the ground between them. He glanced at his rusted sword and then looked at the faces of his three rescuers. He sighed heavily and lowered his head so that his scraggily beard brushed against his chest. Zandria looked away as the setting sun reflected off his bald head, momentarily blinding her. She thought he was struggling to find the right words or simply did not have the strength to speak.

Then Zandria saw it again. As if from deep inside himself, Prince William grew a little stronger. She thought one or two of his brown age spots swirled up and vanished even.

Finally, he began to speak, "There was a time, when I was a young man, that I was not a knight. As I grew, it was noted that I was quite adept with my sword. And by my own humble admission, I was of particular fair and just conscience."

"So, it came to be, on my first year of manhood, I was elected peace keeper of mine and the surrounding villages," he paused to catch his breath then continued, "As happens with young men, there was a maiden in a nearby village that took my fancy. We enjoyed many pleasant days together as my elected position required very little effort under the glorious rule of the four queens. It seemed that nothing could be wrong with the world in those days."

"Never in my lifetime had one of the four queens passed into the golden twilight of the next realm, but in only one summer after I fell in love did we lose the Queen of the Eastern Sky. It was decided that there was to be a festival celebrating her greatness and I decided at that festival to take my bride."

William paused again, this time to wipe a tear from the corner of his eye, "To my greatest sadness and greatest honor, it was revealed at that ceremony that my betrothed was to be the next queen. In the morning, she was carried away with great pomp to the castle Soria Moria and I was left without a wedding. I swore my allegiance to the new Queen of the Eastern Sky and have been her squire ever since."

"That doesn't explain what you are doing here," said Zandria.

"Forgive me for my assumptions. You may have heard of the troll infestations at Soria Moria. Because she had a kind heart, the one I fell in love with, the queen decided not to hunt the trolls, but rather build a new castle further east. So, every day at noon, I honor my queen and await her invitation when the construction is complete. I kneel at the center of my village and praise her."

Kez gave an audible gasp, "I don't know where to begin."

Zandria started to comment, but Kez hushed her. She wanted to point out that there were no villages around.

Kez climbed onto William's shoulder and gently patted his wrinkled head. He said, "I'm not sure which news will be easiest, but I will try it in this order. According to the lore of my tribe, the Palace by the Sea is almost five hundred years old. Surely, you haven't been frozen for five hundred years?"

Zandria still wanted to have her say, ignoring William's pale demeanor and not thinking of his feelings of loss. She blurted out, "And if there was a village here, it's gone now. There's nothing but forest and jungle all around." She was satisfied with herself.

Then she looked at the prince. He was wheezing as if someone punched him in the stomach. A few tears trickled down his cheek as he tried to stand. Olena helped him up and Kez jumped clear to keep the decrepit figure from losing his balance. Olena thought quickly and picked up his sword, so that William could use it as a cane. He wiped his eyes with the back of his free hand and surveyed his surroundings.

"I was afraid of this," he said. "The longer I waited for my queen, the more I neglected my duties. A base element seemed to invade our town and every day without my love, I aged two days. The village fell into disrepair and my neighbors did not feel safe even in daylight with the vagabonds and tramps that came and went. The longer I was apart from my betrothed, the faster I aged and soon it was easier for me to remain in the garden. Alas, the last time I ventured out of this circle, there was a village."

"But how did you get frozen?" asked Olena.

"That is a sad thought indeed. I am certain that the cold came from within mine own heart," he answered.

"Yeah, and it covered this whole part of the forest," said Zandria.

William looked solemnly at Zandria, "I suspect now that as I did this to myself, my town fell to ruin and my friends left. The bitterness in my heart must have spread slowly, if no sign of my village was left before the forest froze." Now the prince turned to Kez, "My little friend, from your previous statement I guess that there is still more disheartening news."

Kez responded, "That is correct, your majesty."

"Please dispense with the formalities. If my villages are gone, then I am certainly no longer a prince. Now deliver your next bit of woe," said William.

"Your maj...," Kez caught himself, "William, the Queen of the Eastern Sky was attacked only a few days ago. I'm afraid she did not survive."

William was winded again and dropped to his knees. This time, tears streamed from both eyes. Zandria felt a cold draft of air come from nowhere. She did not want to be trapped if this crazy old man froze himself again and blurted out quickly, "I'm the new queen though."

The old man stopped crying and stared at her.

She continued although Kez was trying to stop her, "Well, not yet, but we're on our way to Empyrean to make me a queen."

Zandria shot a sideways glance at Olena, but the younger girl did not try to correct her. Apparently, Kez did want to though. He said to her, "Do you think it is wise to tell everyone of our plans. I think we can trust him, but how do you know for sure?"

William stopped crying and straightened himself as best he could while staying on his knees. He grasped the hilt of his sword with both hands and bowed his head. Then Zandria noticed it again, he pulled some strength from somewhere. This time she thought she saw a few wrinkles around his eyes de-wrinkle.

William said, "While my heart belongs to another, my loyalty belongs to the Queen of the Eastern Sky. If it is to be you, then you have my service. With what is left of my body and sword, I shall defend you whatever perils you face on your journey to the throne."

Zandria looked away again. This time the sun reflected into her eyes from a jewel that had not previously been on the hilt of his sword. She knew she was imagining these changes and decided it was better not to say anything.

The old man struggled to his feet and Zandria thought about what good he would actually be if those wolves caught up to them. Maybe, she mused, they could have a chance to escape while the monsters ate the prince. Then she started toward the west again.

"It would be an honor to have you join us then," said Kez. He scrambled through the trees and up the slight incline after Zandria.

Olena took the prince's hand and the two of them slowly began following the others.

The river flowed with uncontrollable force to the sheer drop a few feet away. Adam stopped at the edge, cooling his sore bare feet in the mud. He squatted and scooped a handful of the rushing water to his mouth.

Somewhere behind him, a branch snapped under the weight of someone or something's foot.

Adam stopped, motionless.

Already, he was making great progress. It had only been a day since he climbed out of that filthy hole and he was at the waterfall. He suspected that the girl he was instructed to find spent the previous night somewhere near here. He did not need any interruptions now.

As he waited, a wolf padded silently out of the underbrush and crept down on the shore behind him. It looked as if it were ready to pounce at any moment. Saliva dripped from the corner of the beast's mouth, a mouth large enough that it could swallow Adam's head in one bite.

Adam spoke without turning around, "It's about time you got here. What have you and your men been doing, marking your territory?"

In an instant, the wolf turned into a man and Adam turned around to face him. The bald-headed brute with a bandage across his broken nose did not speak, so Adam continued, "I see footprints that lead right up to the edge. It hasn't been too long since they were here, but they ended up down there."

It was almost a funny scene with a young boy scolding the older man, if they were not plotting a hunt.

"Now I know you and your boys will have to find a way down. When you catch up to me, I'm certain I will have found their trail." Adam stared coldly at the man. He thought about his next words before saying them aloud, this beast could easily tear him apart. He decided to say it anyway, "Don't get in my way. This hunt means more to me than eating a little girl."

With that, he turned from the leader of the assassins and ran to the edge of the waterfall. Without hesitation, he jumped, hoping to himself that the pool so far below would be deep enough.

Chapter 8

Less Than Half
a Day or More

Fury galloped across the open plain, the tall grass brushing at his flanks. In recent memory, it was not often that he could run without saddle or harness. He was free and it should have been exhilarating, except for the lightning.

The dark clouds that hung over the Castle Empyrean spiraled outward. The black and gray sky stretched in every direction growing faster than he could move.

The bolts of lightning struck the ground, sometimes only feet away from him. He could see that some of the most severe strikes in the distance ignited the prairie grass. Black smoke drifted up from the flames and mixed with the clouds, indistinguishable.

Still, Fury was glad there were no more meteors. The storm pelted the castle, but to his surprise, the crystalline fortress showed no damage. To his reckoning, the fiery rocks should have smashed through the glass. He saw some magic in the Northern Woods, but suspected he would never understand all of the mysteries of the ancient castle.

Fury scanned the horizon. Finally, he could barely make out the impression of the Euphoric Mountains. He glanced behind him, but could no longer see the castle. He was not sure how much time passed since he left his mentor and superior officer, Wrath, but he never stopped moving. He knew there was a force working against him. For every two steps he took, it was as if he only moved one. This thought did not discourage him because he could also feel a force of light and love coming from the castle that was pushing him on and protecting him.

The mountains grew nearer and taller. Fury was leaving the plains behind. These plains were not much different than those that separated the Castle Empyrean and his home in the Northern Woods. Under other circumstances, he would have loved to spend many days in the soft grass under a warmer sun than the one now hidden behind the dreadful clouds. But this was not the time and he was not familiar with this land. Because of that, he did not know he was hundreds of miles away from the only safe passage through the Euphoric Mountains.

Instead, Fury was going to have to do something he had never done before. He approached the foothills without a pass or trail in sight. He took the small hills with ease, which boosted his confidence against the imposing wall of rock. His diamond-shoed hooves scattered stony dust that had been undisturbed for centuries. Fury laughed aloud at the lack of challenge from the beginnings of these mountains. He did not know that it was the effect of the mountains themselves that made it seem easier than it was.

The Euphoric Mountains did not have any springs or waterfalls. They were dry and barren. Issuing from the purple and gray, cracked stone was something other than water. The euphoria washed over Fury, but it was not wet. He breathed it in, but it was not air. Even when Fury was crawling almost straight upward on his stomach, he was not aware of his precarious position. Each hoof searched for a hold as the ground faded away below him.

Fury was hanging from the side of a cliff where no Friesian, no horse, should have ever been. If not for the effect of the mountains, he would have been terrified. That was the trick that took the life of many travelers. They would get lost in their own daze, take chances they would normally never take, and then the mountains would claim their lives. Fury did not know how close to death he was.

As his hoof found its next purchase, his muzzle poked into an opening in the wall. Without thinking, he hoisted his body into the crevasse. Fury was wedged firmly, but not stuck. In his stupor, he put one hoof in front of the other on the hidden path. The broken rock pressed into the shiny hair on his sides, only once scraping him hard enough to draw blood.

The passage gradually widened as it sloped downward. Fury would later have no memory of this part of his journey. Moving faster on the way down than the way up, Fury was soon among the foothills on the Dead Forest side of the mountains. Now he was aware of an aching in his head. He felt like he had been asleep for a long time, but he was more tired now than when he was galloping across the plains.

In between the last hard rock of the Euphoric Mountains and the first withered tree of the Dead Forest was a road that divided the two as far as Fury could see. The road looked well-traveled, but showed no signs of life at the moment. Fury suspected that in one or both directions, there must be some kind of town. He heard stories that the Eastern Palace of Soria Moria had once been in this area, too.

That was not his concern now. He had to get back to his task, but the forest looked more impassable than the mountains behind him. Fury was too well aware of his need for haste and decided to follow the road north instead of challenging the lethal-looking branches of the twisted and rotting trees.

In less than half a day, Fury came to an intersection with a road that pointed due east. There was a painted sign on the corner. He took some time learning to interpret the human trick of writing, but this language was different than his homeland. He decided that the words meant there was a town nearby. His best guess was that the town was called Bremen. Fury was concerned that people here may not understand him or why he was traveling without a rider. He hoped he could avoid any of these encounters on his way.

As he continued east, Fury saw that the threatening clouds seemed to stop at the mountains. Still, these lonely woods had their own gray overcast. Fury had not seen the sun since the day he took Snow White to the castle. The Dead Forest was as depressing as the Euphoric Mountains were elating.

No sound, living or otherwise, came from the encroaching woods. That is why Fury was so surprised to hear music. At first, he thought it was his imagination. When he slowed to a trot, he knew it was coming from ahead of him. That was enough of an indication that he was approaching the town named on the sign so many miles back.

Fury continued on for another mile until he could see the first few squatty buildings at the edge of the town emanating that beautiful music. He wanted to go into the town and see where the music was coming from. He knew and loved how humans made music. Prancing around at the many festivals back home was one of his favorite things. Still, he never heard a sound quite like this. It seemed that everything on this side of the mountains offered some kind of enchantment. Fury admitted to himself that he felt like he was under some kind of spell since he began his journey.

This music was no different. The low bass pulsed and thumped with his heartbeat. It connected with his whole body with every hoof step. The sound of the stringed instruments sailed through the air creating their own breeze. There were other sounds Fury could not recognize in the mix, creating something that both amazed and enticed him. As the music pulled him closer, he even thought he could hear singing, but the voices did not sound human.

Then a branch snapped nearby. Fury woke from his daze and froze. He dared not move his body, but strained his eyes all around to see what made that sound. He knew it had to be in the woods to either side. The road was clear of branches and leaves, which meant no one was sneaking up behind him. Now the music was tickling his ears again and he realized he had been holding his breath. Fury started toward the wonderful melodies again.

Another branch cracked and Fury caught a glimpse of white flash to his right. Now the music was forgotten, he knew someone or something was watching him from the woods. Fury took a step off the path and Wrath's voice blared in his head, "Bravery is one salt lick away from foolishness."

Fury knew it was dangerous to leave the path. He was already risking too much heading toward the town. He told himself he was not trying to be a hero, but if something was following him, he had to know. He could not let anything else jeopardize his quest, so he decided to confront his pursuer.

Pushing through the briar at the edge of the road proved quite painful. The thorns and dry twigs tore at his sides and legs. One sharp branch dug in deep at the top of his front left leg. Fury pulled away hard to get free and a thick splinter broke off under his skin. Then, after another step, it was over. The brambles were gone and Fury was surrounded by lifeless trees that he could easily move between, maybe even gallop.

Fury saw the flash of white again. It was moving away from him, now as silent as the Dead Forest. He knew he had to catch it, had to discover if it was friend or foe. He was sure it was a spy of some kind. A friend would not run from him, he thought.

Fury started to give chase and the white shape moved faster. Every time he got close, the shape would disappear behind a tree and reappear from behind another tree in another direction. He knew now that this was no human. It was some beast toying with him. It never occurred to him that there was more than one.

After being led in so many directions, Fury had no idea how to get back to the road. Now, there was no hint of the music. He even lost sight of the tricky animal he was chasing. Fury could feel all of the gloom and despair of the Dead Forest pressing in on him.

Then a thick, soft white tail brushed across his face. He squeezed his eyes, bracing for the attack. When none came, he opened his eyes to see a beautiful white mare in front of him. It took him a moment to realize the creature he was chasing was no ordinary horse. This mare had a short horn rising out of the top of her head that looked like it grew from pure spun gold.

A unicorn.

As a colt, Fury was told they were only stall-time stories, but he always believed in them. Among the few Friesians and occasional other horses that admitted the possibility, it was generally considered that unicorns had been extinct since before he was born. Never in his life did Fury imagine he would meet one face-to-face.

"I am Sayonya. Come with me and you shall find comfort," said the unicorn.

Fury only got a glimpse of her before she dashed back into the woods, but a glimpse was all he needed. Her beautiful white hair glistened. Her tail hung almost to the ground with no tangles. In that brief moment, he also saw his own reflection in her deep blue eyes. Still, it was the horn that amazed him. Even though the sky was overcast, the golden horn glowed with the light of the sun.

Then she was gone. Fury stood for a moment, wondering where she could be in such a hurry to get to. Then he wondered why he was not following her. After all, she was going in what he thought was the direction he needed to go. Besides, she told him to come.

Fury started off after the unicorn, not sure if he was getting closer or even going in the right direction. When he saw a flash of white up ahead, he knew it was her. Then he saw it to his right and another to his left. Fury assumed the amazing creature had magic that let her move quickly through the woods. Still, he did not guess that there could be more than one.

Fury noticed the trees were getting farther apart and suddenly he was in an enormous clearing. The shock of what he saw almost knocked him off his hooves. He knew there was no way he would find Sayonya again. She was hidden somewhere among the hundred other unicorns now grazing in front of him.

Most of the mares took no notice of him, but a few moved around behind. Some nudged him and herded him in among the others. Soon, Fury was surrounded and he surrendered with pleasure. These unicorns were not evil, but they were not going to help him either. Maybe once they roamed all of Empyrean, but now they were only here and this mystical meadow is where they would remain.

Fury was intoxicated by their flowery scent of roses and lilacs. He surprisingly found Sayonya and joined her eating the sweet grass of the meadow and soon forgot about his quest completely. As far as he could tell, there were no males in this herd. Fury was the willing prisoner of a hundred stunning unicorn mares and he was happy.

The group's slow going frustrated Zandria. She was thankful for William's pledge to help, but the old man was having a hard time even walking. She watched as he used his sword as a cane with one hand and put his other on Olena's shoulder.

As they moved through the mix of jungle and forest, Kez kept darting ahead to make sure they were on course. Eventually, they left all signs of the jungle behind and walked beneath the tall, thick trees of an ancient forest. Almost as soon as the jungle was gone, the forest ended. It stopped in a straight line as if the forest grew against a gigantic, invisible wall.

Zandria waved her hands in front of her to be sure there was nothing there. All that she could see now was a vast wasteland. Behind them, the forest stood quiet and green. Zandria could see no reason why it was this way, but knew they had to cross it.

"I don't remember this," said William.

"I'm surprised you remember your own name," said Zandria under her breath.

"It's William," he replied.

Zandria could not believe he heard her and immediately felt bad for saying anything. She turned away before he could see her red, embarrassed face.

The four of them moved across the empty land with Zandria in the lead. There was nothing for Kez to scout now, so mostly he walked at Olena's feet. As they continued on, Zandria noticed cracks etched into the flat ground. She looked to Kez when she saw they were wider in front of them. She saw that he was already investigating.

Kez chose one line and followed it while Zandria and the others waited. As he moved ahead, Zandria could see him able to step down into the crack. After a few more steps, he disappeared completely. Zandria ran forward to find Kez safe at the bottom of the split.

"It appears the cracks are wider here," he said, getting up from the ground and dusting himself off.

It took William some effort, but he lowered himself down into the crevasse. Zandria noticed he did not ask Olena for help. This made Zandria think again that maybe their Prince William was getting younger.

They continued on through the maze of crevasses, now with the rock walls even higher than William's head. Occasionally, the crack ended in a deep, unwelcoming cave. They avoided these passages.

Zandria was glad they spent each night down out of the icy wind that came with the darkness and blew hard as they slept. She was also glad that the pouches the Rainbow Princesses gave them always had something for supper. So they would sit against the close walls, eat, sleep and start over the next day. One morning, she woke up to see William's scraggly beard gone. She assumed he used his sword to shave, but it made him look younger.

Sometimes, the path would end and they would have to climb out and find another crack. Besides the wind, they had no choice but to walk in the cracks because there was now more broken ground than flat. This went on for more days than Zandria could tell.

On the second to the last night in the trenches, Zandria could not get to sleep. She lay with her head on the ground staring at the wall only an arm's reach away. As she sat there not even trying to close her eyes, she thought she heard a sound coming from beneath her. She pressed her ear hard to the surface and could barely make out a continuous pounding. Her only guess was that something deep down was moving and it was moving toward her. Then she thought she heard chanting. She decided it was in her head, but it called to her, urging her down into the blackness. She did not sleep that night.

The next night, still in the same crack, there was no sound. After everyone fell asleep, she let herself drift off and dreamed of thousands of rocks exploding out of the ground. It made no sense to her and she decided not to tell anyone at breakfast.

That day, the path they followed for the last two days, came to another dead end. Kez climbed up first. When he reached the top, he gave a shout.

"What? What is it?" Zandria asked, scrambling after him.

When she poked her head over the edge, she expected more wasteland. Zandria was not sure if the new sight made her feel better or worse. In front of them now was a pale, lifeless forest. Zandria could see no leaves on the trees and no birds in the air.

This time, Zandria did not want to hurt William's feelings, so she asked him first, "What is this place?"

He looked confused, "Forgive me, but when I last set foot in this land, it was all Royal Forest from the spot you found me to the mountains yet to come. I'm afraid I have let you down, as I do not know this place."

Zandria looked at him for a minute wondering why she thought to feel sorry for him in the first place. She decided he was no help and marched off into the woods. Olena, William and Kez followed without another word.

No one spoke for quite a while and the silence of the rotting forest only added to Zandria's mood. She stomped on, grumbling to herself. As she broke branches out of her way and kicked at rocks, she thought about being queen. In her head, she declared she would not allow any worthless old men to serve in her court.

Then the silence was broken by a low rumbling. Olena came up beside her sister and tugged at her arm.

"What is that sound, Zan?" she asked.

Zandria was still in no mood to be friendly and shrugged Olena off, "Probably monsters."

Olena looked at her for a moment and ran back to William. She wrapped her arms around him and hid her face. Kez was at their feet. He gave Zandria a stern look and told Olena, "Don't worry. I'll go check it out."

Kez sprang up into the trees and swung off toward the sound. After a few minutes, he came bolting back.

"You have to see this," he said, pulling Olena's hand. Olena pulled William behind her and Zandria reluctantly followed. Amid the desolate forest, was a green and thriving meadow. The noise that drew them to this clearing came from a hundred horses stampeding across the meadow. Zandria had never seen horses with horns before and let go of the anger that she was holding like a weapon.

The pounding herd came near and the ground shook beneath their feet. The sight was amazing as the beautiful horses raced by. Zandria could see Olena and Kez were enthralled too. Even William's face lit with a smile.

"Unicorns," he shouted over the roar.

"What?" asked Kez.

"These are unicorns. You can tell by the gold horn." The herd moved on to the other side of the meadow, but William was still shouting with joy, "I haven't seen a unicorn since I was a boy and that was in a circus!"

Then Zandria saw it again. A few more wrinkles faded from his face and some hair grew in as she watched. Zandria grabbed Kez and pointed him at William.

Kez spoke in a whisper, answering her unasked question, "Yes, I noticed it a while ago. I think he is getting younger."

Before they could talk more about it, the herd was rounding their side of the meadow again. Olena must have seen something in the herd because Zandria saw her pointing at something. She could barely hear her younger sister over the unicorns.

"Why doesn't the black one have a horn?" Olena shouted.

They all looked and Zandria saw it this time. There was a black horse near the middle of the herd, bigger than the other horses. The herd passed and headed off to the far side again.

William said, "I would know that breed anywhere. That is a Friesian, a protector of the Northern Queendom. Seeing him here makes me fearful for the fate of the Northern Woods."

The herd stopped its racing and started grazing on the soft grass. Zandria watched the enchanted greenery grow in as quickly as it was being eaten.

"Well, maybe we should go ask him," Kez suggested.

"But what if something bad happened?" asked Olena.

"That means we walked all this way for nothing," said Zandria.

Kez led the way to the strong, black horse, but William spoke first, "Sir, I am William, squire to the Queen of the Eastern Sky. Pray tell, the Northern Woods has not fallen to the same horrible fate as our queendom?"

The horse looked confused at first. Zandria did not think he could talk and William let them down again.

Then he answered with a mouthful of grass, "Oh no. It's fine. At least it was the last time I was there. Have you tried this grass?"

William pressed, "No, thank you. Please tell me how you have this knowledge."

Zandria watched the horse swallow his last bite. He said, "I'm Fury, personal bodyguard of the queen. I delivered her to Castle Empyrean myself."

"Then what are you doing here?" interjected Kez.

"I had something to do. I was sent to the East," Fury started, "But you have to try this grass."

"Fury, come try this grass over here," said Sayonya. Then the unicorn turned to the humans, "Please don't disturb us any longer."

Olena looked thrilled about talking to a unicorn, but Zandria felt the mare was quite rude. She also could not believe how the male horse, Fury, would not stop eating long enough to talk with them about such important things.

William whispered to her, "Clearly, he is under some enchantment, but I think we can trust him."

"That's fine," she said, "but what's he doing here?"

Olena walked over to Fury and patted his nose. Sayonya looked concerned, but did not try to stop her. Then Olena gently scratched under Fury's jaw and tried to lift his head. She could not get him to turn away from his feast. Olena walked to his side and examined the healing scratches. There she saw something sticking out. She plucked the poison splinter loose.

"Ouch," neighed Fury.

"That should help," said Olena.

Fury looked back at Olena and then at the others. He looked for a moment to Sayonya, but she stamped off. Zandria could see a different look on Fury's face, now he knew where he was.

"Where did all of you come from?" asked the horse.

William spoke for the group again, "From the East, friend. You mentioned something of a task?"

Fury answered quickly, "The queens are under attack. The Queen of the Eastern Sky has already been lost and I was sent to find the new queen."

Zandria watched Fury looking from her to Olena with dawning realization. Neither girl could keep from smiling brightly.

Kez climbed up on Olena's shoulder and said, "I believe your quest is half finished."

Chapter 9

The Calm and Deadly Night

Zandria was not ready to leave the unicorns, so she was glad when Sayonya allowed them to spend the night at the edge of the meadow. She sat far enough away from the fire to not be blinded by its glare. Under the full moon, she could see the white coats of the mares and their golden horns glimmering. Some of the unicorns were milling about, but most were down on the ground sleeping.

Olena laughed at something and that brought Zandria's attention back to the group by the fire. Kez was standing close to the blaze, waving his arms while telling one of his many funny stories. Prince William and the horse, Fury, listened quietly and Zandria could see that they were completely entertained.

She was not close enough to hear which story Kez was telling, but it still made her smile. With the occasional neigh of one of the unicorns and the crackle of the fire, Zandria came close to forgetting her troubles. She tried to forget about her father and those horrible beasts that were chasing her. When she told William about them, he said he only ever knew of one clan that was not pure evil. Those good werewolves, he told her, were chased off into the far west by the other werewolf packs and never seen again. Thinking about the beasts again gave Zandria a shudder, as if one of them could spring out of the darkness at any moment.

With that thought, she moved a little closer to the fire where Kez was still chittering. Zandria tried to relax and enjoy his story about a group of Nookans and quzzaks that accidentally sailed to an island beyond the sunset. The story did not relax Zandria as her mind bounced from the wolf-men to the journey still ahead. And after that, she wondered to herself, "What happens when I am queen?" She already felt the burden of having to take care of Olena and now there are these others tagging along. She did not want to be angry all the time, but it was hard work making decisions for other people.

Zandria pondered the next day's walk. At least, she thought, Prince William now has a horse to ride, which should keep them from going too slowly. She looked at Fury, studied his muscles and strong looking backbone. She looked to his eyes, which were focused on Kez. Zandria decided she wanted to ask Fury about the Castle Empyrean, the other queens and all the things he had seen there.

Before she could speak, the Friesian's ears, which had been lying back peacefully, poked straight up. Kez stopped speaking in mid-sentence. Fury craned his neck and looked out across the herd. Sayonya was standing out in the middle, looking in the same direction. Whatever affected these animals, Zandria could feel the awareness spreading to all of the unicorns. Something spooked them, but she did not see anything in the pale-lit meadow.

"Prince," Fury said as he stood up, "take the girls back in the wood. Go due north, I think, and don't look back." Fury finished his instructions without looking at them, he was scanning the field.

"Is it what I think it is?" asked Kez.

"Yes," said Fury, "I will follow if I can."

Kez quickly shoveled dirt over the fire and started shooing Olena into the tree line. Zandria looked to Fury's eyes again and tried to follow his gaze. She thought she saw something move at the far side of the herd, but a cloud passed in front of the moon leaving them in blackness.

"Come, dear," said William. He put a hand on her shoulder that startled her in the dark. Then Zandria followed him into the woods. She stopped past the first brambles, unable to resist looking back. She was sure of what was coming, but needed to see it. Zandria needed to see the werewolves.

As the enormous cloud drifted clear of the moon, Zandria could see all of the unicorns were awake and up on their hooves. They looked restless and confused, not sure which way to go. The moonlight began to fill the meadow again. Then Zandria saw it.

On the far side, in the stretch of grass between the herd and the place in the forest where they were earlier today, black figures crouched low to the ground, creeping forward. Zandria strained her eyes a little harder and the last of the cloud moved on. With the help of the full light of the moon, Zandria could see the wolf-men edging closer to the unicorns.

"It's them!" she screamed.

Fury looked back at her and then where she was pointing. He shouted, "Run!", but Zandria did not know if he was talking to her or the unicorns. He rose up on his hind legs, kicking wildly with his front pair and he was yelling, "Heeyaa." Apparently, Fury was attempting to stampede the herd towards the werewolves.

Zandria watched, frozen in place. Before the herd was stirred into action, the closest of the wolves sprang forward. The evil beast tackled the frightened unicorn, sinking its teeth into her flank. Then the other werewolves attacked. One of them did not last long, as his jump landed him on the point of Sayonya's horn.

Zandria cheered, then she was aware of Olena at her side. Despite Fury's warning, none of them had gone far. Zandria looked behind her and saw Kez and William coming back too. They all stayed to watch the magnificent fight before them.

Finally, Fury got the stampede going and charged into the fray. Zandria was afraid to see amid the chaos that so few wolf-men were winning this fight. Still, Fury showed no fear. He used his hind legs to kick a wolf off the back of one of the unicorns. The wolves were jumping and dashing, but now Zandria could see the unicorns move with purpose. They were blocking the werewolves from coming her way and it was costing the beautiful creatures dearly. As the fight continued, Zandria counted ten, twenty, thirty unicorns lying on the ground, unmoving.

Then another cloud rolled in front of the moon. Zandria moved out of the trees to get a look at the sky and saw that this one was larger than the last. She knew they would be in darkness for a while. Zandria tried to look out at the once calm meadow that became a deadly battlefield. She could see nothing, she could only hear it. She could hear the gnashing of teeth, the scraping of claws and another sound that she felt were pure gold horns finding their targets. The whole of the sound was moving away from her and becoming less frenzied.

Then she heard it, a padded, rhythmic sound moving straight toward her. Zandria thought she could see a black shape coming out of the night, coming closer. She had no time to run. Whatever it was, it was on top of her. One of those horrible creatures was about to get her, she thought.

It was Fury. He ducked his head low and scooped her up on his back. "I told you to run," he said angrily. Zandria did not respond, she was too scared to talk.

Fury stopped by the others and let Zandria slide off his back. Without seeing each other, Fury started, "Listen. You have to go. Go north. Two or three of those things escaped into the woods. Sayonya and I are going to try and track them down. Go north and you should find a great road. Try to find the town, I think it's called Bremen."

William interrupted, "Ah, Bremen. It used to be the edge of the Eastern Queendom. Those people built the main road to the Palace by the Sea."

"Good, Bremen. I'll meet you there when this is finished." Without another word, Fury galloped off.

It was finally beginning to set in. Zandria was so enthralled by the battle between the unicorns and werewolves that she did not realize how much danger they were in. Now that they were moving deeper into the forest, she was becoming more scared.

Every sound made her heart race. She was sure that the snapping twig off to her right was one of the beasts. Zandria peered into the darkness, her mind creating shapes out of nothing.

The clouds continued to hang in front of the moon. They moved on as fast as William could go. Zandria fought the urge to run. Earlier, all she could think about was how slow the old man made them. Now, she was glad he was here. She did not want to be running off alone into the claws of a waiting monster. Besides, she thought, an old man with a sword is better than no sword at all.

The girls let Kez lead them. Zandria hoped his eyesight was better in the dark. She could tell he was scared too. He kept dashing ahead and then back between their feet. Zandria had never seen Kez like this. When he was close enough to make out his shape in the dark, she could see that even his tail was curled tight to his body.

They went on in silence, Zandria even held her breath for fear that the sound would attract the attention of the wolf-men. The only noises came from the old woods around them. Zandria was thankful there were no animal noises, only the occasional breeze rustling the dead leaves or the breaking of branches that stuck out in front of them. They continued like this for what Zandria felt was a very long time. Then the trees disappeared. They were in a clearing.

Zandria's anger overcame her fear for a moment and she said aloud, "We've gone in circles. We're back at the meadow." She quickly realized how much noise she made and slapped both hands over her mouth.

As if to refute her statement, the clouds broke enough that they could see this new clearing. The opening was much smaller and in the center of the circle was a house surrounded by what looked like a short picket fence.

"I think it's our only chance," said Kez.

"It looks empty. We should be safe there," answered William.

It seemed to Zandria that these two were sharing a thought and concluding the conversation aloud. Then it occurred to her what they were thinking. She said, "You can't seriously want to go into that house."

"We can hide in there until morning," said Kez. He continued, "It's not safe out here. With those clouds, I can't see the tip of my tail out there. We can get inside and lock the door."

"No way. We need to keep going to the town," said Zandria.

"If I may point out," said William, "We're not even sure we are going in the right direction. At least here, we will have a defensible position."

Then there was a long, echoing wolf's howl. This, more than William's argument, changed Zandria's mind and she led them inside.

The house seemed bigger on the outside, but inside there was only one room. In the center of the room was a candle sitting on the middle of a wobbly wooden table. When they got close to the table, the candle lit itself.

"Hurry! Put it out!" squealed Kez. Zandria and William both blew hard at the candle. No matter how many times they tried, the flame only danced and would not go out. William even pinched the wick with his fingers. The fire was gone for a moment, but came back as soon as he moved his hand.

Zandria was as worried as Kez that the candle could be seen from the outside. She looked toward the window by the door to see how bright it was. Then she was confused because there was no window there on the inside. She looked at the other three walls. She said, "Ka, no windows."

Kez, William and Olena double-checked her observation.

"But I saw a lot of windows on the outside," said Olena.

"As did I," said William. He walked to the door and stuck his head out. "By Empyrean's Gate, there are windows on the outside." They all came outside to see. As soon as Kez, the last one out, was on the porch, the candle went out.

Olena pressed her face to the glass and Zandria looked in next to her. She could see nothing. Not blackness, but actual big, empty nothingness that seemed to go on forever. For a moment, it felt like the nothingness reached out and grabbed her. Then Zandria looked at her sister to see if she saw the same thing.

"Can you see it, Zan?" asked Olena. "Millions of butterflies."

"Not butterflies," said Kez, "it's the jungle back home."

William said, "I saw endless fields of trees like the Royal Forest used to be. I believe we have discovered a very mysterious house. Perhaps going inside is not the best idea."

Zandria did not want to tell what she saw and instead said, "Let's go back in. You said we would be safe inside. Besides, I don't think anyone lives here."

When they were back inside with the door closed, the candle lit on its own again. This time, no one was as concerned. Zandria saw the table which held the candle. It looked homemade, but by someone who did not know what they were doing. The whole thing was wobbly and a bent nail stuck out of one corner. There was no other furniture in the room. Zandria turned her attention to the walls next. They were bare except one where a cold, empty stone fireplace looked like it grew out of the floor. Zandria did not remember seeing a chimney outside.

"What is that smell?" asked Olena. She was making big exaggerated sniffing noises. The way she scrunched her face when she did this always annoyed Zandria. Thinking Olena was being silly, Zandria inhaled deeply, but only got dust up her nose. She sneezed hard and the candle flickered.

Kez was now sniffing the room, too. "I don't know what it is, but it's making me hungry," he said.

"I recognize it," said William. He was leaning against one of the bare walls with his arms folded and his eyes closed. He had a faint grin and, in this light, Zandria thought he did not look any older than one of the Nookan elders in their village. She could not say for sure, but she even thought there were some brown streaks in his white hair.

William continued, "When I was a child, we had these wonderful town faires. My mother would make a special treat. She would mix up three huge bushels of dough and bake enough cookies for everyone over a huge fire behind our home. She called it gingerbread."

"I don't care what it's called," said Kez. "It smells delicious and I think the table is made from it." He climbed up next to the candle and broke off a piece from the edge. He smelled it and took a nibble. After a moment of tasting, he took two more big bites and the chunk was gone.

"Is it good?" asked Olena.

Kez broke off two more pieces and gave one to Olena. "It's great," he said.

William moved the candle over to the mantle above the fireplace and joined them. Zandria did not realize how hungry she was until now. They ate dinner not so long ago at the unicorn meadow and should not be hungry yet. Still, Zandria could not smell what the others said they could. She cautiously broke off the crooked nail and slowly touched it to her tongue.

She expected the rusty-looking metal to be bitter, but it was sweet and the smell of gingerbread quickly flooded her senses. She ate the cookie nail in one bite and was suddenly twice as hungry as she was before the bite.

It did not take long and the whole table was gone. The four of them ate so fast that there were almost no crumbs. Zandria looked at the faces of her friends and could see they were still as hungry as she was. Then she scanned the room looking for something else. In each of the four corners was a chair. They moved in unison, breaking the chairs apart and stuffing themselves like mad, each with their own pile. At this moment, Zandria was not concerned that these chairs were not there when they came into the house.

After Olena finished her chair, Zandria watched her curl up next to the empty fireplace. She lay still for a moment and then was asleep. Kez moved over by her. Zandria laughed at this because his stomach was so full and round that he was waddling. She turned to William and he still looked hungry, but he gave a big yawn too.

Now that the chairs were gone, Zandria wanted something more. She never tasted anything like the gingerbread and could not get enough of it. To her delight, a small footstool appeared where the table had been. She broke it in half to share with William. He only ate part of one leg before he was too drowsy to continue. William fell asleep against the wall where he sat eating.

Zandria ate in silence for a little while longer. It was not until she finished her half of the footstool that it occurred to her she was the only one awake. Even though the others were there, while they were asleep she felt really alone. Something about this place made her uneasy.

She moved over next to William against the wall and surprised herself by how comforted she was leaning on his sleeping shoulder. Zandria wanted the others to think she was strong and knew a good queen would not admit she was scared. If Olena or Kez found her sleeping there, she planned to tell them she moved close to get the last of Prince William's gingerbread.

Zandria fell asleep in this position without taking another bite. In her dream, she was three years old again, laying on her father's chest and listening to the ebb and flow of the ocean. She woke in the morning with tears in her eyes and a strange pain in her arms.

It took a moment for Zandria to understand what was happening. She knew she was no longer next to William because she could barely make out his shape in front of her. He looked asleep, still sitting against the wall. She tried to move her arms to wipe her tears and felt the unexpected sensation of pain again. She could not move her arms. Another try elicited an "Ow!" from Olena.

Zandria could not see clearly, because she could not wipe the tears from her eyes and bright, morning sunlight streamed in through windows that were not there last night. She now realized that she was tied to a chair. She figured Olena must be tied with her, back-to-back in another chair.

Someone moved in front of Zandria and wiped her eyes with a soft towel. Then Zandria could see the figure was an old woman who looked kind, but not quite right. There was something wrong with her, Zandria thought, like this house. The old woman was tan and wrinkled from working outdoors, but her skin hung loose like a costume that was two sizes too big.

"Zan, what's happening?" asked Olena.

"I don't know," Zandria answered. Then she spoke to the old woman, "Let us go, whoever you are."

The old woman looked hurt by Zandria's words and put her hands on her hips. Zandria watched the skin on her upper arms sag and writhe with the movement. Then there was a squirm that made Zandria think something was crawling beneath the woman's skin.

"I am Baba Yaga, of course," said the old woman. She smiled a big toothy smile. Zandria knew her eyes were playing tricks on her. She figured she must have eaten too much gingerbread and it made her see things. She thought she saw something black try to force its way out from behind Baba Yaga's big yellow teeth.

"You know me, dear," Baba Yaga continued, "Everyone in town knows me."

"What town?" asked Olena.

"Why Bremen, dear. You and your friends came from Bremen to ask me for help." Baba Yaga spoke soft and kind.

"We're not from Bremen," said Zandria. "Besides," she continued, "if we were here for help, why tie us up."

Baba Yaga still spoke gently, "Dear, while I was out gathering toadstools and spider eggs last night, you came into my house uninvited. You ate my gingerbread without asking. And I should tell you, too much of it does tend to make one drowsy. I had to bind you because I did not know why you were here. You are here for my help, right? Don't you need some advice?"

"No, we're not here for your help," said Zandria. "This is some kind of trap and you must have drugged us with the gingerbread. You don't even know who we are."

"Oh, interesting," said Baba Yaga. "If you're not here from the town, then I have a pretty good idea of who you are." She snapped her fingers and the fireplace roared with flames. Zandria saw an enormous black kettle now hanging above the fire, one that could easily hold Olena and herself. Baba Yaga spoke again, "Some crows told me two little girls might be coming my way. And since you are not from Bremen, then you have to be the two little girls on a very special task."

"Let us go!" demanded Zandria.

"Well," Baba Yaga paused, "it's too late for that. You did eat enough of my gingerbread to make you sweet enough to eat. It is unfortunate that you aren't here for my help. I can be very helpful." She moved over to the kettle and stirred the boiling liquid. She said, "I don't usually eat people who come to me for help. But since you insist that you do not need me, I am sure there are others who would reward me greatly if I sup on your bones." Baba Yaga cackled and her whole body squirmed again.

The noise must have woke William, because he exclaimed, "Queen's mercy!"

Baba Yaga turned to face him with her arms outstretched. Zandria saw claws on her fingertips that she did not notice before. The old woman hissed. Then Kez jumped from out of nowhere and bounced off Baba Yaga's back. The impact sent the old woman flailing towards the kettle.

She flipped over the side and splashed into the scalding soup.

William got up as quickly as he could. With one flick of his sword, he cut the ropes holding Zandria and Olena.

Glad to be free, Zandria said, "Thank you, Prince. I'm glad you weren't tied up."

"She must have thought her spell would have kept us asleep," he said.

Then Kez added, "Luckily, I think someone else's magic is growing. I believe the closer we get to Castle Empyrean, the more one of you will get the queen's powers."

"So it was really me who saved us," said Zandria.

Before anyone could respond to that statement, Baba Yaga leaped out of the giant kettle. Her boiling flesh fell from her body and thousands of different bugs escaped. Roaches, beetles and grasshoppers swarmed the cottage and still more types crawled out of the limp sack that was her body a few moments ago.

Olena ran outside, screaming, followed by Kez. William ushered Zandria out next and grabbed their magic pouches from the table. He stomped his feet on as many bugs as he could along the way.

When Zandria caught up to Olena, her sister was staring at the fence surrounding the house. What they thought was a white picket fence under the dark of night was actually a ring of human bones when seen under the sun. Olena screamed again and Zandria grabbed her hand, pulling her towards the woods.

There was a loud cracking sound and the four of them turned back toward the house. The whole house rose up from the ground on what looked to Zandria like four huge chicken legs. The house took one step towards them and stopped, then ran off into the woods in the opposite direction. The house splashed into a small swamp behind some nearby trees and sank out of sight.

Before their eyes, dead trees sprouted up out of the ground and erased the small clearing. They were alone and safe, for now in the middle of the woods.

Then Kez asked, "Do you hear that?"

Zandria listened. Ever so faintly, she thought she could hear music.

"It's coming from this way," he said. "Follow me."

Kez led them north through the Dead Forest toward the town of Bremen.

Chapter 10

Music in the Morning, Noon & Night

The music.

The music was enchanting.

As they walked on, the music grew in intensity. Zandria could feel it. It vibrated in the ground and shook the trees, but it was not loud. There was something about the sound that made it unreal.

Zandria was glad that William was keeping up today because the closer they got, the faster she wanted to go. Under the bright morning light, Zandria confirmed her thoughts once more. She knew William was getting younger. He stood up straighter today and did not use his sword as a cane.

The cheerful morning music turned into something soft and slow and sad. With the change, Zandria noticed they all walked a little slower. This gave her time to study William, to notice the subtle changes in his appearance. She wanted to talk to Kez about it, but this morning William seemed to be about the age of her father. This realization brought her mind back to their last day on the beach, the day with the wolves. Instead of going to Kez, Zandria moved close to Olena. She wanted to hug her sister or hold her hand. Then the music changed tempo and Olena started skipping to the faster tune.

As Olena skipped out of reach, Zandria felt empty like what she saw in Baba Yaga's window. This morning, she felt different. She felt like she needed her sister or someone. The thought of being queen scared her more now than the old bug lady or the werewolves. It made her feel like she was standing on the edge of that nothingness and she needed somebody to keep her from falling.

If she thought about it a moment longer, Zandria would have realized that the feeling was only a curse from looking in Baba Yaga's window and not real feelings. Instead, the music invaded her head and she started skipping too. The wolf-men, William, her father and Olena were all forgotten in this blissful sound.

Zandria concentrated on the music now. She figured they had to be close to the town. The vibrations made the little hairs on her arms stand up and gave her a tingle at the back of her neck.

She tried to pick out the instruments, but none of them sounded quite like they did back home. Still, some she knew from the few shows they saw at the Palace by the Sea. She heard a flute, but it was only one of many sounds. There was the boom and thump of drums, but more intense. These drums were so low that it was more of a feeling than a sound. The nearer they came, the drums rustled the dry leaves on the ground. Zandria thought they must have shaken all of the leaves off the dead trees a long time ago.

Now, there was a guitar, but the twanging was more vibrant and faster than the one she heard before. The flute sound twisted into something harsher like when the Nookan Elders blew through polished seashells. This sound was more controlled and varied, though.

Zandria could not even imagine what made the other sounds. She was so excited to see the band. She thought there must be at least fifty people playing together. It had to be an amazing sight.

Then, there it was. Through the last bit of trees ahead, Zandria could see a blanket of green grass. Slightly beyond that were two low huts. She was so excited to finally be at Bremen. Zandria was sure that being in a real town would make them the safest they had been since they left the Rainbow Princesses. She almost ran, but suddenly, the music stopped.

Everything was silent. The music carried and pulled them in for hours now, so no one moved. The enchantment was broken and Zandria was not sure what to do.

Then there was a great cacophony of animals. So many different brays, squeals, howls and yelps that Zandria did not even try to guess what they were.

"The Royal Zoo never made such a din," said William. "There must be quite a menagerie in this town."

Kez took his usual spot on Olena's shoulder. He said, "Maybe we should not make our presence known too early. That racket sounds too much like an angry mob to me."

Zandria listened. Kez was right, she agreed. The animal sounds were not random calls, but animal voices screaming for "Justice. Punishment. Hang the tyrant. Burn the slaver."

"Let's sneak into town and find out what's happening," said Zandria.

"Alright. We should stay low behind those huts," William pointed to the closest thatched buildings as he spoke. He added, "Girls, please stay behind me. We must resist our appetite for running headlong into trouble."

Zandria and Olena did as William asked and the group walked quietly to the hut. William motioned for them to move up next to a full water trough. From there, they could see the entire town.

At one time, Zandria thought, it must have been a wonderful town. There were two and three story buildings. Several had signs that read Inn or Restaurant. As William said, this was where people prepared to take the long journey east. Zandria guessed they did it in style.

But something changed. The buildings looked ransacked and abandoned. Windows were broken and things like clothes and broken chunks of furniture littered the roads. Then there were these little straw huts that dotted the whole town. Zandria thought whatever happened did not happen so long ago because the huts looked brand new. Still, there were no humans in sight, except one.

Zandria could see the town square. She could see an angry mob of animals. She had never seen so many different types of animals together. Even some that should be enemies, like bears and rabbits, stood together shouting at a single man. The man was bound with rope and held by, what looked like to Zandria, big quzzaks.

"Ugh, monkeys," whispered Kez. "I can't abide them. Such filthy creatures."

Olena giggled, but William hushed her.

Zandria watched those things, those monkeys, pull the frightened looking man up onto a platform and hold him in place. He looked like he wanted to run, but dared not. She could hear a group of pigs chanting, "Four legs good." Then the neighboring sheep would answer, "Two legs baaaaad."

Something was not right here and Zandria knew it. At least in her part of the world, animals and humans got along. They each had their own work to do and never took advantage of each other. It seemed that here, the animals felt they were being abused or enslaved. Apparently, they decided to do something about it and either chased off or killed the humans.

Now, a donkey came up on the platform. The crowd got quiet. A moment later, a dog joined him. There was a low growl from the other canines in the audience. Next, a cat slinked up beside the dog. An enormous white tiger in the crowd gave a roar. Then, to a flutter of wings and a myriad of chirps from the surrounding rooftops, a rooster climbed the steps of the platform.

Zandria looked at these four animals and saw something different about them immediately. They looked ragged and worn. Both the dog and cat were shedding so much that patches of skin showed. All eight of their eyes bulged and were bloodshot. The donkey had a sinister bucked-tooth grin that showed many missing teeth. One tooth fell out while he was standing there.

Zandria was now really worried for the man, but there was nothing to do except watch.

The donkey knelt down on his front legs, and the dog climbed up on his back. The cat quickly followed. When the donkey stood up straight, the dog braced herself and then the cat climbed onto her back. When the three animals were ready, the rooster took flight. He appeared to exert a great amount of effort, but eventually landed atop the cat. They would have made for a very unique statue, Zandria imagined.

The rooster addressed the crowd in a dry, cracked voice, "My friends, since the day the great rock fell from the sky, we have been enlightened."

At this, all of the animals bowed and Zandria saw it. Off to the left of the platform, blocked by the standing crowd, was a huge rock embedded in the ground. She saw shooting stars before and wondered if this was what they looked like if they hit the ground. The rock was black and shiny and bigger than any of the animal's huts around town. It had strange spikes and twisting shapes poking out of it in every direction. The top even looked like it had a place to sit.

Then the rooster continued, "For too many years, we have been slaves to humans. They have tortured and abused us. Remember, it took ten days to cleanse this town of Bremen, but we are willing to take a lifetime to bring freedom to all of Empyrean. I will remind you all that a breathing human is a bad human. And here, we have one before us today."

The monkeys pulled the man forward and the crowd growled and hissed. Then they parted so a big brown ox could move to the base of the platform. The ox did not look like he wanted to be there either and mostly stood with his head down.

The rooster asked the ox, loud enough for all to hear, "Is this the man who claimed to be your master?"

The ox did not appear to know how to respond and chose to say, "Um, that is Farmer Mulgart. I worked our fields with him for twenty years."

The rooster addressed the crowd, "Friends, hear that this honest laborer was forced to ground and beaten for twenty years."

The crowd jeered and taunted the farmer. It was so loud that Zandria almost could not hear the ox's next words, "It wasn't like that. We shared the food from the crops. He never hit me. The family and I were traveling east. Farmer Mulgart promised to show me the sea before my last days. He was bringing his new baby too."

The rooster did not acknowledge the ox. Instead, he said, "You did the right thing by coming to our town. We will give you freedom."

The white tiger licked his lips and the bear moved close to the platform. The two big animals were quickly surrounded by a dozen scavenging rats, all waiting for a fresh meal.

"I pronounce this human guilty," finished the rooster.

The crowd roared and the monkeys pushed Farmer Mulgart off the platform and into the mud at the paws of the tiger and bear. The meat-eating animals did not hesitate to pounce.

Olena covered her eyes, but Zandria watched. She saw the wicked rooster fly down to the edge of the platform so he could be face-to-face with the ox.

The rooster, still speaking for all to hear, instructed, "Come, stand before the great rock and be enlightened."

The crowd herded the ox over in front of the fallen star. Zandria watched the dog climb up on top of the rock and sit in the spot that she thought actually looked like a seat. The cat climbed down in front, where the scratch marks looked like she had been clawing at the rock for days. The rooster disappeared around the back of the rock. Finally, the donkey made his way through the crowd and took his place at the side.

The ox kept looking back for the farmer and maybe trying to find a way to escape. Every time he tried to move, the other animals blocked him. Then the donkey put his mouth to one of the twisty spikes sticking out of the rock. He blew in it and again Zandria was reminded of the seashells back home.

The other three animals joined the donkey. The cat scratched at the rock making the guitar sound. The dog banged away at the top, furiously playing the drums. Zandria could not see what part the rooster played, but she was amazed that these four animals sounded like fifty playing something that was not even a real instrument.

As the music wrapped around them, Zandria noticed that the ox was not struggling as much. She also noticed that the music was not having any effect on her or apparently Olena or William either. It still sounded beautiful, but it was not hypnotic now. After a few more minutes, the ox looked as angry as the other animals and was swaying to the tune. The birds and a few other animals tried to sing along, but they could not compete with the four musicians of Bremen.

"I think, perhaps, we should circumvent this town," suggested William.

"I think you're right," said Zandria.

They got up to leave, but Olena did not move. She was looking at Kez and crying. Zandria saw the little quzzak swaying to the music like the other entranced animals. She grabbed his shoulder and spun him around. Kez's eyes were bloodshot and he looked like he went crazy.

"Over here," he shouted. "There are humans over here!"

Zandria did not know what else to do, so she ran. William grabbed Olena by the arm and the three of them raced to the road heading west. Zandria could not believe that Kez betrayed them. They knew him since Olena was a baby. She knew the music was in his head and that fallen star was in control.

It did not take long for a pack of dogs to catch up to them. When they were surrounded, Zandria decided it might be safer to surrender. The rooster and Kez came walking up together.

"Thank you, brother, for alerting us of the interlopers," said the rooster.

"Now that I have seen the way," said Kez, "I must do my part for the cause."

The rooster spoke to the entire crowd, "Friends, we finished one trial this day. Let us save the next trial for later and make it a midnight feast."

There was a lot of cheering from the crowd coming up behind the rooster and Kez. The donkey, dog and cat must have stayed behind because Zandria could still hear the music. She did not feel its intensity as strongly without the rooster playing his part, whatever that was.

"Put them in one of the human buildings and have the bear guard the door," ordered the rooster to the pack of dogs.

The rooster went back toward the great rock, but Kez stayed with the group. The dogs escorted them to a long single story building with a sign on the door that said "Food". Inside, they found an enormous black snake stretched out on the bar. The snake must have recently fed because the middle of its body still bulged. Zandria saw a baby's rattle on the floor and feared that something terrible happened to Farmer Mulgart's baby too.

The dogs watched as the snake slowly slid away. When the last of its lengthy body made it out the door, the bear came up and laid on the front porch. The dogs looked satisfied with the security of their prisoners and left. Kez stood for a moment longer, took William's sword, then walked out without a word.

"Are they going to eat us?" asked Olena.

"Certainly not," said William. "We will escape. Let's try the back door."

The girls followed William past the tables and into the pantry. There was a back door and he flung it open. Their escape was cut short as the white tiger lay there gnawing on a juicy bone.

They went back inside and Zandria said, "I don't see how we can get away now."

"Have faith. We have to realize whatever power holds these creatures comes from that fallen star," said William. "If we can find a way to destroy it, maybe we can save us and them."

Zandria went to the window to look at the rock. She could see Kez right up front with the ox and the music continued. When Zandria turned back, William was in the pantry sorting through food and Olena was kneeling on the floor.

"What are you doing, Olena?" asked Zandria.

"I'm saying a prayer for Furry to come rescue us," she answered.

Zandria scoffed, "That'll never work. Besides, his name is *Fury*."

"It will so," said Olena.

"No, it won't. Even if he knew to come look for us, the music will do bad things to him when he gets too close, same as it did to Kez."

"Then I'll tell him not to listen," was Olena solution.

William interrupted the girls as he came from the pantry with an armful of supplies. He dumped them onto a nearby table, pulled up a chair and got to work. Olena folded her hands and squeezed her eyes shut, so Zandria sat next to William.

"Are you making dinner?" she asked.

"Quite the opposite," William said. "I have a brief knowledge of explosives and plan to put together a little surprise."

"You're going to blow up the animals?"

"No, my lady," he said. "I plan to blow up the star in hopes of freeing the animals."

"In that case, I'll make dinner," said Zandria.

By the time the sun went down, Zandria made a fruit soup and William finished his work. After mixing all the ingredients, he poured it into a jar, then secured the lid with a long string poking out. They all tried Zandria's soup and found it to be too bitter even after she added a pound of sugar to the pot. Olena laughed which left Zandria feeling frustrated. William quickly intervened by procuring some dried beef and several pieces of candy from the pantry.

Zandria did not know if the rooster would really wait until midnight. She thought it had to be getting close, but the only clock in the restaurant was smashed. After their meal, Olena prayed again and then fell asleep with her head on William's lap.

Suddenly, there was a disturbance outside. Zandria peeked out the window and animals were running in every direction. The musicians were distracted, but attempted to continue playing. Then she saw what was happening. One of the werewolves that had been chasing them was attacking the town. He was running back and forth, clawing down dogs, biting chickens. A monkey tried to jump on its back and suffered fatally for it.

Zandria could not turn away from the mayhem. Then the wolf stopped in front of her window. Maybe he could smell her. He started towards her and then stopped. The Bremen musicians were focused again and the music came louder. The wolf-man shook his head as the music stuck in his ears like water after a swim. He looked like the sound was driving him mad and quickly turned back into a human with less sensitive ears.

The sight of the transformation was unsettling for Zandria, but what happened next was worse. As the man stood, scratching his ears, the tiger rounded the corner from behind the restaurant. The magnificent white creature charged at full speed. The man did not know what was happening and was knocked off his feet and out of sight. That was the last Zandria saw of either of them.

Then there was a noise outside the front door. Zandria was sure another werewolf was coming. There was a crash and the bear came bursting through the door backwards. The mighty beast collapsed to the floor, unconscious. William stepped in front of the girls. For the first time, Zandria saw him as the hero he once was. She expected the werewolf to come bounding in at any moment. Instead, in trotted Fury.

"Hurry, get on my back," he was shouting for no apparent reason.

William lifted Olena and then Zandria. As he climbed up behind, Olena hugged Fury around the neck.

"You came," she said.

"I can't hear you," Fury said, still shouting. "I have fluff in my ears. Hang on."

Zandria understood why he was so loud. Fury could not hear the enchanting music with fluff in his ears, let alone even his own talking. She held on tight as Fury turned and galloped out the door. William ducked low to keep from hitting his head.

In the center of town, Zandria saw Kez standing on the platform. She knew yelling at

Fury would do no good, so she pointed where he could see. As they got close, Zandria snagged Kez's tail before he could swing William's sword. William wrested the sword away and slid it in its scabbard. Zandria forced Kez in between her and Olena, very definitely against his hypnotized will.

Now it was William's turn to point. He guided Fury towards the great rock. The animals were still in chaos and no one tried to stop them. They rode past once and William saw what he was looking for. He pointed at a hole on the back side of the rock. As Fury charged, William lit the fuse on his homemade bomb. The donkey, dog and cat saw them coming and scattered. The music stopped and the rooster was nowhere to be seen.

When they were close enough, William leaned over and tossed the explosive in the hole. By the light of the burning fuse, Zandria caught a glimpse of the rooster huddled inside the rock. She was not sure, but it looked like the rock was attached to him, sucking his blood.

A moment later, the rock exploded. Chunks flew everywhere. Some pieces smashed through nearby walls, others crashed on the little huts setting them ablaze. When the smoke cleared, all that was left was the empty crater and a few rooster feathers floating in the air.

Fury turned the corner by the restaurant again, this time to take the west road. Their path was blocked by the leader of the wolf-men.

"He's the last one," shouted Fury as he skidded to a stop.

Olena seemed less worried about the werewolf than getting the fluff out of Fury's ears. She picked out the cottony boughs and said, "Thank you. I knew you would come."

William said, "I fear it was all for naught."

The werewolf attacked. He was running at top speed, straight for them. Fury had no time to react. Right as the wolf was about to jump, the bear barreled out of the restaurant door. The lumbering animal crashed down on the wolf-man. They rolled across the dirt road and smashed through a couple of the remaining huts. Fury did not wait to see who would win the fight. He turned north and galloped for the edge of town.

"We have to get clear of the road," he said, now at normal volume. "If that assassin survives, it will be too easy to track us. Maybe we can lose him in the woods and then head west."

"That sounds like the best course of action," came a voice from Zandria's lap. She forgot that she stuffed Kez in between her and Olena. He looked like he had been asleep for a long time, but otherwise okay. Whatever charm that rock held over him, she thought, went away when it did.

Olena turned back to Zandria and said, "Maybe the other animals are safe too."

"I have a feeling the rooster didn't fair to well," replied Zandria.

"In either case, we're not going back to find out," William added.

Chapter 11

Night Lights
Lead the Way

Without the music from Bremen, Zandria was extremely aware of how quiet it was in the Dead Forest. She heard every pad of Fury's hooves. There were no other living sounds around them except their own breathing. Despite their isolation, Zandria felt they were safer now than they had been in the past few days.

Right now, though, Zandria was too scared to talk. In the last two days, they had two encounters with the wolf-men. If there were any of them left now, she was afraid the slightest noise would attract them. She tried not to imagine any other dangers this horrible place might offer. And she tried, also, not to remember the others they already faced, like the old bug woman, Baba Yaga. So, now for their own safety, they traveled in silence and darkness. There was nothing to light their way, not even the moon could penetrate this part of the forest.

It was some time before any of them dared speak and it was Olena who offered the first whisper. "I don't think we're being followed," she said.

"How can you be certain?" came the whisper from Kez.

Zandria's first reaction was to be angry at them for making noise. Before she blurted out a "Shut up", she realized she was actually relieved to hear the sound. The voices helped ease some of the silent tension she felt.

"I believe she is right," said William in a slightly louder voice. "We have been traveling for a while now with no evidence of anyone coming behind us. Perhaps the bear back in that town released us from our pursuer."

Zandria was a little worried about his volume. Still, the warmth of William's voice made her a little less scared too. He was almost talking in a normal speaking voice and this comforted her.

It was Fury who brought the group to a full conversation. He said, "If everyone is feeling secure now, I have a request."

"What is it, oh noble steed?" asked Olena with a grin. Zandria heard a compassion in her sister's tone that she was far from feeling.

Fury answered as politely as possible, "Could everyone please get off of me now?"

"Oh, horsy, I'm so sorry," said Olena on behalf of all four riders. Kez sprang down immediately. Then William gave an amused sounding chuckle as he lowered himself to the ground. Zandria stuck out her hand, hoping William would help her down first, which he did. Before he assisted Olena, she paused to give Fury a big hug around his muscular neck.

"I'm sorry to be so rude, but it's been a long time since I carried anyone," Fury said. "Plus, when I did, it was only one soldier at a time."

"We understand completely," said William as he took the lead. Zandria thought they were still heading north, but trusted their guidance to the now somewhat less than old man. William continued, "After all, we owe you every courtesy as it was you who saved us this night."

Zandria did not want to be left out any longer and asked, "How did you know where to find us?"

"It is my job to protect you and I sent you toward the town," Fury said.

"Yes, but you came straight to our building," persisted Zandria.

"It's funny you mention that," said Fury. "The unicorns beat most of the werewolves, but a few were trying to slip away. When I sent you on, Sayonya and I went after them. I really wasn't sure if we were chasing them or they were chasing us at that point. After a day's worth of criss-crossed paths, Sayonya returned to her herd. Then, I discovered I was behind them again and the remaining two assassins were heading into Bremen."

"Fantastic," said William.

"But that still doesn't answer how you came right to us," said Zandria. She was sure she knew the answer. She was sure it was Olena's prayer. Somehow it was magic. Zandria was not ready to admit they might share the powers of the queen. She knew that there could be only one Queen of the Eastern Sky and already made up her mind that it was herself.

"That's the strange part. The wolf-men escaped my sight as I heard the first faint sounds of the captivating music. Then, I had a feeling. It was a very specific feeling, like a suggestion that came from nowhere at all. I looked around and saw one cotton bush that seemed to be blooming while all the others were dry and wilted. At that moment, I knew two things. First, I stuck my head into the bush and rustled around until my ears were full of fluff. I knew this would keep the music from taking hold of me. Then I knew to come directly to the corner building at the center of town. Imagine my surprise to find an enormous bear waiting for me."

William said, "I do hope he was large enough to put a stop to that wolf-man."

"That last one was their leader," said Fury. "I suspect it would take more than an angry bear to stop him. Worse still, without his pack, he may prove to be a bit faster now as well."

Zandria could make out Kez scurrying around at their feet, listening to the story. He climbed up on William's shoulder, apparently to be face-to-face with Fury. She wondered what purpose that served in the dark.

Kez asked, "You heard a suggestion?"

"No, I didn't hear anything. No voice, only a thought suddenly in my head," answered Fury.

"The same thing happened to me," said Kez. "The day I came to you girls on the beach, I was looking for some bananas and then decided to come see you. I forgot that until now. In fact, I forgot it even by the time I reached your hut. First, there was nothing and then there was this need to go. Like a suggestion from nobody."

"Ah," said William suddenly. Zandria saw the response startled Kez so much that the quzzak jumped from William to Fury. "Sorry little friend," he continued, "That is only a small example of their abilities. The four queens can communicate over great distances as the need arises."

"I prayed for you to save us," said Olena.

"And your praying made me think it," chimed in Zandria quickly. This was another opportunity for her to remind everybody that she was going to be queen. She started to say, "I.....OW!"

Something stung Zandria on the cheek and she stopped moving. At first, she thought maybe Olena was mad and threw something. Then Olena shouted too.

"Something bit me," she said.

Zandria peered into the dark, but could see nothing. Then she felt a sting on her left forearm and slapped her right hand over it on instinct. When she pulled her hand away, she expected to see a grotesque bug that could only survive in this dreadful forest. Instead, she saw a speck of light flicker and then fade out.

"What was that?" she whispered to herself.

Fury was next. He received a sting or bite or whatever it was and gave out a whinny. This time Zandria knew what to look for. She saw a tiny dot of light hovering around the horse's hindquarters.

She saw William continue to move a few paces ahead, but now he stopped walking too. Zandria could see the glowing specks begin to circle him as well. There were only a few at first, but now she guessed there were hundreds.

"They're so beautiful," said Olena, then, "Ow!"

Soon there were enough of the miniscule flying creatures that Zandria could see everything around her as clear as day. The bugs circled and swarmed them. Outside of their illuminated sphere, the rest of the forest remained in darkness.

"Three tolls of Empyrean's Bells," exclaimed William. "We've stumbled into a nest of wood fairies. Don't worry, they're not poisonous. They do have a nasty bite though. Ouch."

Zandria thought of the fairies that she met under the waterfall. She was certain that all fairies should be like the Prismata. These little creatures were not only disappointing in that regard, but also very annoying.

Fury was swatting wildly with his tail. He suggested, "Maybe this is a good point to turn west and get clear of them."

"I agree whole heartedly," said William, waving his hands in every direction.

William and Fury led the way. Then Zandria and Olena tried to run ahead, but the wood fairies quickly enveloped them. It was obvious to Zandria that they were not going to get away too easily. Under any other circumstance, she would have been glad to have a night light to lead the way.

After a while, the fairies must have grown tired because they stopped their biting. Zandria thought maybe they startled the fairies, which led to the attack. She wanted to believe that the beautiful little creatures were actually friendly and only protecting their nest. Now that they were calm, she thought, they would see the strangers as no threat to their home.

As they walked on, a bunch of fairies started flitting through Zandria's hair. Now she knew they were friendly. She said, "I think they're trying to braid my hair."

Then Zandria found out the truth. The pesky wood fairies were not trying to braid her hair. They started pulling it and tying the strands in knots. She ran to William for help and he swatted most of them away.

"I thought fairies were supposed to be nice," said Zandria. "No wonder they stopped biting. They were trying to think of something meaner to do."

William put an arm around her shoulders. He said, "I think that's the last we'll see of them. The sun's coming up."

Zandria looked to the west and saw the sky turning pink. Then she noticed the fairies scattering. Soon they were back in a pocket of darkness waiting for the sun to reach them.

"Why would the sun scare them away?" asked Olena.

"Such spiteful creatures can't bear to be in the presence of something that outshines them. That's most likely why they attacked you girls and they definitely don't stand a chance against the sun. If we keep moving, we should not have any more problems from them," said William.

They followed Prince William's advice and walked toward the morning sun. They did not get very far when William stopped in his tracks. Zandria was afraid he was frozen again.

"What's wrong?" asked Olena.

William pointed in front of them and said, "It can't be."

Zandria looked ahead, squinting her eyes. She could not believe she did not see it before. The glare of the sun in her eyes hid the huge castle behind the trees until they were right in front of it. It looked like one lone tall tower sticking up out of the ground, but it was bigger than any building she had ever seen and wider than all of Banookanook. Zandria looked up the cracked and mossy walls to the crumbling parapets. There was a small river between them and the ancient tower.

"Soria Moria," gasped William.

Zandria was disappointed in the state of the place, "Please don't tell me this wreck is the castle we're looking for."

"Don't you remember, Zan? This is Soria Moria, the queen's old castle," said Olena.

Zandria did remember the story that William told, now. She said, "Yes, but didn't you say something happened to it?"

William still looked in shock and did not answer.

Kez answered for him with a shudder, "Trolls."

"Ka, trolls," said Olena. Zandria watched her take William's hand. This must have snapped him out of it.

William said, "I hoped we wouldn't have come this way."

"Why?" asked Zandria. "It's been hundreds of years. The trolls still couldn't be inside, could they?"

"That might be true," said William. "Still, for me, it seems like only a single year since I was here last."

"I can imagine the shock," said Kez. "It must have changed so much."

"Nevertheless, we should go inside. At the very least, we may rest securely from the recent trying times we've had. Perhaps, we might find something useful that Re..." William could barely finish his sentence as tears welled up at the corners of his eyes, "That *she* left behind."

Fury added, "That sounds great and I bet the stables are amazing. One problem, how do we get in? Bridge's up and the moat's full."

They were all studying Soria Moria and none of them saw the figure come up behind them.

When Zandria turned to William for direction, she noticed the boy. She let out a sound of surprise and that drew everybody's attention.

"Hello," said the boy. "I help."

"Who are you?" asked Zandria.

She looked at the boy dressed only in short green pants. His feet were bare and wide with webbing between the toes. This peculiar sight made Zandria inspect him more closely. Where his hands should have been looked like a second pair of feet, wide and floppy. He was skinny and his bones were visibly pressing against his pale, slimy-looking skin. His head sat on his thick neck like an enormous egg. The sides of his head stretched out almost as far as his shoulders. His black hair was short and ringed a large, bald dent in the top of his head. Zandria thought it looked more like a huge soup bowl because it was full of water.

"I Kappa," answered the boy.

"That's a funny name," giggled Olena.

"Kappa no name," he said. "Kappa me."

Then the Kappa was quiet. No one said anything and then he smiled a wide smile. Zandria would have said he smiled ear-to-ear, except he had no ears. Still, his mouth was as wide as his head. They waited in the awkward silence and the boy blinked at them with his eyelids closing side-to-side, instead of top-to-bottom.

"Well then, um, Kappa, how can you help?" asked William.

"Kappa bridge open. Kappa prize get," said the boy.

"Oh, I see," said Kez. "He wants some sort of prize for helping us. From the looks of him, I'd say he's an excellent swimmer. Can you swim over and lower the bridge?"

The Kappa said, "Kappa swim bridge. Kappa water like. Kappa prize win."

"Okay, Kappa. If you help us, we'll give you something," said Olena.

"Kappa girl like," grinned the unusual looking boy. Then he stood looking at them.

"What are you waiting for?" said Zandria.

The Kappa looked at her and then did a back flip standing in place. Zandria was amazed that he did not spill a drop of water from his large, bowl-shaped head.

Then, without a word, he bounded high over them and did a twisting dive into the still water. A moment later, the Kappa splashed out on the other side. He flopped on his wide flipper feet to the side of the drawbridge and slapped hard on the old wood. There was a creaking and a shudder, then the bridge fell hard. It slammed on the ground, splintering the edges and spanning the gap to the castle.

Fury stepped out onto the wood. "Feels safe," he said.

The Kappa climbed up onto the bridge and stood next to Olena. "Kappa girl like," he said.

Olena started looking in her pouch for something to give him. Zandria pushed past them and tried the heavy iron door.

"It's locked," she said with frustration. She looked at the oversized keyhole. It was like no keyhole she had ever seen, but somehow familiar. William came up to inspect, but looked to be at a loss.

Olena offered the Kappa some food and then a shiny rock she picked up somewhere. The Kappa pushed each item away and said with each rejection, "Kappa girl like."

"Well, I don't know what you want," said Olena.

The Kappa started turning cartwheels. He went end over end further away from them without spilling a drop from the bowl on his head. The entire time he was tumbling, he was chanting, "Kappa girl like. Kappa girl want. Kappa girl like. Kappa girl want."

"Oh dear," said Kez. "It seems Olena is to be his prize. Maybe we should get inside."

"We are trying," stated William.

The Kappa had been doing so many acrobatics that he was now far enough away that he had to shout to be heard. He yelled, "Kappa girl like. Kappa girl want. Kappa girl eat."

Then he started running towards them.

Fury moved to block the bridge and Olena ran to William. The prince drew his sword with the precision of the young man he once was. Zandria kept staring at the keyhole.

As the Kappa came closer, he opened his mouth wide. It was filled with double rows of razor sharp teeth. Kez jumped up on the door handle next to Zandria

"Do something," he said.

Then it dawned on her. "It's not a weapon," she said. Zandria reached into her pouch and pulled out the Glass Axe. She turned it around and held it by what she originally thought were the blades. "It's a key," she cheered.

Zandria shoved the Glass Key into the lock. It was a perfect fit. She twisted it and swung the door open with Kez still attached. Everyone dashed inside as the Kappa reached the bridge. Zandria and William pushed the door shut as the Kappa pounded against it. She could hear him snarling on the other side. Then Zandria used her Glass Key on the inside to relock the door while Fury helped William hold it shut.

Chapter 12

Late Afternoon Sun Peaking Through

The door held firm as the Kappa continued to pound his webbed hands against it.

Zandria could hear him sobbing on the other side. "Kappa girl like," he repeated over and over as his pounding grew less frequent.

William took Zandria by the shoulders and moved her away from the door. They were in a wide hallway that curved out of sight in either direction. A pair of tall wooden doors stood opposite of the main entrance. One of the doors was slightly ajar, but inside was only darkness.

William said, "It should be safe to assume that the creature knows no other way inside, since he only attempts to breach the front door. We should be quite secure in here."

"Yeah, unless there really are trolls," added Fury.

Zandria looked from the horse to William with concern.

William tried to reassure her, "This place looks to have been deserted for quite some time."

There was another pound from the Kappa, only much softer. Zandria almost forgot he was there, but when she listened, she could hear him whimpering. She tried to imagine him sitting in front of the door, weakly slapping the thick iron in frustration. He must be crying like a boy who lost his favorite toy, she thought.

The thought of the toy made her think of her Glass Axe, but actually it was a key. She turned it over in her hand, examining the crystal form. She wondered now how she could ever have thought it was an axe. She knew when she was queen, she would not be able to make those kind of mistakes. Still, she felt Ruby and the other Rainbow Princesses tried to trick her by telling her the gifts were not what they appeared to be.

Zandria stuffed the Glass Key into her pouch and said to William, "You've been here before. Would you show us a good place to rest?"

Before William could answer, another voice chimed in, "Of course, please follow me."

Surprised by the squeaky, high-pitched voice, Zandria looked around afraid that another Kappa may already be inside. She looked to her companions to make sure they heard it also. William stood open-mouthed and Fury was quickly glancing down each hall. Only Kez and

Olena were looking at the floor. Olena was doing her little giggle that sometimes had a special way of irritating Zandria.

"Isn't he cute," said Olena.

Zandria saw what she and Kez were looking at. At their feet was a man, no bigger than Zandria's hand. Except, he was not quite a man. He was made of wood. His body was tiny and two straight arms and two straight legs were attached with little pegs. Altogether, she guessed, he was no more than three inches tall.

He walked over to Zandria with a slight wobble because he had no knees. Then he said, "Please my lady. I will show you the way."

Zandria bent down and looked at his small round head. She wondered where his screechy voice came from because he had no mouth or even a face.

"What are you?" asked Kez.

"Forgive me. I am Sylvan," he said with a bow. His little body folded in half at the hip joints and then he stood back straight. "The Mistress of Soria Moria has invited you to join her," he squeaked.

"Mistress of Soria Moria? That's preposterous," William said with a look of outrage.

Sylvan turned his body toward William. Zandria tried to picture his expression in her head, but could not guess his response.

Then Sylvan said, "I see. Of course, the care of this keep is in some dispute. I understand if you thought that *other* woman was in charge. However, there is only one true Mistress and her name is Vasilissa the Beautiful."

Zandria looked to William for confirmation. His face was contorted with confusion. She was beginning to feel a bit confused herself. She knew the ruler of Soria Moria used to be the Queen of the Eastern Sky. She also knew that the queen abandoned this castle hundreds of years ago. By her reckoning, Zandria felt Soria Moria belonged to her now. She wondered who these two women were that could be having such a dispute.

"I have never heard of this Vasilissa the Beautiful. That is not the name of the Queen of the Eastern Sky," said William.

"Quite right," squeaked Sylvan. "The signs indicate that the queen has passed into the twilight. My Mistress, Vasilissa, is the next in line and therefore, the rightful heiress to Soria Moria and the Eastern Queendom. The lady Psyche is but a pretender."

"But I'm the..." started Zandria.

William interrupted her, "What are you talking about. We have been traveling for some time and have heard no news of the queen."

Zandria quickly understood that it was not wise to tell everyone their secret. She thought it was possible that Vasilissa could be dangerous.

"I thought everyone moved to the Palace by the Sea. It seems that Soria Moria has fallen into disrepair," said William.

"Forgive me. I am but one servant and the chores are many. Still, I do what I can," said Sylvan. "You should find the Great Hall to your liking."

William seemed to be an excellent diplomat and continued talking to Sylvan. "Sir, your stature does not do your spirit justice. If you maintain this entire fortress by yourself, I am astounded."

"You are too generous," said Sylvan. "Please allow my Mistress to repay your kindness."

Sylvan wobbled off into the darkness of the interior doors. Fury nudged open the thick wooden door. What Zandria thought was the dark interior of the castle proved only to be a short hallway.

At the other end of the passage was a luxurious and well-lit room. Judging from the expansiveness of the room, Zandria deduced this was the Great Hall. The room was lit from end to end with candles of various size and scent. There were long couches against the walls overloaded with fringed pillows. In the center of the room was a table full of food. Zandria saw everything she could imagine plus some foods she could not have imagined. At the end of the table, there was even a trough for Fury. It was divided in half with one side full of water and the other with some type of grain.

"Now this is more like what I remember," whispered William.

"Please, enjoy yourselves. I will inform my Lady that you are comfortable. She will join you shortly," said Sylvan. Then, he added, "I suspect Psyche will be right behind her, no doubt."

Zandria detected no attempt to hide the annoyance in his high-pitched tone. She watched the amusing figure display another of his folding bows. Then Sylvan disappeared through a different darkened passage.

Without further discussion, they all attacked the buffet. Zandria did not care what the others thought about her using her hands and leaving the utensils in their place. She noticed that no one else bothered to pick up a knife or fork either. Apparently, the sights and smells were too compelling for all of them to be slowed down by courtesy.

While Zandria stuffed meats and vegetables into her mouth that she had never seen before, she looked around the room. Ragged cloths that were once beautiful tapestries still hung from the ceiling. The doorways were framed in gold that matched the trim on the table and chairs. Overhead, most of the ceiling used to be an ornate dome of stained glass. What was left now was basically the leaded frame and a few pieces of cracked, colored glass, that refracted the afternoon sun.

As Zandria moved on to dessert, she watched the strange patterns move across the wall. She tried to picture what the dome would have originally looked like. She did not know that the colorful dome was built to be an enormous kaleidoscope. The rings in the frame used to turn as the day progressed, forcing the sun to cause an ever-changing pattern on the wall. The few hints of color Zandria saw were only a vague memory of the dazzling display of ages past.

As they finished the last sips of their strangely fruity drink, Zandria thought she was hallucinating. The trays and plates and bowls began rising from the table. They floated off down a wide hallway, which she guessed led to the kitchen because of the clank and splash that must have been the dishes dropping into a giant washtub.

"What's happening?" asked Olena.

Zandria was glad she was not the only one seeing this, but it still made her nervous.

"Bad magic," said Kez to the continually clearing table.

"No. Not bad magic," said a new voice.

Everyone looked around for their next surprise visitor of the day. Zandria knew this was not Sylvan's voice, or thankfully the Kappa's. This voice was much softer, kind and feminine. William saw where it came from and pointed. In one of the dark corners of the chamber, sat a girl. Zandria guessed she was not much older than herself, but there was something strange about her.

"My name is Psyche and despite what you have been told, I am the ruler of Soria Moria," said the girl.

Psyche stepped from the shadows and Zandria thought she carried herself like her feet never touched the floor. She saw that Psyche was of exceptional beauty. At first, this made Zandria jealous, but she knew in a few years, she would easily catch her. Psyche was tall and slender. Her straight golden hair hung down past her waist. Zandria knew that Psyche's every movement was full of the grace of a true queen.

"The Invisible Hands are my servants," Psyche continued. "They will see to your every need while you are my guest. I daresay they will be of far better service than that little wooden doll."

"But Sylvan's so cute," blurted Olena.

Psyche turned on Olena and her eyes flashed with a momentary rage. Her face seemed to warp into something frightening and Zandria could have sworn she rose off the floor. Then it was gone and Psyche was again the look of compassion and gentleness. The transformation happened so fast that Zandria did not think anyone else noticed.

"Child," began Psyche, "Sylvan, as you call it, is a creation of a dubious witch called Baba Yaga that roams my Royal Forest."

"Baba Yaga," said Zandria.

"Royal Forest," said William at the same time.

"So you have encountered the woman," said Psyche. "I can tell by the looks on your faces that she is no friend to you."

"She was horrible," started Zandria.

"Yes, but you said Royal Forest. How long has it been since you've been outside?" asked William.

"Outside?" Psyche looked embarrassed. "I can't quite remember. Yesterday? Yes, it seems to be yesterday. But today, I could not go out because of the sleeping trolls."

"Oh, I think it was longer ago than yesterday," said William with a look of growing concern.

"Yeah. That forest is all dead," said Olena.

William moved to Olena and put a hand on her shoulder to quiet her. Zandria knew he suspected something, but he was not saying it yet.

Behind them, Zandria heard Kez ask Fury, "Did she say *trolls*?"

Before they could continue the conversation, there was a scream that almost made Zandria feel like she was jumping out of her skin.

"Siiiiiikeyyyyy!"

This new voice came from another girl rushing out of the door that Sylvan went through a little while ago. As she came forward, Zandria noticed that this girl had the same strange way of walking that Psyche did, where her feet barely seemed to touch the floor.

"Vasilissa, you stop it now," said Psyche.

Psyche's words halted her charge, but Vasilissa remained furious. Despite the anger, Zandria saw that she was every bit as beautiful as Psyche. In fact, they looked so much alike, Zandria thought the two could be sisters. The main difference was Vasilissa had deep brown hair wrapped high on her head. But they both had the same porcelain skin. Zandria was afraid if she stared too long, she would look right through them.

"How dare you pretend this is your throne," said Vasilissa.

"You know with the queen gone, I am the rightful heiress," said Psyche.

"I am the next in line to be queen. Sylvan told me so," said Vasilissa.

The girls looked, to Zandria, as if they already had this argument a thousand times. Then dawned on her that they had. She looked to William and now understood what he hinted at earlier.

"How can you trust that little witch doll?" said Psyche.

"He's not a witch doll. My mother gave him to me for protection when I was sent to Baba Yaga," said Vasilissa.

"Well, I came here because the Oracle said I was chosen," said Psyche.

"My people said I was chosen when I escaped from Baba Yaga," said Vasilissa.

The two girls could no longer contain themselves and began slapping and pulling each other's hair. Soon they began twirling around and rising in the air. Zandria saw the look of shock on Olena, Kez and Fury's faces. She considered herself pretty clever because she was not surprised.

"They're ghosts," Zandria explained.

"Ghosts? But how?" Kez looked puzzled.

William answered, "At one time, they may actually have been in line for the throne of the Queen of the Eastern Sky. They probably even lived here. The sad fact is that without the power of the queen, they continued to live mortal lives. Most likely, they died here. Now their souls are trapped in this place, full of jealousy and hate, because they didn't get what they wanted. This fate could befall anyone." With those words, William looked solemnly at Zandria.

"But how did you know, Zandria?" asked Kez.

"Their feet. When they walk, their feet don't touch the floor," she said.

"Are they dangerous?" asked Olena.

"I shouldn't think so. Not to us anyway," said William. "Not unless their screaming wakes up the sleeping..."

A loud roar from somewhere deep in the catacombs of the castle interrupted him.

"Trolls," William finished.

The ghosts stopped arguing immediately. Fury stood at attention. His tail swooshed once in the silence. A crashing boom shook the walls. Small pieces of rubble fell from the ceiling bouncing off the table or clicking on the stone floor. Zandria watched the girls drift back down to her level.

"That is why we can't leave this place," said Vasilissa. "I have to get to Castle Empyrean, but the trolls won't let us out."

"Once you're in, they make sure you're trapped," said Psyche. "You'll stay here with us now, but we'll make sure you're comfortable."

"But we have to get out," demanded Zandria.

Psyche and Vasilissa looked confused and scared.

Vasilissa said, "They can't get in here. You'll be safe."

"No. We'll be dead like you." Zandria was angry with herself for leading them into Soria Moria in the first place. She had never seen a troll, but knew she would never want this castle now. If she got out of here, she swore her first act as queen would be to have this place torn down.

Zandria was so worried about herself that she did not realize the effect her last words had. Both Psyche and Vasilissa were in tears, sitting slightly above the floor with their heads in their knees.

They were sobbing with the sudden truth that Zandria gave them. She understood what she did. For possibly five hundred years, both of these spirits believed they were going to be queen. Neither realized they were dead and they were both so selfish that they were willing to fight each other, their only companion. Zandria knew she took their only dream away and she felt sick because of it.

William knelt down beside the weeping girls. The thumping of heavy footsteps sounded like a troll was right outside the door.

He said, "My exquisite maidens, I wish there was something I could do for you both, but sadly that time has passed. Still, there is something you can do that may ease your restless spirits. I am honor bound to deliver these two to the same Castle Empyrean. You must tell us a safe way out of here."

Olena took Zandria's hand and together they watched the double-doors for the coming terror. Zandria thought she could hear laborious breathing on the other side.

"There is none," said Vasilissa when she could momentarily stop her sobbing.

"Wait. There is one," said Psyche slowly, "but it is too dark, even so that a torch will not light the way."

"My light will show them the way. It can light even the darkest spaces," said Vasilissa. She stood up with renewed confidence. "Sylvan, please bring my light," she called.

After a moment, Sylvan made his way into the room. Zandria thought he looked absurd carrying a human skull that was easily five times bigger than he was. She would have laughed aloud had the skull not looked so ominous. It was shiny black, so shiny that she could see her reflection in it even from a distance. When Vasilissa touched it as she took it from Sylvan, the eyes glowed red like an unnatural fire burned inside.

"This is the light that I stole from Baba Yaga when I made my escape," said Vasilissa. "It guided me safely back to my mother, but not without risk. It's light will draw the old witch like a moth to flame. That is why it has been extinguished for so long."

"That risk has been greatly diminished. The old woman was dispatched very recently," said William.

"Then may it's light guide you to safety now," said Vasilissa.

She handed the glowing skull to William. Then she started to float back toward the ceiling. Psyche joined her there.

Psyche looked at Zandria, which made her feel guilty again. Psyche said, "Please don't feel bad for us. You saved us. I only hope we can do the same. My helping hands will open a Taenarum Tunnel. There are many of these across Empyrean, often where you need them most. Be careful not to go too deep though, because most of them lead to the underworld."

With that, the Invisible Hands began removing stones from the back wall. It only took removing a few large blocks to reveal the secret passage. Zandria could only see blackness inside. It was darker than a moonless night in the Dead Forest. It reminded her of looking in at Baba Yaga's window. She felt so empty, but Olena was still holding her hand and pulled her toward the entrance.

Vasilissa spoke again, this time to Sylvan, "My mother gave you to me to help when I was in need. Now there are others that need you more than I." Vasilissa turned to Zandria, "Sylvan will be there when you need him. Let him lead the way and he will take you through to the mountains."

Then Vasilissa and Psyche floated up further. They faded into sparkling gold dust as they passed through the beams of late afternoon sun peeking through the shattered dome.

Sylvan hobbled into the tunnel, saying in his unique pitch, "Follow me please."

William went second with the skull held out in his left hand and his sword drawn in his right. Kez took his perch on Olena's shoulder as the two girls followed William. Zandria looked back to see the outline of Fury coming in last. From the eerie red glow of the skull, she could see that Fury moved with his head down in the cramped space. She hoped they would not be in this tunnel too long.

Chapter 13

Only a Day Behind

The water was cold and took Adam by surprise when he finally hit it. The waterfall was so high, he had no idea when he would reach the lagoon. Adam was still reeling from the cold shock and did not expect to hit the bottom of the pool so quickly. His feet jarred against the mushy surface sending a jolt right up to his teeth. He thought a lagoon at the base of such a huge waterfall would have been deeper. Adam recovered and swam to the top. He burst through the surface gasping for air.

The first thing Adam noticed was that his swimming caused no ripples. Then he saw that the thousands upon thousands of gallons of water falling from above caused no waves either. He knew this lagoon was enchanted.

Then he suddenly felt like he was being watched.

Adam was aware of how exposed he was with his head poking up out of the center of the pool. He quickly swam for the shore opposite of the waterfall. As he sat on the muddy shore, he stared at the cliff face. He sensed whoever was watching him hidden safely behind that rushing torrent.

Without further concern, he shifted his attention upward. He could barely make out the shapes of a few wolf-men gazing down at him. Judging from the distance he fell and his surroundings now, he gained at least a day on them. If he could pick up the girls' trail, there would be almost no chance of the wolves catching him.

The oversized shirt he took from the hut was now soaked. The sleeves covered his hands. He decided to cut them off and pulled out his small knife. He did not want any additional distractions.

Adam made it to his feet to look for signs of anyone going this way. He spotted a few footprints at the edge of the vegetation and followed them. It only took a moment to lose the trail amidst the dense combination of forest and jungle. Adam suspected whatever magic surrounded that pool extended its reach to block his progress now.

Pulling the long knife from its sheath, Adam began cutting his own path in as close to a northerly direction as he could. Up to the cliff, he knew his prey was heading southwest away from the Palace by the Sea. He planned to make his way back north to the Great Road. He knew where the girls were supposed to be going and thought he could make better time on the open road. He was sure to cross their path eventually.

It took him less than a day to make it to the Great Road. To his disappointment, he found he had been moving northeast and now stood in front of Edge Town right outside the gates of the Palace by the Sea. He could see people still clearing the destroyed market, but no one took notice of him. Adam turned west and began running. Edge Town quickly faded behind him.

After only a day, Adam reached the strange barrier that marked the beginning of the wasteland. He looked out across the vastness, knowing he was partly responsible for it.

The dwarves told the story like it was some sort of triumph. There were only twelve of them. So at night, they would sneak into the small towns and villages that used to dot the Royal Forest. There, they would steal as many children as they could to bring back as slaves in their mine. Adam was only a baby when they took him, so he had no memory of his parents, what town he came from or if it still existed.

Over the course of one hundred years, generation after generation of slave-children died in the mines. Those that did not die from exhaustion either grew too tall or too rebellious and were executed. Adam was currently one of the oldest slaves, which apparently earned him some special favor with Lord Vanril, the leader of the dwarves. Maybe that was why he was chosen for this mission.

Now Adam surveyed the devastation caused by the decades of mining under the Royal Forest. At first, the dwarves celebrated the ruin of the beautiful forest. As they continued mining and creating their army of Rockhorns, the land above became known as the Dead Forest. Then, as they depleted the minerals and nutrients, most of the Dead Forest dissolved into this uninhabitable wasteland.

Adam's heart sank for being part of this. Still, it gave him one more reason for completing his mission. Lord Vanril, along with a grimy snail called General Gusk and a crazy looking gypsy called Sasha, instructed him to stop a certain girl from reaching the castle. Before Adam even climbed out of the hole, he had a plan of his own.

Somehow, the power of the Eastern Queen stopped the wasteland from spreading further east. Adam decided this last shady refuge would be a good place to spend the night before challenging the barren land.

He woke up refreshed by a dream he could not quite remember. As Adam wiped the sleep from his eyes, he focused on the encroaching wasteland. Then reality returned and any pleasant thoughts he dared to have vanished.

With only a small breakfast scavenged from the fringe of the forest, he took off west on the Great Road. This time Adam did not run, but kept a brisk pace. He knew he could not keep going too fast or he would succumb to this lifeless desert. He was certain staying on the Great Road would give him a time advantage, but he would have to find shelter somehow along the way.

The first night in the wastes, Adam found there was no possibility of simply lying down on the roadside. He moved off the path and huddled down in the cracked ground. He could see farther away from the road that the cracks were deep enough to walk in, but he wanted to stay close. So he lay down in the dirt with his head and back barely blocked from the unrelenting night wind.

One night, he moved toward a crack for sleeping and instead found a gaping hole. This was one of the places where the slave mining came close enough to the surface to rip open the ground. Adam knew the wasteland was covered with these tunnels. Most of them ran down into utter blackness and had not been mined in years.

As he stared into the hole, he became aware of a faint rhythmic sound. It was a distant pounding echoing up through the labyrinth of mines below him. Zandria heard the same sound that night, but she did not know what it was. Adam knew the monotonous thump thump thump could be only one thing. Or rather, he thought to himself, ten thousand things. It was the sound of five thousand pairs of feet marching.

Then the pounding was joined by a low hum. Adam would never have guessed the Rockhorns had their own language, let alone voices. Whatever that language was and whatever the words meant, the Rockhorn army was chanting as it marched underground toward the Castle Empyrean.

His ten-day head start was gone. If the Rockhorns were moving, Adam could not afford any more delays. He was tired from running all day and still needed to sleep, but knew he must start earlier and faster in the morning.

The wasteland was unbelievably long and the destruction he and the other slaves caused sapped his will. With every step, Adam doubted his strength to continue. It really was a race now. Adam did not care about the werewolves anymore, his only hope was to beat the army to the castle.

One morning, the urge to give up was so overwhelming, then he saw something in the distance. It looked like a woman stumbling down the middle of the Great Road. She was heading straight towards him and she seemed to be carrying something. As Adam drew closer, he could see that she had been attacked. Her clothes were ripped and there was a cut on her right cheek. She was desperately clutching a bundled blanket to her chest.

When he was next to her, she collapsed at his feet, sobbing, "Please help me. Please."

"What is it? What happened to you?" Adam asked.

Before she could answer, whatever was inside the blanket kicked and cooed. It was a baby! Adam could not mistake that sound. He heard it in the mines every time the dwarves kidnapped more slaves. Being one of the oldest, it was sometimes his responsibility to care for them.

It had been a little while since he held a baby, but he gently took the child from the weakened mother. The baby boy instantly smiled and giggled at Adam. This alone was enough to give him renewed strength. Adam coddled the child and sat next to the mother. She was still crying, but sounded greatly relieved.

"They're mad. They're all mad," she said.

Adam looked at her, "Who?"

"The animals back at the town. They've gone crazy. They have my husband."

"Town? How close is this town?" Adam asked. He tried to hide his excitement of being almost through with the wasteland.

"I don't know. I walked for a day maybe," she said. The woman looked in shock. "We were heading east, taking our ox with us. The animals grabbed my husband, but I took the baby and ran."

Adam tried to make sense of what she said. "We have to get to this town."

"I can't. I can't go back," she said.

He could see the fear in her eyes. "Listen," he started, "none of us will survive out here for very long. Think of your baby. What's his name?"

"We..." she tried to stop crying. "We haven't named him yet. We were going to take him to the Palace by the Sea for a naming ceremony."

"Well, we have to get back to that town. Then we can plan how to get you to the queen," Adam lied to protect her. "Besides, if they are only animals in the town, they couldn't be bad. We'll have to talk to them. Let's go before it gets dark."

Adam held the nameless child in one arm and helped the woman up with the other. He led them west, not knowing what to expect.

After one last night in the wasteland, he finally saw the town from which she escaped. It stuck out of the side of the Dead Forest, straddling the Great Road. From here, he could see no signs of life and everything was quiet. He could tell the woman was afraid, but she did not doubt his confidence. She squeezed his hand tightly as they passed the large wooden sign that said "Welcome to Bremen".

The town was empty, but before then, it looked like a war was fought there. Adam surveyed the damage. There were feathers and fur everywhere and countless varieties of tracks and paw prints in every direction. At the center of town, it looked to Adam that there had been a huge explosion. Lying close by was the body of one of the wolfmen.

"Whatever happened here, it's over," Adam said.

Then there was a noise from one of the buildings. Adam spun around to see a few animal faces peeking out the doorway. An instant later, a big brown ox clambered out into the street.

"Lady Mulgart! I was so worried. I'm so happy you're alive," said the ox. "And the baby's okay too!"

Adam had not thought to ask her name, but he knew the ox could only be talking to the woman he saved from the wasteland. A sickly looking cat, two monkeys and a white tiger followed the ox to inspect the visitors. The monkeys were busy helping the cat stay on its paws, so Adam chose to speak to the tiger.

"What happened here, friend?"

"I, Virgata, am ashamed even to think about it," said the tiger.

"I'm sorry," said Adam. "We are trying to find her husband. Then I must continue on."

Virgata, the majestic white tiger, lowered his head. He said, "Many humans and animals were lost here these past days. I recognize this woman and it saddens me to say her mate will not be found."

Lady Mulgart dropped to the ground for the second time since Adam knew her. She held her child close and the ox did his best to comfort her.

"What was the cause?" Adam asked.

"There is much chaos in my memory, but I will try to sum up," said Virgata. "Most everything began when the rock fell from the sky. Four animals, this dying cat here being the last survivor, took some power from it. Then there was music of which I cannot describe. I think that was truly the cause of it, as even I was not myself while it played."

Adam looked to the woman. She was already gaining her composure. He was impressed by her strength and wondered if that is what it means to be a mother.

The tiger continued, "Then things got quite out of paw. There were these girls, followed by werewolves. At some point, the rock exploded. I believe the old man, who was not quite as old when he left, caused that. And I..."

"Girls?" said Adam. He was surprised that he caught up to them so soon, if it was them. "What girls? Where did they go?"

"Oh, the girls," said Virgata. "I'm not surprised. They seemed to have a power that contradicted the rock. Maybe that is why the wolf humans were after them."

"Did the wolf-men catch them?" Adam was concerned, because he was sure these were the girls he was looking for.

"By my incisors! No. I put one down myself. My friend bear, rest his soul, sent the crooked nosed one scampering off down the west road before he breathed his last."

"Yes, but the girls?" asked Adam again.

"To the north, my impatient fellow," said Virgata. "They escaped to the north. If your eyes are keen, you should pick up their trail. After all, they were rescued by a Friesian."

Adam turned to Lady Mulgart and said, "I have to go. You should be safe here now." Next, he addressed the ox, "Look after them."

"Of course," said the ox.

The tiger spoke up, "We have much amends to make. The care of these two will be but the first step on a long journey that the animals of Bremen shall share."

Adam started to run up the north road. He knew he was taking a risk by detouring, but there was a chance he could get to the girls.

"Boy," called Lady Mulgart.

Adam stopped and looked back at her.

"What is your name?" she asked.

"I'm called Adam, if that means anything," Adam said.

"It does to me," said Lady Mulgart. "I wanted to thank you, Adam. Besides, I still need a name for my child."

Adam did not know how to respond. This was the first time in his life that someone treated him with kindness. He was at a loss for words, so waved instead. Then he took off again to look for the girls whose names he did not know.

Virgata called after him, "Watch out for wood fairies. They're ferocious this time of year."

The sun was already setting when Adam left the town of Bremen. He did not mind being in the Dead Forest and he did not mind being alone in the dark. Even the occasional sting of a wood fairy did not bother him. The thing that upset him most was that he was having difficulty tracking the girls. Luckily for him, they had a large horse and some other little creature scurrying around their feet. Whenever he thought he lost the trail, one of the two animals left hoof prints on the ground or fur on a broken branch. Adam did not believe they gave much thought to hiding their course. It would be all too easy for any werewolves to find them as well.

When the sun rose the next morning, Adam was standing in almost the same spot as Zandria did the day before. He was looking at a once mighty castle silhouetted against the morning sun. He did not give a thought to what it might have once been as the girls did. His only concern was if they were inside, he needed to be as well.

Approaching the drawbridge, Adam saw a creature slumped in front of the enormous door. This thing looked miserable with its floppy hands and feet and a dented head full of water. It was the creature's expression that made Adam think it was the most pathetic thing since that angry little snail, General Gusk. The fish-boy, as Adam decided to call him, did not move when he got close. He only sat with his back to the door mumbling. Adam leaned in to understand him.

"Kappa girl like."

"What girl?" asked Adam calmly.

"Kappa girl like," was the only thing the Kappa would say.

Adam lost his patience quickly. He grabbed the Kappa by the shoulders and slammed him down on the ground. Adam noticed that the water did not spill from the creature's strange head, but only started dripping one drop at a time.

The Kappa got wide-eyed and screamed, "Kappa no water, Kappa no more."

Adam made sense of the gibberish. He understood instantly if the Kappa lost the water from his bald bowl, he could not survive. He pulled the Kappa back upright to stop the drip.

"If you want to live, Kappa," said Adam. He dipped a finger in the headwater, twirled it around and then flicked a drop away. The Kappa looked terrified. "Tell me where the girl went."

The Kappa seemed ready to cooperate. He said, "Girl home go. Girl door lock. Kappa girl like."

"So, they locked you out, huh? Gee, I wonder why?" Adam said sarcastically. He tried to turn the handle, but as the Kappa said, it was locked. Adam knelt down and stuck his small knife into the unusually shaped lock. He was sure he could break it open. To pass the time while he worked at it, Adam chatted pointlessly with the Kappa. "You're a Kappa, huh?"

"Kappa me," said the Kappa.

"What does a Kappa do?"

"Kappa swim. Kappa help." The Kappa appeared to be in better spirits. Adam was glad he was not whimpering anymore.

"So, why does Kappa like the girl?" asked Adam.

"Kappa girl eat," he said matter of factly. Adam felt a burst of anger and surprise. He jammed the knife into the lock and pulled it out to see that he bent it. He pointed the twisted metal at the Kappa's face.

Adam said, "No, Kappa's not going to eat the girl. The girl is mine and she's going to help me get revenge on some really bad people. If you get in my way or try to hurt either of them, I'll drain your water right now."

Then Adam tossed the ruined knife into the moat. He slammed his fist and the iron echoed dully. A moment later, there was a knock from inside, only it sounded like it came from a much larger fist. The thick door visibly vibrated from the heavy thunk.

Adam and the Kappa looked at each other, then back at the door. Suddenly, the door exploded outward. Adam was closer and the force of the blast sent him flying. He landed on his back in the grass on the other side of the drawbridge.

He recovered quickly and saw the Kappa was not as lucky as he was. The fish-boy was smashed beneath the weight of the immense door. Adam saw the last of his water dripping down into the moat. Then Adam looked up to see what caused the door to fall.

"This can't be good," he said.

It was a troll.

Adam had never seen one, but the dwarves were full of stories. He guessed this one was at least twenty feet tall because it had to duck all three of its heads to come through the opening.

Adam pulled himself from the ground and yanked his remaining knife from its holder. He did not want to fight this monster, but if the Kappa was telling the truth, he had to get inside.

The troll's three heads were looking around, presumably to see who was knocking at its door. The snake-like head on the right shoulder spotted him first. Then the center human head looked at him. It was followed by the feathery black head that looked like a crow.

Adam took a moment to study the troll for any obvious weaknesses. The beast had short, thick legs and arms so long that its knuckles dragged the ground. The rest of its body was covered in rags, probably stolen from the castle beds and roughly sewn together. Adam saw how the three heads moved independently, but the body moved like a single person as it lumbered towards him. He knew the troll was strong, but clearly not fast.

He soon discovered the troll was also extremely clumsy. Even with a total of six eyes, it must not have seen the door lying in front of its extremely large feet. The troll tripped over the battered iron door and fell head first into the river. There was a massive amount of splashing and Adam got soaked. Still, the troll could not manage to get any of its heads above water and quickly sank to the bottom.

Adam waited a few minutes, but the troll was gone. As he crossed the bridge to enter the castle, he was surprised to find the Kappa barely alive. Knowing he could never move the gigantic door, Adam knelt down by the Kappa.

The Kappa tried to speak, water bubbles foamed at the corners of his mouth. "Kappa troll no like. Kappa swim. Troll no swim."

Then the Kappa closed his sideways eyelids. Adam felt some small pity for him. His pity turned to hope for the safety of the girls as he left the Kappa. Adam walked into Soria Moria at the same time Zandria and Olena met a dragon at the top of the Euphoric Mountains.

Chapter 14

Not on My List for Today

Zandria did not like being in the tunnel. Although William was right in front of her with that creepy skull, she still felt like she was being swallowed by the dark. They kept going down. She wondered if this was some final cruel trick of the ghost girls. Maybe, she thought, there was no way out on the other end.

All the while they were in there, Zandria could not stop thinking about the blackness. Ever since they left home, she felt surrounded by it. The same black that was in Baba Yaga's window was here now, engulfing her. Zandria even remembered it deep in the Prismata's cave. Now it tried to swallow her whole.

She could not hide it from herself. She saw it in the way she treated other people, especially her sister. Zandria always thought she was a good person. Down in this tunnel, she did not believe that was true. She was looking at herself as if she was staring in that window again. She could see her hurtful attitude and how she was prone to jealousy. She knew she had to change these things, but lying to herself was easier. Maybe everything would be better when she was queen.

Then she heard it again. The chanting from deep underground called to Zandria. She remembered the sound from the wasteland. It was low and in a language she did not understand. That did not keep her from getting its meaning. The voices wanted her. The sound squirmed through the darkness and pulled at her.

Suddenly, Zandria could not see the red glow of the skull anymore. She did not dare to call out into the emptiness. She was alone. Somehow, she got separated from the others. The calling voices did not get louder, but their message grew stronger. Zandria squeezed her eyes shut in a futile attempt to block out the sound. It was equally as dark inside her head.

She was scared. She did not want this. She wanted the darkness out of her heart. She wanted to be a good queen. She wanted to scream.

The next thing she knew, a warm, rosy light pressed against her eyelids. Zandria slowly opened her eyes. The light was not coming from the skull, but rather, the morning sun climbing over an unending wall of mountains. It was the start of a new day. She looked around and saw they were standing in front of a hole at the base of a gnarled old tree.

They made it. Zandria wanted to jump up and down and scream. Except this time, her screams would be of joy. She felt so happy to be out of the tunnel, so happy to be in the light. She almost forgot the feelings she had down in the darkness.

There was one other thing she noticed. Olena was still holding her hand. She remembered Olena taking her hand when they entered the tunnel inside Soria Moria. She did not realize it, but her sister must have held on to her the entire time. She must have led her out of the darkness.

Zandria looked around and saw her friends staring at her. She smiled with relief and their looks of concern faded into smiles as well. Then, Zandria hugged her sister.

"I'm glad to be out of there too. It was so cold," said Olena.

"It feels good to stretch my neck," added Fury.

William moved to Zandria and presented the skull to her. The eyes were no longer glowing. He said, "I think we can put this away for now." He gestured to her pouch. Zandria took it and quickly slid it out of sight.

Now Zandria could take a moment to see where they were. The Taenarum Tunnel led them the rest of the way under the Dead Forest. They were standing on the side of a road that ran north and south as far as she could see. On the other side were the foothills to one of the most amazing sights Zandria had ever seen.

"The Euphoric Mountains," William informed her.

Zandria could not believe how the ground could reach so high up into the sky. The shades of purple and gray gloriously reflected the rising sun. The sharp, uneven breaks from peak to peak hinted at hiding countless mysteries.

Sylvan wobbled into the road and turned south. He said, "We can be to the Great Road by nightfall if we go this way."

"Too dangerous," said Fury. "If there are any more werewolves, they'll be watching that way."

"But that is the only safe passage through the mountains. At least that used to be true," said William.

"And still is," peeped Sylvan.

"I wish somebody would've told me that," said Fury.

"There is one other way," replied Sylvan, "a secret way."

"Please tell us," said William.

"Better. I will show you. Look there."

Zandria looked in the direction Sylvan's little wooden arm pointed. All she could see straight across from her were a few short hills and a sheer rock wall.

"I don't see anything," said Olena.

"That's because it's hidden," said Kez. "Turn your head this way."

Olena turned her head slightly sideways like Kez demonstrated, then her eyes got wide.

Zandria followed their example and she saw a narrow path appear in the mountainside as if by magic.

"I think we should go that way," Olena said with a smile.

Zandria suspected it was not as safe as the Great Road, but at least there was almost no chance of running into any wolf-men. She crossed the road with everyone, but Kez looked back. She turned to see that he was looking at Sylvan still in the road. Now that they were in the open, the miniature wooden man was not setting their walking pace. Zandria knew his tiny legs were too slow.

"Gentle Sylvan, please don't be offended if we carry you," said Zandria. After her experience in the tunnel, she chose her words deliberately. Zandria really wanted to make an effort. She did not want the darkness to win.

"That would be acceptable," said Sylvan.

Olena looked delighted to run over and scoop him up. She nestled him in her pouch with his arms hanging on the side so his head would poke out to guide the way.

The rocky path was easy going and soon all of them were chatting like they were on a leisurely hike. All of them, that is, except Sylvan. Zandria felt quite giddy and could not understand why Sylvan was not joining in the pleasantries.

"Why are you so quiet," she asked at Olena's pouch.

"This place is called the Euphoric Mountains," he said. "I'm certain Prince William could attest to its powers. Alas, they only have an effect on living beings."

In any other mood, Zandria would have been saddened by Sylvan's plight. Because of the essence flowing down from the mountaintops, she simply said, "Ka."

They continued on for a while. Gradually, the path sloped up and then eventually leveled out. The secret path zigzagged in front and behind them. That way, they were always hidden, but they never knew what was coming next either.

"I believe we are in the heart of the mountains now," William said. He looked in awe and, Zandria thought, the youngest since she had known him. "No one has passed this way for hundreds of years, if not longer."

Zandria found what he was saying interesting, but she could not keep other thoughts to herself any longer. "How are you getting younger, William?" she asked.

Kez laughed, "That's an excellent question. I've been meaning to ask you that as well."

William looked thoughtful for a moment. "Indeed, that is an excellent question," he started. "Here is my best account. Being frozen in ice was a result of my lonely heart growing cold. As such, my icy heart never grew old, only my body. I don't really feel old. I think it is simply a matter of time for the age of my body to catch up to the age of my heart. I believe I have another ten or twenty years to go."

"I've never heard of such a thing," said Kez. "Apparently anything is possible outside of Banookanook."

Zandria was astounded. She knew he was changing, but this is the first time they approached him directly about it. His explanation made sense. She was glad it was not her imagination after all. Now, she even noticed his full head of hair was starting to grow toward his shoulders.

She did not realize they stopped to have this discussion. Therefore, Zandria was the first to start walking again. She turned the narrow corner and walked into a wide basin near the top of the Euphoric Mountains about the same time that Adam entered Soria Moria.

At first, Zandria was relieved to be out of the enclosed passage in which they had been climbing the mountain. The massive bowl-shaped formation was bigger than the hall they dined in at Soria Moria. She figured it was a perfectly natural occurrence, never having seen mountains or their tops before. The walls and floor were smooth and curved. Then she realized there was no exit on the other side.

"There's no way out," exclaimed Zandria. She was almost in a panic, but it was balanced by the anger she felt for wasting so much time coming this way. Zandria fought her urges and tried not to give in to her passion. She started taking deep breaths when William came up next to her.

"Stay calm, my dear. There has to be a way out," he said.

"Oh, there is," said a thick, gravelly voice that echoed and slid around the basin.

Fury moved up into a defensive position as Olena and Kez ducked back into the passage behind William. Zandria looked around wide-eyed, fighting an unexpected need to cry.

"I'm blocking it," came the voice again.

Then the wall on the opposite side began to crumble. Only, Zandria saw, it was not crumbling, but rather something underneath was shaking off years of dust. As the small rocks and dirt fell away, Zandria could see an enormous creature ruffling its shiny purple scales from its neck to the tip of its tail.

"Well braid my tail," exclaimed Fury, "it's a dragon."

Of course, Zandria heard stories of dragons, she even told a few herself. Like the unicorns, dragons were supposed to be extinct. Then she realized the area where she was standing was not a bowl shape, but a nest shape. She imagined the rock was melted and shaped like this by the dragon's fiery breath.

The dragon shook himself loose from the sediment. It stretched its two front legs out and the enormous joints popped. Zandria stared at the three claws on both feet, each longer than she was tall. She knew if it decided to eat them, there was no way they could out run its fire in the windy pass.

"I have not had company for a long time," it growled. "I must have fallen asleep. Feels like five or six hundred years' worth. Oh well, I guess a short nap is better than no nap at all."

This made Zandria smile. Maybe he, she guessed *it* was a *he*, was friendly after all. On the other hand, maybe, it was more likely that the mountains affected him in the same way. In either case, when he shifted, Zandria could see the path behind him.

The dragon's voice boomed this time, "I will be happy to let you pass. You have to say but one word."

"Please?" Zandria heard timidly from Olena behind her.

The dragon turned his face toward them and slightly parted his mouth. Serrated teeth showed from the front to the back. Zandria suspected this was supposed to be a smile, but it was difficult to read his lizard-like face. She looked from his threatening mouth to his solid orange eyes. There was no emotion conveyed there.

"Your courtesies are without measure, my morsel," said the dragon. Then he rose up on his hind legs. Zandria could hear the muscles stretch being used for the first time in hundreds of years. He spread out his wings that moments ago were pressed so tight to his body that she did not know he had any. If Zandria had ever seen a bat's wings, she would have thought the dragon's looked like a giant version of theirs. Then he curled his tail up and his long neck down so his body resembled a letter "S".

"Alas, no," the dragon continued, "The one word I am looking for is my name."

Zandria felt cheated. "How are we supposed to know that," she yelled at him. William held her back, even though she did not know what good it would do to run at the beast.

"How indeed? That is why I will give you three guesses. I promise, I will not devour you until, I mean, unless you miss all three," he said and parted his lips in that strange smile again.

William gestured Zandria to come close and the group huddled to confer.

"Listen, girls," said William. "There is no way we could ever guess his name. The dragons were already gone in my time. I wouldn't know where to start."

"What's your plan then?" asked Fury.

"Regardless of the outcome, Zandria and Olena have to get to that other passage. They have to continue on to Castle Empyrean."

"So you want to try and fight our way out?" came Fury's next question.

Olena interrupted, "Why don't we ask Sylvan?"

William grinned at Olena, "Why didn't I think of that." Then he bent over further to where Sylvan was sticking out of Olena's pouch. "What say you?"

Sylvan began, "I am the Master of My Domain and keeper of all knowledge under the reign of the fair and beautiful Vasilissa."

"That's great. So what's the big guy's name?" asked Fury.

"I do not have the vaguest idea. I've never been up here," said Sylvan.

Zandria felt helpless now.

"Well, draw your weapon, Prince," said Fury.

William put his hand to his sword, but Zandria rushed over and stopped his hand with both of hers.

"I don't know what to do, but being eaten by a dragon is not on my list for today," she said. "I've been through too much. We've been through too much. Sacrificing ourselves now feels like giving up. I don't know how to be a queen, but I know that quitting is not a part of it."

The others looked at her like she was a stranger. At that moment, Zandria did not feel quite like herself either. The thought of not making it out of these mountains sparked something in her. She went to a dark place in her heart and did not like what she saw. Right now, she did not even care about becoming queen. This was about survival.

"What should we do, Zan?" asked Olena, with a mixed look of admiration and hope in her eyes.

"Well, this is not our world," she said. "I mean, we didn't grow up with this stuff. Between the three of these guys," Zandria swung a hand past William, Fury and Sylvan, "we should, at least, come up with three good guesses before we get burnt up."

"Your wisdom exceeds your years," peeped Sylvan.

"That sounds like it's worth a try," said Fury.

"Even Kez knows about these things," said Olena.

Zandria looked to Kez. This entire time, he was silently staring at the purple behemoth. She said, "He's a quzzak from a jungle by the sea. His guess is as good as mine or yours, sis."

"Well then, what do we know about dragons?" asked William.

"He's big. Maybe it's Titan," blurted Fury.

"Wrong," came a startling sound. Zandria realized the dragon was listening to their every word. "Two guesses remain," he said.

"That's not fair." It was Olena's turn to shout.

The dragon blew a puff of smoke from his nostrils to show his indifference to Olena's rules. Then he flapped his wings once and that set everyone momentarily off balance. Zandria was convinced that fighting was not even a possibility.

Zandria said, "How about I signal you when we are ready with our next guess."

"Fair enough," said the dragon.

She turned back to her friends as Fury said, "Sorry about that."

"It's not your fault. Now, what else can we say about him. He is very much like a giant lizard," said William.

"Lizardo?" suggested Zandria.

"Dragons are rumored to have been very regal," commented Sylvan. "It needs to sound more majestic, like Lizandro."

"Lizandro then?" she asked.

The others nodded and she waved to the dragon. Kez had moved out in front of the group and she had to step over him. He had a blank look on his face like he was thinking of something else.

"What is your second guess?" asked the dragon.

"Is it Lizandro," guessed Zandria.

"That's not it," whispered Kez before the dragon responded.

"You are down to one last opportunity," said the dragon.

Zandria moved past the unflinching Kez back to the others.

"Maybe it has something to do with his pretty purple color," proposed Olena.

"That's not it," said Kez, still looking like he was lost in thought.

William ignored the quzzak, "What are names that mean purple?"

"Lilac," said Olena.

"Where did you ever..." began William.

"That was the name of one of the Prismata," she explained.

"Prismata," mumbled Kez.

Zandria wondered where his mind was, but had to stay focused on their situation. She looked to the dragon. She was surprised to see him still holding his upright pose, like a statue.

"Any other suggestions?" she asked.

"I am at a loss," said William. Fury's expression was almost as blank as Sylvan's permanent one.

Zandria slowly turned back to the dragon. She gave him the signal for her final guess.

"That's not it," said Kez. His tone indicated that he was back to the present.

"Well," said the dragon.

"It's..." Zandria started.

Then Kez climbed up her legs and grabbed the front of her shirt so he was in her face. His face was switching between panic and excitement. He yelled at her, "That's not it!"

"Then what is it!" Zandria shouted back, frustrated by his erratic behavior.

Kez twisted around to face the dragon, holding tightly to Zandria. She could feel him shaking. Then he said, louder than she ever heard him in her life, "Evorin. Your name is Evorin."

The "rin" part echoed around the basin and then it was quiet.

Zandria could not move, fearing what would come next.

Then Evorin said, "That's impossible."

The dragon named Evorin lowered himself to all four legs and moved his head close to Kez. He spoke in a whisper that was still loud enough to vibrate the ground beneath Zandria's feet. "No one has ever guessed my name," Evorin said. "You may pass."

"But how did you know, Kez?" asked Zandria.

Kez hopped down from her front and darted to the now cleared passage. "No time. I'll explain later. We have to move now."

Zandria grabbed Olena's hand. She noticed Sylvan duck down inside her pouch as they neared Evorin. Zandria did not take her eyes off the dragon as they moved by him.

Before William and Fury could follow, Evorin slid his tail in front of the path. There was no way for them to get through.

"William," screamed Olena.

"You can't do that," said Zandria, kicking Evorin's tail.

"Three guesses. Three passes. I have not decided what to do with these two. They will earn their toll or be but a scant meal to put me back to sleep," Evorin said.

Zandria was trying to climb over the tail, but William pushed her back.

He said, "You have to keep going west. Do not give a thought to us. Get down out of these mountains."

"Run girls," Fury added. "You only have to cross the plains. You're so close."

Kez was pulling at both girls' legs, "We have to go before Evorin changes his mind."

The girls turned and ran down the twisting path without looking back. A sound that passed for dragon laughter lingered behind them. Zandria thought the strange euphoria coming from the mountains made it easier to deal with their loss, but the sensation vanished when they reached the foothills. They dropped to the ground on top of a small hill in sight of the grassy plains. Both girls cried themselves to sleep, while Kez attempted to stay awake, keeping watch.

Zandria awoke the next morning to the smell of smoke. Her first thought was that Evorin flew down from the mountains to finish his meal. Then she realized it was not a bad burning smell.

It was the smell of breakfast.

Chapter 15

Good Morning

Before Zandria opened her eyes, she was sure Kez raided her pouch. She knew there was not much food left in there, but there was enough to make a decent breakfast. Her first reaction was that this was something they needed after yesterday's ordeal.

She slowly opened her eyes, letting a tired smile creep across her face. Her pleasant mood suddenly vanished when she focused on Kez still sleeping, curled up with Olena. If he was not cooking breakfast, then who was?

Zandria bolted upright and looked around. She hoped against hope that William and Fury escaped that cheating dragon, Evorin. There was no sign of either of them. She thought maybe William was gathering some of the tall grass nearby for the fire. That would explain why she could not see him, but not Fury. Zandria knew if at least one of them was not close, then neither of them were. She did not want to admit to herself that neither of them made it down the mountain.

Sitting a safe distance from the fire, Zandria saw Sylvan. She guessed he must have climbed out of his hiding place when whoever the cook was made the fire. Either it was someone he knew, she thought, or someone that appeared to be trustworthy. Zandria decided not to wake her sister and question Sylvan first.

She crawled quietly over to the wooden doll, not wanting to make too much noise. She felt it was possible that this stranger could be dangerous. Zandria did not want to attract any attention yet. She leaned forward, resting on her elbows, so her face was next to Sylvan. Looking at him amused her like a child's toy is supposed to. He was sitting, folded like an "L", with his unbendable legs sticking out in front of him.

His head spun around, Zandria guessed he was turning a make believe face in her direction. She looked at the smooth round surface out of courtesy, in case he believed he was looking at her.

"You may find this strange," said Sylvan. "I've always loved the feel of a warm fire."

"Why is that strange," she started, then, "Oh."

"I realize it could be my undoing, but I find the heat very comforting," he said.

Zandria was not sure how to respond to this, so she skipped to her question. "Do you know who started the fire?"

Sylvan did not answer, but only pointed.

Zandria followed the tiny arm to see a boy coming up over the rise of their hill. She guessed right about the person gathering kindling for the fire, but it was not William. The boy was carrying an armful of the thick, reed-like grass. Zandria got to her feet.

At first, Zandria was taken aback because he was dressed like a Nookan, but he looked nothing like them. She knew everyone in her village and this boy was not from Banookanook. For starters, his skin was light, lighter than hers. Her first instinct was that he looked a lot like William, but that passed as he got closer. Her next thought was that she and he were about the same age. She believed this only because they were about the same height. She conceded to herself that he might be a little taller.

"Good morning," said the boy as he dropped the bundle at his feet. Zandria noticed the healing cuts around his ankles, and, as she scanned up, matching wounds on his wrists. She could not imagine what could make those marks because she had never heard of slavery before.

"Who are you?" she said.

He looked directly in her eyes and she was instantly uncomfortable. Zandria had never been around a boy her own age and did not understand the butterflies now swirling in her stomach.

He said, "I'm Adam."

"Is that all?" she asked. Zandria purposely let her suspicion win against that strange tingle of excitement.

"Isn't that enough?"

"No. I mean, who are you? Where did you come from?" she said.

Their conversation must have woke Olena and Kez, because the quzzak said through a yawn, "What are you doing here and why does it smell so delicious?"

Adam smiled at this and any mistrust Zandria felt melted away into more of those infuriating butterflies. She asked herself, "Why would a boy make me feel like I was going to throw up?"

The boy knelt next to the fire and tossed on some of the newly gathered grass. He built up some rocks to make a cooking pit and was roasting a small animal. Zandria studied him and thought he was both strong and intense. Still, there was a softness to him, like he had a great heart.

"Why don't you come eat," Adam said. "I caught this guy down by the edge of the plains." Adam must have noticed a look from Kez, because he added, "Don't worry, it's not a talker." Zandria knew he was trying to distinguish between the intelligent beasts and the type generally accepted as okay to eat.

Somewhere under her butterflies, she felt hunger pangs. She tried to fight her unexplainable trust and get more information from Adam. She said, "I'm not eating anything until you tell us where you came from."

"If you insist," he said. Then Adam tore off one of the creature's six legs and began eating.

"Zan, I'm starving," said Olena. "Maybe we can talk after we eat."

"I'm not," Zandria said and turned away from them. This was the first time she really looked out at the plains. Behind her to the left and right, was a wall of purple and gray mountains. In front of her was an unending field of grass. She was impressed with the openness of it and had not felt this at peace since she last stood ankle deep in the ocean by her village. After thinking of the waters of Banookanook, she could not imagine these plains any other way then as a sea. Even the way the wind blew the unusually tall grass made it look like waves.

Then Adam stepped up next to her. He presented some breakfast as a peace offering. "I've been following you for a while," he said. "I have to make sure you reach your destination."

"And what destination would that be," said Zandria, faking ignorance.

"Castle Empyrean, your majesty," Adam said with a wink.

"How do you know about that?" Zandria was shocked.

"I didn't," he said. "At least not for sure until now."

"You tricked me," she said. Zandria hit him on the shoulder with the side of her closed fist. She wanted to be mad, but the gesture seemed more like two friends joking with each other. She knew the smile she tried to hide did not help her position either. "Who do you think you are?"

Adam fought a smile of his own. Zandria hoped he was sharing these confusing feelings. She could feel an immediate bond forming between them and decided to accept whatever answer he gave as the truth.

"It doesn't matter who I am or where I came from," he said. "What matters is that I'm here to help you."

Zandria felt vulnerable. Without Fury and, more importantly, William to guide her, she told herself she needed somebody. The boy was mysterious. She could not guess why he wanted to help, but it did not matter. Right now, security was the same as trust for her.

She said, "How can you help us?"

"Well, I met some traders this morning and arranged a transport." Adam pointed to the north.

Over the next large hill, Zandria saw a post sticking up with a flag on it. The flag was a deep yellow with a black shape that resembled a familiar wing in the center. She thought the wing looked very much like Evorin's. The post reminded her of the mast of a ship like the kind that sometimes came from the ocean to the Palace by the Sea. However, Zandria knew that was impossible because there was no water around for miles.

Kez and Olena finished eating and then came to see what Adam was pointing at. Olena was hugging Sylvan to her chest like a beloved doll.

"So, we are to go sailing," squeaked Sylvan.

After putting out the fire, Adam ran toward the flag. Zandria followed quickly, excited to see what could be waiting for them. When she crested the hill, she was amazed to see a full size sailing ship.

Zandria could not believe her eyes. From stem to stern, it was exactly like the boats she would watch back home. The flag she could see from the distance was at the top of the tallest mast. There were two shorter poles, one in front and one behind, hanging with men readying the sails. She did not see one anchor, but several groups of men removing ropes that were staked into the dirt.

Most of the men were dressed in common work clothes. Some wore hoods that could presumably be pulled closed against the wind. There was one man that stood out from the others. He wore black pants and a black bandana over his bald head. His shirt was as richly yellow as the flag flying overhead and the wide sleeves billowed in the breeze. Zandria had no doubt this was their captain.

When the man saw his visitors, he grabbed the nearest rope. He swung across the deck and landed both feet on the top step of the plank that extended from the deck to the grass at the base of the hill.

"Welcome aboard The Dragon's Wing. I am Mildoo Vol," he said with a bow.

Olena bowed back with a giggle. Zandria inspected the crew's faces. She saw them to be grim and rough looking men. Zandria turned to Adam.

"I thought you said they were traders," she said. "They look more like pirates to me." She knew this from some pictures she saw once. The story went that the pirates sailed from across the eastern sea. The palace was still being constructed and the Nookans helped save the day.

Mildoo Vol started strutting down the boarding plank. He said, "I assure you, we have never pirated from anyone who did not have something of value."

Then he flashed a sincere smile and another exuberant bow.

Zandria did not know if this made her feel better or not. She thought if she was going to trust Adam, then this went along with it.

Then, a one-eyed man came up to the rail and said, "Captain Vol, the wind's up."

Mildoo Vol said, "As soon as our guests are aboard then you may give the order to haul away." He extended an arm to usher them aboard. Zandria looked to Adam and he mimicked the Captain with his opposite arm. She had no idea how wide these plains were and was so tired of walking. She saw her only choice as riding with these pirates. So she, Olena and Kez walked up the ramp between man and boy.

The girls ducked quickly out of the way as men dashed back and forth. They were shouting about untying this and swinging that. Even before the boarding ramp was stowed, the sails were tied in place. A strong gust of wind rolled down from the north across the face of the Euphoric Mountains. The breeze filled the sails and they took off with an unexpected burst of speed.

"Hang on, young ones," said Captain Vol. "Evorin must be awake today."

"What did you say?" asked Zandria.

"It's an old expression. It means the wind is blowing hard," said the Captain.

"But how did you know about Evorin?"

"That's a legend among our people. Supposedly, Evorin used to be a dragon that turned into the North Wind. So when the gusts are coming hard, we say the old boy's awake," explained Mildoo Vol. "If this keeps up, we might be to your castle by nightfall. But that rarely happens."

"He is real, by the way. We met Evorin yesterday," said Olena. "I think he ate our horsy."

Captain Vol gave a deep belly laugh. A few of the deck hands nearby chuckled. He said to his men, "Boys, it's been too long since we've been to port. After this trip, we should see our families. I'd forgotten the joy of a child's imagination."

There was a cheer across the deck as the ship cut through the prairie grass on its three rows of short, hard wheels.

Zandria did not feel the same happiness as the pirates. She could not believe that Olena could talk so carelessly about losing their friends. She moved over to the rail and watched the grass ripple away from the ship. Adam came and stood next to her.

"I'm sorry about your friends," Adam said. "Sylvan told me about them earlier. If it's any consolation, I saw no sign of them when I came through the mountain pass." Adam paused. "No dragon either," he added.

"We didn't make it up," Zandria was letting her anger get the better of her and did not feel like stopping it.

"I know. That horse left hoof marks on about everything since Bremen," he said.

"Exactly how long have you been following us?"

"Listen, Zandria, I said that doesn't matter." Adam was on the defensive.

"How long?"

Adam closed his mouth for a moment. He looked like he was trying to decide what to say next. Zandria was growing impatient. She wanted to be more understanding, but other people made it too easy to give in to the darkness.

Before she could say another word, Adam said, "Since the beginning." He lowered his head.

"The beginning?" Zandria was furious. "You've been following us from Banookanook? From our home?" She felt betrayed even though she only met him this morning.

"Yes, I've been to your home."

"Who are you? What do you want?" She started to cry.

"I don't really know *who* I am," said Adam. "It's hard to explain, but there are people who want to keep you from reaching that castle at any cost. They sent the werewolves after you and they sent me. They thought I could trick you, maybe be your friend and lead you the wrong way. Now they've sent an army to destroy all of Empyrean." Adam paused to read her face. "You've heard their marching in the darkness. I can tell by the look in your eyes."

The wind whipped Zandria's hair in her face. She turned her back to Adam, partially to get the hair out of her face and partly so she did not have to look at him.

"You can't stop me," she said coldly. She had visions of pushing him overboard, grisly imagining what the fast spinning wheels would do.

"I don't want to. Not now. I had to agree to their plans to get away. If you become queen, that will undo their plans. Then I will have revenge. They stole my life. I had a mother and father once. I can never get that back. By helping you, I can at least take something from them."

Zandria did not want to listen to Adam's problems right now. She only heard one thing he said. "What do you mean *if* I become queen?"

Olena walked up and asked, "Whatchya talking about?"

"He said *if* I become queen," Zandria shouted at her.

"Don't yell at me because of it," said Olena. "Besides, he's right."

"What's that supposed to mean?" asked Zandria.

"Me and Kez were talking. It's possible I could be queen. You keep saying it's you, but she was my mother too."

Zandria lost control. She did not try to push the blackness out of her heart and instead drew strength from it. She said, "You're not the queen. You're a baby. All I've had to do was take care of you my whole life. I'm sick of you and your whining."

Then the one-eyed deckhand pushed between them. He spotted something out on the plain and Zandria was too mad to talk anymore.

"We've got one," he shouted and everyone looked to the grass.

There was something out there keeping pace with the ship. Whatever it was, it was hidden by the grass, but it was almost as big as the ship. Zandria tracked it as it moved with unbelievable speed.

Then they crossed a burned patch where there was no grass to hide in and Zandria saw it. This creature had a thick brown body and six legs. Zandria could not believe it was a giant version of the animal they had for breakfast that morning.

Captain Vol joined them at the rail. He said, "Gents, it's a mother dirt bandit. We'll be paid well for that one. Bring the canons around."

Before anyone could move, a lightning bolt struck the ship. Everyone looked to the sky to see what was happening. It was overcast, but no sign of a storm. When Zandria looked up, her already sore heart sank. She looked into the face of Baba Yaga soaring above them in what looked like a large stone bowl. Somehow, she got back into her skin. Now she fired two more blasts of lightning from a long bony finger. Zandria knew better though, she thought it was probably a centipede inside that finger instead of bone.

Mildoo Vol responded quickly. "Forget the dirt bandit boys. We're under attack."

The pirates moved on instinct. In a matter of moments, they were firing small spiky cannonballs at the old woman. Most of the shots missed because of her wild movement, but a few struck her vessel and bounced off.

"What do you want from us?" screamed Zandria.

Baba Yaga answered in a voice that should have been impossible to hear over the clamor. Still, Zandria heard it like the bug lady was whispering in her ear.

"I've come for my eyes," she said.

Zandria did not know what this meant. She was scared that the woman meant her own eyes for looking in the window.

Then Olena grabbed Zandria's arm. Zandria, still mad at her sister, pulled away saying, "Get off me."

"No, wait Zan," said Olena. "She wants the skull thingy."

Olena must have heard Baba Yaga as well. It made perfect sense to Zandria now. Vasilissa warned them that Baba Yaga would come looking for the black skull with its glowing red eyes. Zandria was arrogant enough to think they had seen the last of the bug filled woman. The magic of the skull must have pulled her back together and called her to them.

Zandria stuck her hand deep in her pouch and pulled out the shiny black object. Its eyes blazed in the presence of its owner. Zandria looked around, not sure what to do with it. She thought maybe Captain Vol could help, but he was busy pulling levers and spinning wheels to make The Dragon's Wing go faster. Still, Baba Yaga kept up with them. Then Zandria looked overboard to see that the old woman was not the only one staying close. The dirt bandit was right behind them.

The sun was dipping down in the east, but the deck was still lit by the eerie red glow as Zandria raised the skull.

"You want it? Come and get it," said Zandria.

Then, she threw the skull out into the field. It disappeared in the thick grass, but she could tell where it landed by the light shining up out of the hole it crushed in the reeds. She saw the dirt bandit change course to see what else invaded its domain. Then Baba Yaga whooshed over within inches of Zandria's head. She crashed her bowl into the waterless sea and hobbled frantically toward her precious object. The entire scene was rapidly fading away, but Zandria could see the monstrous dirt bandit rise up, then dive down on Baba Yaga. Zandria hoped that was the last she would see of her.

Zandria had a mix of emotions that was not helped by Mildoo Vol's next statement. He said, "We have a slight problem."

He did not have to explain further. Zandria could feel the wind rushing against her and knew they could not slow down. She looked into the coming night ahead of them and could see small fires spread across the plain. She did not know these fires were caused by the same storm that dropped the poisoned rock on Bremen.

Then in the distance, something was sticking up out of the ground, reflecting the hundreds of fires. There was no moon or stars from above to illuminate the object. Then she realized it was not quite night. The darkness was caused by ominous black clouds that swirled and spread out high above the object.

At the same time Zandria felt its name, Olena, standing next to her, whispered, "Empyrean."

"Ay, the Castle Empyrean," said Mildoo Vol. "As I was saying though, we have a problem. Thanks to that crazy old woman, we can't stop."

It was the one-eyed man's turn to talk. He said, "It gets worse Captain. The lookout says there's some kind of ridge ahead and we can't miss it."

Captain Vol let a look of panic escape and then masked it with an exaggerated smile. He announced, "Everyone brace yourself for, well, for I don't know what."

Zandria, Olena and Adam ducked down at the rail. Kez crowded in beneath and Zandria watched Olena stuff Sylvan safely in her pouch. She wished she could have been outside the ship to be able to see it hit that ridge.

In Zandria's imagination it was much more magnificent and much less frightening than in reality. The Dragon's Wing moved as fast as it could without tearing apart. Loose rope ends flailed in every direction and one or two of the thirty wheels shredded out of existence. The land boat ramped up the gradual incline then leapt from the ridge.

For what seemed like an incredibly long time, the only sound Zandria could hear was the rustle of the sails. The ship was flying in midair into the unknown. Then, with a painful crash, they hit solid ground. Zandria banged her head on the rail during the impact and passed out.

Chapter 16

Same Day, Different Place

Wrath woke with a strange feeling. It was not the perpetual darkness that hung over the castle in the form of unwelcoming clouds. His joints were sore and his head felt heavy. He raced to the Northern Wood and back in only ten days. The last time he came from his home, it took six days one way and he thought that was fast. Wrath stopped counting his birthdays after he was in his sixties, but today he felt all eighty of them. It was the first time in his life that he felt like an old horse.

There was something else, too. The war horse stretched his back and four legs, then let his bare hooves rest on the dirt. The diamond smith was carving him some new shoes because he wore the last set down to shards. Wrath liked to be bare hoofed, it made him feel more connected to Empyrean. Today, he was so connected, he thought he could feel the ground breathing.

No, he thought, it was not the ground. There was something under the ground. It was not breathing, but rather a vibration. Wrath planted a hoof firmly and cocked his head sideways as if he could hear it also. The vibration was definitely someone or something marching. He felt that same sensation in countless parades over the years. What worried him was that the marching was coming from underground.

He looked across the field at his army, most of which was still sleeping. He managed to gather a force of three hundred Friesians and their riders. Only the swiftest came back with him. The rest arrived last night. He chose their camp to be on the north side of the canyon that surrounded the Castle Empyrean. Even though the drawbridge was smashed by meteors, he wanted to keep any attackers as far from the front door as he could.

Wrath knew from the start that the horses of the Northern Wood would not be enough to face whatever enemy was approaching. By the force of the vibration, he guessed they were outnumbered more than ten to one. He hoped Fury and Apis would be more successful in their tasks.

He knew Fury was reckless, but he was a good student. Wrath sensed the potential in him to someday be a great leader of the Friesians. His concern was if Fury's fool hardy and careless behavior would let him reach that point.

Fury was supposed to find the new Queen of the Eastern Sky. Wrath knew that would not be an easy task without a wizard to interpret the signs. He told himself it was not like the queen would come out of nowhere and walk right up to him. Wrath feared Fury would not find her in time to save them.

Suddenly, the vibration in the ground stopped and that brought Wrath back to the present. He missed his student and friend, but this was not the time to be worrying about him. He worried about what was happening under his own hooves. The ground was still, even more than its natural rhythm.

"I don't like this," said Wrath to no one as he stood alone.

Then the ground shook violently. Wrath looked to the glass tower hoping to see it unaffected. It was safe, so he turned to his soldiers. The ground shook again. All three hundred horses were instantly awake and their men quickly joined them. Wrath thought this must be the attack they were waiting for. Still, more shaking came from underground.

In the distance, to the east and west, Wrath saw the field rupture. Two identical splits twisted around and joined on the north side, completely surrounding the small army. The ground did not give up its unpleasant swaying. Wrath did not have a chance to issue any orders before the ground inside the cracks sank a few feet. Then the ground outside their field burst upward. The surrounding field angled up leaving them in a massive depression. Then the shaking stopped.

Wrath inspected their situation. The shifting ground left them encircled like a giant arena. There were steep rock walls on three sides. He could see cracks and gaps where single horses could get through, but the only clear opening was to the south. Wrath knew that was no escape because it opened to the bottomless canyon that surrounded Castle Empyrean. The sheer immensity of the newly formed structure made his army seem very tiny and isolated in the center.

The next thing Wrath expected was the actual attack. When none came, he sent several lieutenants to scout the walls. The reports were all the same. The horses said the walls were impassable except in a few narrow places. The one thing he could not see from his position were the hundreds of caves that opened along the base of the walls. Wrath did not think himself so foolish as to send anyone into those dark depths.

While they waited, the vibration started again. Wrath steeled himself for battle. His nerves were becoming frayed. It had been a long time since he did any fighting other than practice. Still, he would rather die fighting than waiting. Then he noticed this vibration was not coming from underground, but rather on top of it. Wrath looked to the west ridge to see what was coming.

Apis the great black bull appeared at the crest. Beneath him, a thousand men and women from the Southern Valley streamed through the narrow openings. Wrath was glad for the reinforcements, but, at the same time, disheartened because they were not warriors.

Most of the sun-darkened people were farmers. They carried their simple tools, hoes and rakes. Some brought basic hunting equipment like spears and bows. Then Wrath saw several groups of old men carrying wicker baskets. He thought this was no place for these terribly old men until they sat down with their baskets. The men started playing flutes that were stuffed in their waistbands. The baskets seemed to come alive as their contents squirmed out. Soon the ground slithered with hundreds of snakes all under the control of a group of old men and their strange flute music.

The last of Apis' army came over the top with him because they could not fit through the wall. Six of the fiercest women Wrath had ever seen rode on the backs of six of the largest and strangest creatures he had ever seen. The beasts were at least thirty feet long each from the tips of their thrashing tails to the front of their pointed, teeth-filled mouths. They crawled low to the ground and the women guided them with harnesses attached to their thick, wide heads. Wrath turned to one of the nearby Southerners to find out what these gold colored creatures were called. He received a one word answer, "Crocodiles."

With the combined forces of the Northern Wood and the Southern Valley, Wrath saw that they did not fill the wide open space even a third of the way. Wrath made his way to Apis, near the center.

"Thank you, great one, for bringing your people," he said. "I fear our numbers are not enough for whatever lies beneath us."

Then something happened that Wrath never expected. Apis the silent bull spoke in a silky, echoing voice, "We will fight with the strength of the sun at our backs. The day will not be lost in vain. More good news will reach your ears."

Apis turned his head skyward and a stunned Wrath slowly followed his gaze. The horse received a second surprise. A small dot was fluttering in from the west, barely visible against the dark sky. As it approached, Wrath could not understand why it was not getting any bigger. When it was close enough, he saw that it was one of the guardian hawks from the heights of Empyrean. Now Wrath understood why it was so small, these hawks did not grow much larger than a human hand.

The breathless hawk landed roughly on Apis' back. He rested for a moment to catch his breath and then gave a bird bow to Wrath. The little hawk spoke between gasps of air, "Forgive the late arrival. I am Aeran, Captain of the Guardian Hawks."

Aeran looked battered and worn. He was missing a few claws and most of his tail feathers. Wrath said, "Rest friend, your injuries seem great."

"Alas, I was not wounded on this journey. These scars are mementos of a previous flight that left me almost mortally wounded." The little bird perched proudly.

"Then what urgency is it that causes you this further pain?" asked Wrath.

"As I lay recovering under the care of my savior, the Queen of the Northern Wood, word reached me of your mission," said Aeran. "Knowing only three of you escaped the castle and knowing there were four directions to be reached, I had to perform my duty. Without thought for myself, I left the comfort of my hospital nest and flew directly to the West."

Wrath was impressed, "That is a brave thing you have done. You have earned much needed rest. Before you go, please tell me what news you brought back with you."

Aeran said, "I will tell you of the response, but first let me say that I do not intend to lie down. I have roosted on my laurels for too long and know that my place is here defending those blessed ladies."

"Then you are welcome to stay. Please, what news from the West," Wrath said.

"It is good news. Five hundred of the Court Gardeners Squad and another two hundred stablehands are marching this way now."

Turning to Apis, Wrath said, "That brings us to two thousand. By all accounts, a sturdy army if not that most were farmers, gardeners and stableboys. Still, I will not go to pasture without a fight."

"Then, for the defense of Empyrean," said Aeran, puffing up his chest.

"For Empyrean," said Wrath. "Now Apis, see to it that you and your people meet with the dwarves in the armory."

"I do not require armor," said Apis.

Wrath looked at the size of the bull and said, "I suppose not. If I am required, that is where you will find me."

When the dwarves finished dressing Wrath in his battle armor, even he was astonished. The skilled artisans of the Seven Families led by Professor Erbadin hammered and shaped their purest platinum specifically for him. He watched his reflection in a water trough. Every piece fit perfectly to his body, but he hardly felt the weight at all. His flanks and legs were well covered in solid plates. Across his chest and neck was a very flexible mesh. Wrath's helmet allowed his ears to poke out, then it came to a point down the length of his nose. It was not ornate, but simply stamped with the apple crest of the Queen of the Northern Wood.

Wrath had not worn armor since before his student, Fury, was born. The dwarves did an excellent job of making him look like a general, he thought. He was instilled with a new vigor that pushed away the aches of old age that he was feeling this morning.

He did not have long to admire himself though. One of his riders ran to him in a panic.

"Something is coming from the east and it's moving fast," said the human. Wrath wished he had time to learn the names of the men he was going to war with. Whatever was approaching now would not allow him that luxury of time.

As Wrath neared the east ridge with a handful of other Friesians, he saw an unbelievable sight. He knew it was a ship because he heard enough stories of the plains' pirates. He thought they were supposed to roll across the ground on wheels like immense carriages. This one was flying through the air. He instantly deduced that it lost control, ramped off the newly reformed ground and was now soaring right at them.

Wrath skidded to a halt on his fresh diamond shoes. The other horses scattered as the ship hit the ground in front of him. The tallest mast fell forward, barely missing him. The ship's inertia was lost in the impact and everything was still.

Wrath was afraid no one survived, then a bald headed man in an extremely bright yellow shirt jumped up holding the broken steering wheel. He shouted at Wrath, "Look to the children," and then passed out.

Wrath trotted past the broken rail to find three children and a small unusual animal. The animal, with a face like a furry old man, was holding the hand of a young, curly-haired girl. She was crying, but otherwise seemed okay. The other child, an older boy, was kneeling beside an older girl. She looked very much like the first girl and she looked very much at peace as she lay unconscious.

Wrath spent enough time in the presence of the queens to know immediately in his heart who one of these girls was. He did not know their names or from whence they came. All he knew was that he had to get them to safety and hopefully find a way to get them into Empyrean.

Chapter 17

A Day for Parting

The crash was frightening and being grabbed by a bunch of strangers and carried off to their camp was no better. Still, the worst part for Olena was being yelled at by Zandria. She played the hurtful words over in her head as she lay next to her unconscious sister.

Olena saw Zandria hit her head when the ship wrecked. She wanted her big sister to be all right. Kez told her to get some sleep and then took his own advice. But she stayed awake. She loved Zandria and did not want her sister's last words to be "I'm sick of you".

She thought about this most of the night. She thought about Zandria once blaming her for losing their mother. She thought about always having to be the servant or monster when they played games. And she thought about how Zandria insisted she was going to be queen.

Olena believed it was possible that she could be queen. Zandria always made her think she was not as smart or pretty as her big sister, but that did not matter. Olena knew they shared one thing. Since her mother was next in line, to her, that meant she had as much of a chance as her sister. She did not want to hurt Zandria's feelings, but she liked the idea of finally getting her turn to be queen.

Outside their tent, Olena heard movement that distracted her from her difficult thoughts. She could not believe how many horses there were that looked like Fury. She liked that the old one in the fancy armor came to check on them a lot. The horses and humans pulled them from the wreckage and put them in this tent. She heard someone call the lead horse Wrath.

This time, Wrath did not poke his muzzle into the tent. He was cut off by a voice that Olena recognized. Mildoo Vol spoke in a low voice, but she could still hear them.

"What can I do for you, Captain?" said Wrath.

"As it is, General, my friends and I are without transportation. I seem to think I could be of some service if you could get me swiftly away from here."

Olena liked Captain Vol and was sad to hear he wanted to leave. Wrath must have given the man one of those looks. Olena knew the look without seeing it because she often received it from Zandria when she did or said something that her sister did not like. Olena thought the captain got the look because he spoke quickly to clarify himself.

"Please don't misunderstand. As simple traders, we thrive on a free market. It is in our best interest to help you in your cause to keep it free. The problem is that my associates are at least a day's ride from here."

"Captain, are you volunteering to help us?" asked Wrath.

"I merely think it would be beneficial to both parties," said Mildoo Vol.

"Very well. Go with this rider here and he will introduce you to one of my fastest stallions," finished Wrath.

Olena heard two pairs of footsteps walk away. Then she ducked under her blanket and faked sleeping because she knew what was coming next. Wrath stuck in his head to check on them for the fourth time that night.

She waited until she was sure the horse was gone before she sat up again. Olena did not want to answer any questions and especially not by herself. She was afraid she might say the wrong thing. The horses were the same as Fury, so she knew she could trust them. Her concern was that they were getting ready for a fight and she did not want to say anything to make that happen sooner.

When she was carried to the camp from the wreck, she could easily see the huge glass tower. It reminded her of the trees that grew close to the beach. The tower went straight up and had a cluster of smaller towers springing out of the top. She knew this was the center of all of Empyrean.

She knew they finally made it. Olena did not want to stay in this camp any longer. She wanted to go inside.

She started to roll down her blanket, then there was a rustling underneath. Olena flipped back the blanket to find Sylvan struggling to get out of her pouch. She helped him the rest of the way out and he stood silently in front of her.

Olena whispered to him, "I'm leaving now. You stay here."

Sylvan's head slowly moved from side to side meaning he did not agree with that decision. Olena was confused. She did not know if Sylvan was telling her to stay or saying he did not want to be left behind.

She whispered again, "I have to get to the castle. It's what William wanted. It's what my father wanted. Maybe it's not what Zan wants, but she made it clear she doesn't want me around anymore either. So, I'm going. Do you want to come with me?"

Sylvan bowed with approval. She surprised herself by being glad that he wanted to join her. She was also glad he did not speak and wake anybody up with that squeak of his. Olena grabbed Sylvan and her pouch and crawled out the back of the tent.

Olena crawled past several rows of tents. Between rows, she would poke her head up and make sure she was moving toward Empyrean. She was near the edge of the camp when she was startled by, "Where do you think you're going?"

She stood up and slowly turned around, knowing she was caught. To Olena's relief, it was Kez. She knew she was in trouble, but at least Zandria was not with him.

"You're going to the castle," accused Kez.

"That's what I'm supposed to do. Please don't try to stop me."

"I'm not going to stop you," said Kez. "I'm coming with you."

Olena got down on her knees and hugged the quzzak. She said, "Thank you."

Kez struggled against her smothering grasp, "I can't believe you were going without me. You didn't even try to wake me up."

"I didn't want to bother anybody. I know I'm a pain," Olena said, finally letting Kez go.

"Child, that is so far from the truth. Zandria did not mean those things," said Kez.

"Then why did she say them." Olena did not wait for an answer, "It doesn't matter. I'm still going."

"I've been with you your entire life. Zandria has a whole army now, so you're not getting rid of me that easily," said Kez. He climbed up to his comfortable spot on her shoulder and they walked away from the camp.

Olena walked for quite a while, doing her best to keep even distance between the camp and the rock wall surrounding it. She moved on in the darkness as straight toward the castle as she could.

Olena thought she saw something fly above her. That made her instantly think of the dragon

Evorin. She asked Kez, "You never did tell me how you knew Evorin's name."

"It was simple really. Lilac told me."

Olena started to say "Who" and then remembered the purple Rainbow Princess. It seemed like so long ago when they were in that cave under the waterfall. It was true. Lilac's gift was a single secret word whispered to Kez. The Prismata told him he would know when to use it and she was right.

Then Olena noticed the flying thing again. This time it came straight at her and landed at her feet. She was delighted to see a tiny bird, but he looked to be in bad shape.

"My lady," said the bird, "I am Aeran, Captain of the Guardian Hawks, sworn protectors of the Castle Empyrean and its queens."

"Pleased to meet you," said Olena.

"Sorry to interrupt you. I was merely flying my patrol and noticed you heading directly for the canyon edge," he said.

Olena was surprised and looked a few feet ahead. She could barely tell in the darkness, but it looked like the ground ended. "But I have to get to the castle," she said.

"Then allow me to be your guide, my lady," said Aeran. "There is but one way for those with the misfortune of being born without wings."

It took the rest of the night, but Aeran led Kez and Olena all the way. First, they squeezed through a narrow break in the surrounding wall. Olena saw how the ground sloped up all around and understood how Mildoo Vol's ship jumped through the air. As they followed the edge of the canyon, Aeran showed them the intersection of the North Road and the Great Road. Eventually, he led them up an ancient path that ended in a barrier of thorns as the morning sun fought to break through the impenetrable cloud cover.

"On the other side of this, you will find the gates of Empyrean," said Aeran.

"How are we supposed to get through this?" asked Kez.

"I normally fly over it. Maybe we can find a way through."

Then the horrible sound of thousands of chanting voices filled the air. Aeran fluttered and Kez's tail pricked up. Barely audible over the chanting was a lone horn. Aeran lifted into the air.

"That is the call of General Wrath. They are under attack. The battle has begun. I'm sorry, I must return."

Then Aeran flew away, leaving them standing in front of the painful looking thorns.

"Now what?" asked Kez.

Olena answered without doubt, "We crawl."

Zandria woke to the sensation of Kez crawling across her leg. Her head hurt so much when she tried to open her eyes that she could barely make him out. She tried to focus on something closer and saw Adam's sleeping face. She felt safe with him despite their argument. Ignoring the aching bump, she rolled over to rest her sore head on his shoulder. She fell back asleep before Kez was out of the tent.

The dream of the rocks exploding from the ground came again. This time, the rocks were chanting. It was the same language, the same words, that Zandria heard in the depths of the Taenarum Tunnel. She tried to wake herself, but the sound did not go away. It was louder and clearer than it had ever been.

She opened her eyes to an empty tent. No Adam, no Kez, not even Olena. She remembered the crash of The Dragon's Wing and hitting her head. She did not know where she was now or where this tent came from.

Zandria heard a faint horn blow against the chanting. She went outside and found Adam talking to an armored horse. The chanting was unbearable, but she could still hear them talking.

"This is a tragedy," said the horse.

"But how could you not know where she went?" asked Adam.

Zandria knew instantly that they were talking about Olena. Her heart sank, but at the same time, the darkness surrounding her heart was relieved to be rid of her.

She interrupted them with her own question, "What is that noise?"

"Wrath told me," Adam referred to the horse, "that it's coming from underground. His scouts don't know what it is yet. Zandria, your sister's gone."

She did not feel quite as mad at Adam today and decided it was okay to talk to him. The dark seed inside of her wanted to respond with "Finally". Instead, she said, "Where'd she go?"

"We're not sure. I do know she was here after Captain Vol left. She did not go with him. I've sent for the hawk captain. Maybe he can help," said Wrath.

"So, your pirates ran away," Zandria scoffed at Adam.

"He went to get help," said Adam. "We're about to go to war here."

Zandria looked around her for the first time. The camp was full of men and horses. She saw dwarves as well as other creatures she did not know rushing their preparations.

"Captain, I'm here," Wrath called to the sky.

An unbelievably small hawk dropped down and landed on the tip of a spear that was leaning on a nearby rack.

"Aeran, thank you for coming so quickly," said Wrath.

"I heard your call General and could not fail you. I bring good news. The gardeners are marching up the western slope. They arrived faster than I would have thought," said Aeran. "And they brought a rather large canon."

"That news is good," said Wrath. "But we have a more pressing issue. A child is missing."

Aeran looked confused, "She's not missing. I delivered her and her fuzzy friend to the castle gate myself."

"What?" said Adam.

"You are certain she is safely inside?" asked Wrath.

"I left her at the briar. All that was left was to cross the bridge and..."

"The bridge was destroyed, Captain," interrupted Wrath. He turned to Adam, "She is too far away for me to help her now. The enemy is upon us and if they truly have five thousand soldiers like you say, then we are dreadfully outnumbered."

Zandria thought of her sister being alone, but could not bring herself to feel anything. She said, "I have to get inside. Is there any other way?"

"There is only my way," Aeran said stretching a wing.

"There is another possibility," said Wrath. "It is quite dangerous, but I will take you to it myself."

Adam looked at Zandria. He did not speak, but she could tell he wanted to come. She nodded and he climbed up on Wrath's back. Then he helped her up. She had a clear view of the camp from this height. It looked quite small in the middle of this barricaded field. Wrath started galloping past the tents. To the east, she saw the wrecked ship that raced them across the plains. The broken ground and rocky walls behind looked strangely familiar to her. Zandria looked to the west. Hundreds of men in blue uniforms lined the surrounding wall in the distance. They were positioning a massive canon and seemed to be loading it with a pumpkin that was bigger than five of them combined. Then Zandria realized why the land looked so familiar. This was the place in her dream where the rocks broke through. She was glad to be leaving it behind.

Wrath dashed away from the camp and covered the open field as fast as he could. He took Zandria and Adam to the edge of the canyon that protected Empyrean. As Zandria dismounted, she looked over the edge. There was no visible bottom, only a point where she could see no further and it turned to white mist.

"Look across the way," said Wrath. "The Castle Empyrean does not float in mid air. It grew from the canyon wall. That is why it is protected on one side by impassable thorns."

A mile away, Zandria could see the natural barrier and knew Olena was there. Right now, she did not care if the little girl was safe or not. Then Zandria looked down the canyon wall. A long way down, she could see where the crystal stretched from the side before turning skyward.

"Along this edge, you will find a hidden staircase," explained Wrath. "It will be neither easy nor quick. My only hope is that there is still an entrance at the bottom."

"What does that mean?" asked Adam.

"Empyrean is alive. As your face changes with the passage of time, so do the secrets of the castle. There is nothing left but the attempt and not trying is the same as failing." With that, Wrath left them.

Zandria was already scouring the edge for the hidden staircase. She found a stone sticking out barely wide enough for her two feet at the same time. Over and down slightly was another small stone. This was it. She found the hidden staircase. There was no guardrail, no wide landings. There were only these little outcroppings that followed the curve of the wall down and down.

Zandria said, "Ka, you've got to be kidding me."

Chapter 18

A Day for Fighting

As Wrath left Zandria and Adam at the canyon's edge, he thought about the strange pair. His feeling was that both of them were filled with anger. He was sure they had their own reasons and from the look of the boy, he was justified. Wrath thought about the girl a moment longer before his mind turned to battle strategies.

Whatever it was that bothered Zandria, he suspected, was not completely of her own doing. He wished he could have talked to the younger girl. Still, he believed Zandria truly felt about her sister the way he felt about his own students, the way he felt about Fury. They could be aggravating and annoying. They could mess things up, fail to follow directions and complain too much. But without question, he loved every one of them, as Zandria had to love Olena. She could not have love in her heart and still be of royal blood. The enchantment that wrapped her heart in darkness would either break away by Empyrean's magic or consume her.

The lieutenants quickly surrounded Wrath upon his return. Even the western gardeners in their pristine blue uniforms made it to the camp with the exception of those needed to operate the canon. Wrath saw Apis standing alone and moved to him.

Apis said, "The time is now."

Then the ground began rumbling. Men and dwarves and the southerners with their cat-like features grabbed their weapons. Barely able to keep their balance, riders mounted Friesians and crocodiles. The snake charmers were rapidly blowing tunes on their flutes to call the cobras and asps to attention.

Far out of Wrath's sight, a snail crawled up out of one of the tunnels on four spindly legs that extended from the back of his shell. Later, Wrath would hear a wild looking gypsy call this creature General Gusk and Gusk would refer to her as Sasha.

General Gusk surveyed the queens' army and then clicked his antennae together.

The rumbling instantly grew more severe. Tents toppled and weapon stands fell over. Then the first of the Rockhorns, as Adam called them, burst from the cave. Soon they were coming from all directions and could not get out of the tunnels fast enough. More of them began breaking through the ground. If Wrath could have seen inside

Zandria's head, he would know her dream was coming true.

A small, pointy piece of rock poked up between Wrath's front hooves. He thought the rock was growing but quickly realized it was rising out of the ground. The tiny horn did not change size, but the head it was attached to was enormous. When the stone creature was completely out of the ground, it stood as tall as Wrath on his hind legs. Wrath took a moment to see the carved spear in place of one of the Rockhorn's hands. The other that was swinging towards him was shaped like a thick war hammer. Wrath dodged the blow. He knew the battle had begun.

In an instant, all was chaos. The camp was indistinguishable as they were overrun by five thousand hand-carved Rockhorns. They only had two thousand men, women and beasts, so Wrath feared the battle would not last long.

Wrath saw that the giant crocodiles were quite effective, smashing Rockhorn after Rockhorn with their tails. One exploded right in front of him and his armor was dented by bits of stone and shattered jewels. The western gardeners and southern farmers did not fare as well. They were being mercilessly slashed and pounded by the Rockhorn's weapon-hands.

The canon fired from the ridge and a massive pumpkin flew through the air. It landed in the middle of a group of three Rockhorns and broke open when it hit the ground. The pumpkin was filled with mice that burst out and swarmed their enemy. The mice picked the Rockhorns apart, piece by piece. The canon was reloaded and fired in a different direction.

Professor Erbadin, the leader of the seven dwarven families of the North Wood, signaled Wrath. Erbadin was the oldest dwarf Wrath knew and the one who personally sculpted his helmet.

"Professor, what can I do for you?" Wrath shouted as he came near.

"I am in need of a ride, Mighty Friesian. There is someone we must meet," said Erbadin.

"I am at your service, my lord." Wrath knelt down and the Professor grabbed a heavy axe before climbing on. "Which way?" asked Wrath.

The dwarf pointed north and Wrath took off. After a moment, they were joined by twenty other Friesians carrying the rest of the dwarves that came to aid their queen. Then Wrath saw what they were heading towards. There was a small group of dirty, rugged dwarves giving commands to the Rockhorns.

"It is as I feared," said Erbadin. "Lord Vanril has returned." Wrath knew the name from his history lessons. Lord Vanril was the betrayer. He divided the ten dwarven families when Snow White became queen. Wrath did not have any more time to think about it as Professor Erbadin leapt from his back. The old dwarf sailed through the air and tackled Lord Vanril. The other dwarves jumped into the fray following Erbadin.

Wrath saw General Gusk cowering in his shell near the brawl. He trotted over to the snail and back-kicked him as hard as he could. The spiral shell spun through the air and disappeared into one of the deep holes left by a Rockhorn.

The gypsy woman Sasha seized her moment. She yelled, "Rise my children. It is time to feast."

Wrath and his herd were trapped by the rock wall as a hundred werewolves stormed out of the caves. The attack was vicious and Friesians fell on both sides of him. Wrath tried to lead his soldiers to safety. He reunited with the main force in the center of the field. Sasha's assassins were relentless, attacking in both wolf and human form.

Wrath did not notice the man with the bandage across his nose break off from the group. The leader of the werewolves was heading in the direction that Zandria went.

Even without the wolves, Wrath could see they were losing. One of the crocodiles was defeated and the pumpkin canon was out of ammunition. The poisonous snakes were not effective against the Rockhorns and only stopped a wolfman when they could catch one. The farmers and gardeners knew no battle tactics and were dropping beneath the waves of Rockhorns. They were surrounded on three sides and being slowly backed to the canyon's edge.

Then there was a deafening roar and the fighting momentarily stopped on both sides. Wrath looked around to see what new evil this enemy unleashed. Instead, he saw a lone figure on the east ridge. When he looked closer, he knew it was not one, but two figures. On top, was a young man he did not recognize. The young man, with long brown hair, was exceptionally handsome by human standards, Wrath thought. And he looked like a warrior with his sword pointing to the sky.

The figure holding the man was unmistakable and made Wrath's heart surge. It was Fury. Wrath stared at his friend, proud to be with him at the end. Wrath was exhilarated, but knew that Fury and a single human would make no difference.

A moment later, Fury was joined on one side by a huge white tiger and on the other by a stunning unicorn. Then, an enormous dragon flew over the top of them and gave another of his deafening roars.

The young man on Fury's back yelled, "Charge!" A flood of unicorns and other animals spilled over the ridge. A cast of condors followed in the dragon's wake. Then the battle resumed. Wrath knew he had to bring his army together with Fury's.

The dragon flapped his wings, scattering the werewolves. He shot fire from his mouth that melted scores of Rockhorns to nothing. Then the dragon turned his attention to the east wall. He smashed it flat with one swipe of his tail.

This cleared the way for a small fleet of ships to roll into the arena. Wrath saw Mildoo Vol at the prow of the lead ship. Their canons fired into the Rockhorns, taking them out one at a time.

Finally, Wrath and Fury were side by side, galloping through the mayhem. The old war horse could feel the tide turning in their favor.

"You couldn't wait for me, could you ol' nag," said Fury.

"Knowing you," laughed Wrath, "You were probably asleep under a tree somewhere. Tell me student, was that Sayonya?"

"You know her? You old stallion, I always knew you had a way with the mares," said Fury.

"I was barely older than a colt when I knew her."

They leapt over a crumbling Rockhorn. Wrath intended to lead his troops to encircle the Rockhorns.

"I want you to meet someone else," said Fury. "This young fellow back here is Prince William."

"Your majesty," said Wrath, "Thank you for coming to our aid."

William looked to Wrath from atop Fury's back, "Please, I am not nearly as majestic as you. More importantly though, did two girls pass your way?"

Wrath dodged a pouncing werewolf. The wolf was quickly knocked back by three Bremen dogs. He said, "They were here and gone before the fighting. Each is making her own way to the castle, but I cannot speak to their present condition."

William looked like a strong young man, full of vitality. However, Wrath saw a momentary flash of old age and worry in the man's eyes.

William said, "Then it is all we can do to hope that they are safe." He swung his powerful looking sword, cracking a Rockhorn in half.

The battle raged. Wrath felt like they were winning, but he could get no clear picture. For every shattered Rockhorn, he saw a wrecked pirate ship or fallen gardener. There was one of his on the ground for every one of the enemy. He saw the white tiger that Fury called Virgata lead his menagerie of animals in attack after attack. Sayonya and her unicorns matched evenly with the werewolves. Eventually, Professor Erbadin returned, but Wrath could not tell from his stern face if he defeated Lord Vanril. Aeran's hawks and the condors ruled the sky.

The only enemy leader Wrath did see was Sasha. She was at the edge of the canyon guarded by a pack of her strongest werewolves. When Wrath got close, he could hear her reciting a spell and emptying potions off the edge.

Most of the Rockhorn attack was now focused on the dragon Evorin. Wrath saw Apis lead the bulk of their army to fence in the stone warriors.

Then, the saddest moment of the day occurred. Wrath watched helplessly as Apis was mauled by ten wolfmen. He shook them off and gored as many as he could. Then four Rockhorns joined the attack. All told, it took more than twenty werewolves and Rockhorn to drive Apis to the ground before he could not get up again. Even then, a solitary wolf-man gnawed at the bull's motionless body.

There was nothing for Wrath to do there, so he and Fury broke off from the main group to try and stop Sasha. They could not get close to her, but watched from a spot on the curve of the canyon edge. They could see Sasha's charms and powders falling into the bottomless pit. The white mist below swirled with black smoke that started to climb the walls like oily vines.

A massive bolt of lightning struck the castle. The fighting stopped for a second time. Then more lightning struck the field and meteors began to fall. One burning rock split Mildoo Vol's new ship in half. Virgata and Sayonya were ordering everyone to retreat.

"Here we go again," said Fury.

Wrath did not move. He knew the evil that was coming up out of the canyon had been trapped there for thousands of years. He watched Sasha continue to rant until she was struck by a bolt of lightning. Then she was gone.

Fury nudged his old teacher, "We have to find shelter."

As they turned away, a meteor struck the spot where they had been standing a moment ago. It tore the ground away and tumbled into the canyon. Wrath looked across the battlefield and saw most of his allies taking refuge in the Rockhorn caves. Their stone enemies had no emotion and knew no fear. They simply stood in place while the sky crashed down around them. One after another was smashed, but Wrath no longer felt like they were winning.

Something long forgotten was coming. Wrath knew it was evil and he knew there was nothing he could do. Everything was now in the hands of two little girls.

Chapter 19

Midnight

Olena crawled through the thorns, the little barbs picking at her hair and clothes. She felt like she should know a word that would make the brambles move, but nothing came to mind.

Kez followed close behind her. When they started in, she saw his tail wrapped tight. She asked him why he was doing that.

"Sometimes, this thing has a mind of its own. I'd hate to get it wrapped around one of these branches," he said.

"You're funny," said Olena and continued crawling.

Sylvan was leading the way. His small body was impervious to the thorns. He did his best to guide a clear path. Olena was glad he was with her. She was glad Kez was there too.

She knew Kez almost her entire life. He was always fun and always took care of her. She felt that Kez liked her better than Zandria, but her sister always did have a hard time making friends. Olena missed William and Fury dearly, but did not know what she would do without Kez.

Then she remembered her father did not like quzzaks for some reason. William reminded her of her father. Thinking about both of them at the same time brought tears to her eyes. She stopped and caught her breath.

Kez could not make it through the last opening to reach her. So, Sylvan came back to comfort her. She knew he was no ordinary toy, but now she realized he was capable of love.

"It is not fitting to see tears on the face of Olena the Beautiful," he squeaked.

The sound of his voice alone was enough to bring a smile to her face.

"I thought you only called Vasilissa *the Beautiful*," she said.

"I may only have one beautiful lady and you are it," said Sylvan. "Her time has passed and I will never leave your side."

Olena hugged him and put him back on the ground. She felt a small hand on her leg and reached back to squeeze it. Although Kez could not quite reach her at the moment, she knew he was part of the hug too.

"I'm okay," she said. "We should keep going."

Sylvan turned back to his task without a word. Olena saw that it was easy for him to move through the small spaces. She loved him even more because he took the time to find bigger openings for her.

It took most of the morning, but the three of them finally made it through. At first, she was excited, but instantly gave up hope. She was standing on the precipice of the canyon that surrounded Empyrean and there was no bridge. She could see the door only a short distance away. Far below, she could make out the remains of the drawbridge splintered on the outcropping where the castle grew from the wall.

"We're never going to make it," said Olena.

"Don't be so sure," said Kez. "Who is that?"

Kez was pointing at Empyrean's open gate. In the archway, Olena saw a tall skinny man with braided hair and pointy ears talking to a short, stocky man. The stocky man, who turned out to be Snow White's coach driver, left with his instructions and the tall man turned to look at her.

He shouted across the chasm, "My name is Tym. I've been expecting you."

"Hi Tym." Olena was delighted to see him, but had no idea how to get to him.

"Wait there," said Tym, "We're getting some rope."

After a moment, the stocky man returned with a bundle of rope. They held their end and threw it once. Twice. Three times. It was no good. Olena could see the rope was not long enough.

"Maybe you have something in your pouch that will help," suggested Kez.

"Good idea," she said.

Tym shouted, "We'll be back. Stay there." Then he and the stocky man went back into the castle.

Olena did not respond to Tym. She was busy searching her magic bag. She still had the mirror and the bronze ring, but neither felt like they would help right now. She had a few trinkets and souvenirs that she picked up along the way. There was even a crust of leftover bread. The only other thing she had that might have any power was the mayblossom that Ruby, the red fairy, gave her. Her heart told her this was what she needed.

Olena took it out and presented it to Kez and Sylvan in the palm of her hand. "I think this will get us there," she said.

"As lovely as it is, I do not see how a mayblossom will help," said Sylvan.

"It seems like we should plant it and see what happens," said Olena. She sat the flower on the ground at the edge of the canyon and scooped some dirt around its edges.

Instantly, the six pink petals in the center of the delicate flower doubled in size. A second later, the three red petals on the outside expanded. The flower continued growing in little bursts until the soft pink middle was like an overstuffed pillow for Olena. Maybe it was the amazing smell hypnotizing her, but Olena decided to sit down on the pink petals without thinking about it.

"Come on, let's go," she said.

Sylvan climbed up without hesitation and she put him in his spot on the edge of her pouch. Kez was more reluctant.

"How exactly is that thing going to get us over there?" he asked.

"Have faith. It'll be a surprise."

"You don't know, do you," said Kez.

"Nope," answered Olena. "That's why it's a surprise."

Olena knew Kez trusted her, so she stuck out a hand. He took it and climbed onto her lap. As soon as he was seated, the three big red petals underneath them started spinning fast. In a moment, they lifted off the ground. Olena grabbed the stamen poking up out of the middle and pushed them toward the gate. The beautiful, giant mayblossom hovered in that direction.

"Wee!" cheered Olena as they flew out over the canyon.

Then Kez got her attention. "Isn't that Zandria?"

Olena looked to the far side of the canyon. It did look like Zandria and it looked like she was walking down the wall. Olena knew it had to be some kind of trick, but there was Adam right behind her. They kept moving over and down. They were climbing on something. Then farther back and further up, Olena saw a man climbing over the edge. Before he took the first step, he turned into a wolf.

"Kez! It's a werewolf. She doesn't know he's there. We have to warn her," said Olena. She tried changing the direction of the mayblossom, but it would not turn. Then they tried screaming, but Zandria and Adam were too far away to hear them. The next thing Olena knew, they were landing in

Empyrean's courtyard. She ran to the doorway and peeked out.

"We can't see them from here," Olena said. She looked around and chose a door at the top of some short steps. "Maybe if we get inside, we can get around to warn them."

Olena ran for the door. Kez chased behind her saying, "Shouldn't we wait for that pointy eared fellow?"

Then they were in Empyrean.

Zandria could not believe how long it was taking them. It felt like they were on the stairs the entire day. She took each step one foot at a time. There could be no stumbling here. If she missed a step, that would be the end.

It was not enough that she was scared of falling and mad at Olena. Every time she looked at Adam, those butterflies came back too. She thought it would be easier to give in to the darkness. But it only wanted her to go down the fast way.

She liked Adam being close, but not too close. There was not much space on the ledge and sometimes they even had to move with their backs to the wall. There was no room to hold hands. For one thing, Zandria was sure if one of them fell, that one would pull the other one down. Aside from that, she simply did not know if she could stand it.

It did not matter at this point, but she kept thinking that there might not even be a way in when they get there. She told herself she was going to be queen. She told herself there better be a door for her. Anything else would not be acceptable. Zandria started her journey not believing in magic. Now she believed in the magic of Empyrean and her own magic. The castle was not allowed to change now. If there was no door, she did not know what to do.

At one point, Adam said, "What was that?"

"What?" Zandria said.

"I thought I saw something flying up there." He pointed to the side of the castle facing the wall of thorns.

"I don't see anything," she said. Still, she felt something. She felt like someone was watching them. Maybe someone was looking down from the castle. Right now, they were only about halfway down and that was too far to see anything.

When they were almost to the bottom of the steps, the white mist was rising to greet them. Every couple of steps, it would bubble up, blocking her view of the next foothold.

Then a bolt of lightning struck the tower. It shook the castle so hard that pieces of rock broke off the canyon wall close to them. After a few more steps, burning chunks of rock started dropping from the sky. They reminded her of the late nights when her entire village would gather on the beach to watch the falling stars. Next came more lightning.

Zandria was five steps away from the wide part where the castle protruded from the wall. The way those stars were falling made her want to jump. She thought she could make it. Plus, she did not want to be hanging on the ledge if one of them came too close. She looked down, trying not to imagine what would happen if she missed. Then Zandria closed her eyes and jumped.

She was on solid ground. The mist parted briefly and she could see streaks of crystal in the stone on the short stretch that stuck straight out. There were also broken pieces of wood that must have fallen from above.

For the first time since the start of the staircase, Zandria looked back at Adam. She had not had the nerve to look around too much except at the narrow steps until now. She saw him preparing to jump from a greater distance then she had, but that was of little concern. A short way behind him, a werewolf was following them and it was getting close.

"Adam. Jump. Now," demanded Zandria.

He did not look back, but jumped. When he hit the ground, he rolled over to see what scared her. The wolf had to span three steps at a time to stay on the wall. It always had one paw in the air, so Adam took advantage of this. He began throwing the broken wood to try and knock the wolfman down.

"Get inside," ordered Adam.

Zandria turned to go and was face-to-face with a solid glass wall. There was no door. At least, she did not see one at first. As Wrath warned, the castle had a tendency to change on its own. Zandria found the door on the side out over the canyon.

"This way," she told Adam. He was still watching the werewolf getting closer, but he was out of wood to throw.

Zandria eased out, gripping the jagged crystal. There was not really anywhere to put her feet. She slipped, but Adam caught her wrist to steady her. They scooted around the short distance together and ducked through the door.

Then they were in Empyrean.

Kez and Olena with Sylvan in her pouch wandered through the hallways. There was no clear path to follow and no one around to guide them. Olena noticed that every time they turned a corner, the hall behind them would change.

They kept going, though. They would go up staircases and turn back down. Through curved halls and hallways that doubled back on themselves. Olena could feel the magic working on her. Empyrean was a maze that did not want to let her in on its secrets.

At one point, they were in a hallway that was so long, it could not have existed inside the castle.

"I think this hall is longer than the whole outside of the castle," remarked Kez.

Then a door opened beside them and Tym with the pointy ears poked his head out. "There you are. Follow me," he said.

As Olena and Kez walked through the door, the entire castle shook.

"What was that?" asked Olena.

"I believe lightning struck the outer wall," said Tym. "Let's move quickly."

He led them on more wild twists and turns. Olena could not have repeated the course even if she took a hundred years. Then they were in a little room at the top of some stairs. To one side was a pair of double doors. Tym pulled a key from his hidden pouch and went to unlock them. On the other side was an opening to a little balcony.

Something urged Olena to see how high up they were and she went to the rail. So far down below, she could barely make out the stocky man surrounded by piles of rope.

"We must be at the top," she said to Kez.

Then Tym had the doors open and stepped inside. He must have thought they were right behind him because he looked surprised when they were not there.

"Hurry. Get inside. It's almost midnight," he yelled.

"But what does that have to do with anything?" asked Kez.

Then the bells of Empyrean chimed for midnight.

Olena could feel it in every part of the castle. Before the sound got inside her head, she wondered why she could see no bell towers. Where was this magical sound coming from that caused her to swoon? The last thing she could focus on was Tym disappearing as the doorway faded into a solid wall. Then she flipped backwards over the balcony rail.

Zandria and Adam stood in a low ceilinged room. Everything was made of crystal and the floor was an enormous criss-cross of beams. Zandria could see straight through to the mist below. She saw black smoke rising up and swirling in the mist. Hanging in the open spaces between the beams were every imaginable size and shape of bell. There were so many that Zandria did not even try to count them. This was Empyrean's hidden bell chamber.

Adam pointed to a staircase that led up into the castle on the far side of the chamber. "We have to get over there," he said. Then he went first, walking the balance beam between the bells.

Zandria looked to the bottomless pit again and saw the black smoke fighting to get in. She knew this smoke was made from the same blackness that ate at her heart. She was so close to it now and so scared. She thought she would lose her mind if it touched her. She did not want to give in to it and hoped Empyrean's power would keep it out. Then she knew it would not stop other things as she heard the click of claws on the glass behind her.

"Run," Adam screamed from the far side.

Zandria bolted out to the center of the beam, out of the werewolf's reach. Then she realized she was standing on a beam smaller than the stairs she climbed down. She almost lost her balance and stopped moving for a moment. The wolf slowly padded toward her.

As the wolf-man was in striking distance, the bells started swinging on their own to ring in midnight. Soon, the sound was so intense, Zandria thought her ears would pop. The assassin turned back into a man to cover his ears. The last she saw of him was a bandage across a nose on a face that was burned into her memory. This was one of her father's attackers. Then a large bell swung hard and knocked him from the beam into the roiling blackness below.

When the bells suddenly stopped, Zandria was still standing over the middle. The magic sound got into her head, but more importantly, it felt like it cracked a shell that was hardening around her heart. She looked down and the dark was no longer calling to her. In her heart, she knew what she had to do. Her head was clear, too. She even suddenly knew the fastest way through the castle to the throne room.

Zandria grabbed Adam's hand and led him up the stairs. This time, she did not mind the butterflies so much.

After a fast run through the maze, Zandria and Adam turned a corner into a short hallway. This was not the same room that Olena stood in, but it had the same two openings. On one end, a pair of double doors opened from the inside by a man with pointy ears. At the other end was a balcony. Zandria was surprised to see Kez sitting there alone with his head down.

She started to say, "Kez, what are you doing?"

"There's no time. Get in here," said the pointy eared man. Behind him, Zandria could see several wizards and court attendants. In the center of the room stood three radiant old ladies. She had no doubt who they were and knew this was the moment she anticipated for so long.

Before she went in, something made her want to go to the balcony. It was a feeling like a suggestion jumped into her head. Later, she would remember it as a spark of light reigniting her heart. Suddenly, Zandria was filled with love and rushed to the balcony.

She saw that Kez did not have his head down. He was actually looking over the edge saying, "Hang on. Help is coming." Zandria looked over the rail to find her sister hanging from the lip of the balcony. She was dangling by one hand and her fingers were slipping off the smooth surface.

Zandria did not hesitate and flung herself over the rail toward Olena. Adam caught her right arm at the last second as she caught Olena with her left. He helped pull the girls back from the drop. They fell safely to the floor together, hugging and crying.

"I never want to lose you," said Zandria. "I'm so sorry."

"I knew you didn't mean it. Thank you for saving me," said Olena. "I think you're going to be a great queen."

Then two wizards rushed over, mumbling to get the queen into the throne room. Zandria stood up, ready to go. The wizards stepped past her and grabbed Olena by the arms. They lifted her to her feet and rushed her over to the other queens.

Zandria was so happy for her sister right now that she started crying again. It truly did not matter to her that she did not become queen.

Now she watched the pale queen with the black hair and deep red lips whisper instructions to Olena. Adam and Kez moved close as the four queens formed a circle in the middle of the room.

From the balcony opening, Zandria could see the black smoke rising up outside to envelop the entire castle. The force of it was pressing against the crystal and cracking it.

Inside, the floor in the center of the room danced and spiraled up into a short pillar. The four queens each put their right hand on it. Olena stood on her tiptoes to reach.

Then the dark skinned queen said, "I am the Queen of the Southern Valley. I bring my precious drop of water, from which all things live."

She was followed by the fair one in the white gown, "I am the Queen of the Western Sun. I bring my righteous flame from which all evil is purged."

Next came the one with the red lips, "I am the Queen of the Northern Wood. I bring my fertile soil from which all things grow."

Finally, it was Olena's turn. She looked unsure and glanced at Zandria. Zandria smiled at her, then Olena said, "I am the Queen of the Eastern

Sky." She paused nervously. "I bring my breath from which all things start anew."

As soon as Olena finished her last word, a bright white light erupted from the top of the pillar. It shot straight up and out of the top of Empyrean, cutting through the evil black smoke. A new tower sprang from the inside of the courtyard wall. Then the shaft of light widened to encompass the four queens. The light kept growing wider until it wrapped around Zandria, the whole room and then all of Castle Empyrean. The blackness fractured as the light shone against it. Then the light exploded touching every part of the four queendoms of Empyrean all at the same moment. For an instant, there were not any shadows even in their small hut in the village of Banookanook.

Then it was gone. The light was gone and so was the darkness. The pillar sank back into the floor and the three older queens fell back into their thrones. Olena did not look like she knew what happened, so Zandria rushed up and hugged her.

"You did it, sis." She corrected herself, "I mean, you did it, your majesty. You saved everybody."

Then Zandria turned to Adam and kissed him on the cheek.

Chapter 20

A Good Day

That morning, the sun rose and for the first time in a long time, the sky was clear over Empyrean.

Everyone slept easy for a short while and woke early to cheers coming from the courtyard. The surviving army gathered in front of the castle. The pirates gathered wood from their wrecked ships and helped Professor Erbadin and his dwarves build a temporary bridge when the queens called back the thorn barricade. Now more than a thousand humans and animals from across the four realms of Empyrean waited to welcome the fourth queen.

The four queens gathered their heroes in the courtyard. Zandria and Adam stood on the top step in front of them. Kez held Sylvan on his shoulder. William rode atop Fury and they lined up next to Wrath, Sayonya, Virgata and Mildoo

Vol. Aeran and his hawks circled the courtyard, but Evorin could not fit inside.

Cinderella stood behind Olena and said, "Allow me to present the youngest Queen of the Eastern Sky, Olena the Beautiful."

The cheers and cries of joy were so great that Empyrean shook once more. Then the wizards launched fireworks over the courtyard from the newly grown tower.

That evening, after the celebration, the queens held a feast for their friends.

It was a fine meal and many stories were shared. They spoke of Professor Erbadin returning to the Northern Wood to immediately begin construction of a new bridge. They celebrated Mildoo Vol uniting the plain's traders. They discussed how the battlefield would be deemed sacred and the ornate remains of the Rockhorns would stay as memorials. There was much debate as to the whereabouts of the enemy leaders, General Gusk, Lord Vanril and the gypsy Sasha. The belief was that they were gone for a long while, if not forever.

Time was taken to mourn their fallen comrades. Isis assured everyone that Apis was quite stubborn and would return soon in a new form.

There was one story told with great enthusiasm at that table, which Zandria did not hear. The tale of how William and Fury brought Evorin down from the mountain will be saved for another time.

They even commented on the Forgotten Evil. It was generally believed to be sealed once again beneath Empyrean. As long as four queens were in power, there would be no other opportunity for escape. To that end, it was decided that Olena would remain at Empyrean for some time, always with at least one other queen.

With Snow White's permission, Wrath made an announcement. Sayonya invited him to return with her and he would resign his post. Wrath said, "I can think of no better hooves to fill my shoes than the brave Fury." Naturally, Fury accepted.

Then Olena made some important decisions for the East with the guidance of Snow White, Cinderella and Isis. First, it was agreed that much effort should be put into the rebuilding of the Dead Forest and the wasteland along with their surrounding towns. William was asked to oversee this project and to be Prince of the Royal Forest. He modestly declined, but Olena insisted in that special way that a six year old does. William asked that among his towns, Bremen be given strictly to the animals and Virgata the white tiger named mayor. When Olena and the others agreed, Virgata graciously offered that humans would always be welcome.

In regard to the wasteland, Adam requested to lead a rescue party into the mines. He wanted to make an effort to free any other children that may remain.

Lastly, Olena said, "Before we go to bed, Zan, I wanted to give you a special present. I will have Soria Moria completely restored for you."

"But no trolls or kappas," joked Zandria.

"I promise," said Olena.

"There may be a ghost or two," offered Sylvan.

They ended the evening with much laughter and hugging.

Adam escorted Zandria to her bedroom with the elf Tym as their guide. The clear vision Zandria had only the night before was gone and Empyrean was as much a maze to her as anyone now. Tym gave them a moment of privacy to say goodnight. This time, it was Adam's turn to kiss Zandria on the cheek.

Finally, Zandria was left alone in her wonderful bedroom. The crystal walls were decorated with flowers and ancient paintings. There were two couches bigger than her old hut. The bed was so soft that Zandria was almost invisible when she sank under its covers.

Zandria fell asleep imagining she could hear the waves rolling against the shore. She dreamt something beautiful that never actually happened. She and Olena were playing in the sand of Banookanook. Their mother and father walked out of their home and they all splashed around in the water. In the middle of the night, she woke from this dream crying.

When she finally got herself under control, she tried to go back to sleep. Zandria lay quietly for a long time, unable to drift off. Then she heard a noise in an otherwise silent Empyrean. At first, she thought maybe it was a strange echo, because it sounded like her own crying. She quickly dismissed that possibility.

The noise was coming to her from a distance. It would not let her fall back asleep. With a combination of curiosity and frustration, Zandria got out of bed. She left her room barefoot and dressed only in her new nightgown. She followed the sound down dark corridors, not paying attention to her way back.

At last, she came to a door and was certain the noise was coming from inside. Before she opened the door, she listened closely. She decided it was definitely someone crying. Apparently, no one else in the entire castle could hear it though as no one was around. Zandria put her hand on the glass knob and chills ran up her spine. For an instant, she did not want to know what was on the other side. However, this was the new Zandria and she was going to live life without fear. She opened the door and walked into the room.

Zandria said, "Mother?"

About this book

Where do fairytale princesses go after their happily ever after?

The land of Empyrean is home to all the myths and folklore of childhood. The princesses of once upon a time became the four great queens of this land ruled by magic.

Now their land is in danger. One of the queens has disappeared. Without the fourth queen, the Forgotten Evil will be freed from its ancient prison.

Two sisters, Zandria and Olena, live in a tiny village by the sea. Their world is about to get bigger. With his dying breath, Zandria's father tells her that she is to be the new queen. The sisters flee their home, chased by werewolves, facing danger at every turn. With the help of some unique allies, they must travel to the crystal castle, claim Zandria's birthright and stop the Forgotten Evil.

Will the sisters reach the castle in time to save Empyrean? Or will they lose each other forever?

Take the first step into the land of Empyrean to join Zandria and Olena on the Journey of the Fourth Queen!

About the author

As a best-selling author and publisher, Mark has won various awards for writing and book cover design.

Growing up in Kansas, Mark graduated from Sumner Academy of the Arts and Sciences and received his Bachelor's in Film from the University of Kansas.

Mark has written under a few pen names with numerous novels, screenplays, short stories and digital series to his credit.

www.ingramcontent.com/pod-product-compliance
Lightning Source LLC
Chambersburg PA
CBHW061936170626
46813CB00006B/2418